Sunstar and Pepper

S U N S T A R

and

P E P P E R

Scouting with Jeb Stuart

BY

EDNA HOFFMAN EVANS

ILLUSTRATIONS BY A. E. PARK

The University of North Carolina Press

CHAPEL HILL · 1947

To Mother and Dad

WHO HAVE STOOD BY

CONTENTS

CONTENTS

Sunstar and Pepper

CHAPTER ONE
Pepper Meets General Stuart

"If you want to have a good time
Jine the cavalry—"

T H E boy lounging against a column on the wide porch
lifted his head sharply as the gay tune, accompanied
by the jingle of sabers against stirrup irons, the tinkle
of bridle chains, the thump of a banjo, and the steady
rhythmic beat of trotting horses came floating through
the June sunshine.

Leaping over the broad steps, Potter Pepperill ran down the long sloping lawn fronting the Magnolia Hill plantation house to the white gate to watch the riders pass. The Civil War had been raging for a little more than a year, but cavalry troops were still a thrilling novelty to Potter. His gray eyes sparkled with anticipation and the breeze stirred his dark brown hair as the boy leaned far out over the gate to catch an early glimpse of the riders.

Nearer and nearer came the merry song as a troop of nine soldiers trotted into view, singing as they rode. The morning sun glinted from highly polished weapons and the shining brass buttons on trim gray uniforms.

The big, golden-bearded officer who was in the lead checked his horse and flourished his plumed hat to Potter.

"Is this the way to Ashland?" he asked, smiling at the boy.

Potter snapped to attention and saluted smartly, as his soldier father had taught him to do.

"Yes, sir," he answered. "Ashland's eight miles down the road."

"Thank you." The officer returned the salute and then spurred away after his staff.

Potter's gray eyes followed them wistfully, his heart throbbing in time with their rollicking song, until their gray uniforms had disappeared in a swirl of dust far down the road.

"I reckon Jeb Stuart's captivated you, too, with that 'Jine the Cavalry' tune of his, eh, Pepper?" A laughing voice behind him brought the boy out of his reverie.

Young Potter Pepperill, better known as "Pepper," turned to see his older cousin, Brian Cromartie, leaning against the fence beside him. Brian's extra years gave him three inches of height over his cousin and he made the most of them, despite the crutch he carried under one arm to ease the strain on a right leg and foot that were swathed in bandages. Already a seasoned soldier at twenty years of age, Brian was home on sick leave after a minie ball had cut him down at Seven Pines, the bloody battle which had been fought a week earlier.

"Why do you say that, Brian?" Pepper wanted to know. "Who were those soldiers?"

"Son," said Brian impressively, "I'm ashamed of you. Didn't you recognize Jeb Stuart and his staff? You know, they're camped just above Ashland."

Pepper's jaw dropped.

"Jeb Stuart," he exclaimed. "And I talked to him and didn't know it. Why, he acted just like any other officer."

Brian threw back his head and burst into a roar of laughter.

"Ho, ho," he said at last, almost choking. "How else did you expect him to act?"

"I don't know," Pepper admitted. "Reckon I've heard so much about him that I just expected him to act different." He heaved a deep sigh and then added, "Sure wish I could ride with him."

"Huh," Brian snorted, "horse cavalry. They look pretty, all right, but give me the infantry every time.

Now in Stonewall Jackson's command we're called cavalry, too—'foot cavalry.' We earned that name, I'll tell you! When Jackson says march we start, and we don't stop until we get there."

"Uh-huh," Pepper agreed absently. "I want to hear more about Jeb Stuart."

Sixteen-year-old Pepper was as staunch a Confederate rebel as any boy in the South in the spring of 1862, and the glimpse he had just caught of the famous cavalry leader made him tingle all over. This was easy to understand, for Stuart was the pride of the Confederate cavalry—the idol of every man in gray. Already, although the war between the North and the South was only a year old, Stuart's hard-riding, hard-fighting troopers had won a glowing reputation for reckless daring.

Loyal infantryman though he was, Brian was quite willing to talk about the famous cavalry leader.

"I reckon Stuart's the youngest general in the army," he began. "Got appointed brigadier general last year just after the battle of Manassas. He's only twenty-nine years old, but there's not a smarter officer in the whole army—except General Lee and Stonewall Jackson, of course. And say, did you notice the staff officers with him?"

Pepper shook his head.

" 'Fraid not," he admitted, "but I've heard that he has a lot of mighty queer officers on his staff."

"That's the truth," Brian chuckled, "and most of 'em were with him today."

"Who were they?" Pepper wanted to know.

"The two big troopers just behind the General were Rooney Lee and Heros von Borcke. Rooney Lee is General Robert E. Lee's oldest son."

"Von Borcke," repeated Pepper. "That's a funny name."

"It is," agreed Brian. "He's called 'Stuart's big fighting Dutchman.' He belongs to the King of Prussia's crack Dragoon Guards back in Europe, but he got special permission to come over here and join our army."

"Good for him!"

"He ran the Yankee blockade to get here," Brian continued. "Then he hung around the War Department in Richmond until they sent him out to Stuart. The Dutchman turned up in full hunting kit—pink coat, white breeches, top boots, and his long dragoon sword. He wanted to be sure to catch the General's eye."

"Did he?" Pepper inquired eagerly.

"He sure did," replied Brian. "Stuart was so tickled that he took von Borcke right along to Seven Pines. During the battle I saw the Dutchman fighting with his long sword and yelling like a demon, but it wasn't until afterwards I found out who he was."

Pepper's gray eyes were sparkling as he listened.

"John Pelham, the young looking officer, is only twenty but he is Captain of the Artillery," continued Brian. "And, of course, that was Sam Sweeney with the banjo. You'll never see Stuart without him. Sweeney joined the army after his minstrel troupe got stranded in Richmond. Stuart heard Sweeney play his banjo and detailed him to the escort right away."

"Good idea," commented Pepper.

"You bet," his cousin agreed. "The fellow with the thick black whiskers growing right up to his eyes is Lieutenant Henry Hagan, the best forager in the army. He can smell out a ham or a chicken at half a mile. They say Stuart made him a lieutenant just to see him swell up with pride. But he's a real soldier, though."

When Pepper made no comment, Brian continued.

"The scholarly looking soldier was Talcott Eliason, Stuart's staff surgeon. The last two men were Captain Farley and John Mosby, Stuart's best scouts."

Pepper drew a deep breath.

"I'd like to join the cavalry," he said, "and ride with General Stuart."

"You can't do that, Pepper. You're too young," Brian said quickly, shaking his head. "The war will be over and won long before you're old enough to enlist."

Pepper sighed and turned away without a word. Down in his heart he was afraid of that very thing. With drooping head, he walked slowly across the broad lawn and turned thoughtfully into the white gravel drive that led to the plantation stables.

An eager, gentle whinny greeted Pepper as he entered the airy sun-filled stable.

"Mawnin', Marse Pepper." Uncle Elijah, the white-haired old Negro hostler, left off currying the big black horse just long enough to bow a greeting to his young master. "Sunstar done heard you a-comin' ev' since you fust put foot on de gravel. Smartes' horse in all Virginny, Sunstar am."

"You bet he is, Uncle 'Lije," agreed Pepper, running his hand lovingly over the horse's glossy neck.

Sunstar nudged his master with his soft muzzle, snuffing at his pockets for the lump of sugar that Pepper always carried for him. Sunstar and his father's sword were Pepper's most prized possessions.

The boy rewarded Sunstar's search with the desired sugar lump and then settled himself comfortably on a bale of hay to watch Uncle Elijah continue his currying.

"How's Aunt Delila's rheumatism?" he asked after a time.

"Hit's troublin' her some of a mawnin'," the old slave replied, busy with his brushes. "She done had de misery pretty bad in her back yestiddy. Uncle Snag-tooth fix' her up a charm bag to chase away de achin', but it seem like de ole rheumatiz done git wuss, 'stead o' better."

"That's too bad," said Pepper. "Tell her I'll ride down and see her soon."

"I'll sho' do dat, Marse Pepper," grinned the old man. "Delila be mighty proud to have you come. An' we's got us another new gran'chile baby fo' you to see. We's named him Robe't E. Lee Stonewall Jackson Gin'ral Stuart."

"That's some fine name, Uncle 'Lije," said Pepper, smiling wistfully at the mention of his hero's name. "I'll be down to see them both real soon."

As Pepper rose to go, Uncle Elijah caught him by the sleeve.

"Jes' a minute, Marse Pepper," he whispered. "I'se got sompen else to tell you."

"All right," Pepper said, sitting down again. "What's on your mind?"

"Shhhh," hissed the old darky, looking cautiously around to see that no one was near. "I'd get skinned if'n anybody caught me tellin'."

"Nonsense. There's nobody on the plantation to hurt you."

"It ain't that, Marse Pepper," answered the old man. "Hit's dat Yankee I'se afraid of."

"What Yankee?" Pepper demanded, jumping up in surprise.

"Shhhh," Uncle Elijah's eyeballs rolled fearfully. "De no-'count Yankee white trash dat's been a-stirrin' up trouble down in de quarters. He done tol' us he's gwine cut out our hearts and fry 'em fo' breakfast if'n we tol' on him."

"Quick, Uncle 'Lije, tell me about him! You know I won't let any Yankee hurt you. Since Uncle Buford's away and Cousin Brian's wounded, I'm the man of the plantation now, and it's up to you to tell me about anything that goes wrong!"

"Please, Marse Pepper, don' scol' me. I'll tell you.

Jes' you sit down dere again on de hay and I'll keep on a-breshin' whilst I whisper de tale to you."

Pepper sat down again and tried to look unconcerned, so that no one passing by might suspect the startling nature of the old man's conversation.

Uncle Elijah moved closer, busy all the time with his brushes.

"Hit's dis way, Marse Pepper," he whispered. "A li'l rat-faced white man wid a big black mustache done come into de quarters last week and start talkin' to all de niggers. Done tol' 'em to run off to de Yankee army so dey kin git guns and fight de rebels."

"The low-down hound!" exclaimed Pepper.

"Yessuh," agreed Uncle Elijah. "Most ob de folks wouldn't pay him no mind, but he come back an' come back, an' he talk and he talk 'til some ob de young nigger bucks git to sayin' maybe he's right."

"Humm," said Pepper thoughtfully. "Where did he come from?"

"I ain't right sure, Marse Pepper," was the reply. "But las' night de breeze done blow open de long coat he always wears and I seed a blue Yankee uniform underneath. Looks like he done snuck across de lines to stir up trouble."

"Does he come every night, Uncle 'Lije?" asked Pepper eagerly. Already he was forming a plan.

"No, suh, not every night. But he wuz here las' night, just a-talkin' bigger an' faster than ever."

"Listen, Uncle 'Lije." Pepper bent close to whisper

his plan to the faithful old man. "If he comes tonight I want you to come tell me. Don't let anybody see you, and don't tell anyone else about this. I'll handle it myself."

"Yessuh, Marse Pepper," the old man agreed solemnly. "I come tell you an' I'll sho' be right keerful, 'cause I don't want no Yankee a-cuttin' out my heart and a-fryin' it fo' breakfast. No, suh!"

CHAPTER TWO
Pepper Captures Two Yankee Agitators

THAT evening after supper Pepper followed his mother, his aunt, and Cousin Brian out to the broad veranda, where they sat under the massive white columns, enjoying the cool evening breeze and watching the glowing colors of the sunset in the western sky.

"Virginia is a beautiful state, especially in the spring," remarked Mrs. Cromartie, looking up from her sewing and gazing out at the shining green leaves of the magnolia trees which gave the plantation its name.

"Yes," agreed Pepper's mother with a sigh. "It is such a pity that war has come to spoil it."

"Oh, war's not always so bad," Brian said, drawing designs on the porch floor with the tip of his crutch. "And besides, it can't last much longer." Brian looked slyly over at his cousin. "It will be over too soon—that's what Pepper is afraid of," he added.

Pepper said nothing. He only shrugged his shoulders and grinned to himself. If Brian knew everything, he wouldn't be so cocky, Pepper thought.

"Pepper's father and grandfather were soldiers," Mrs. Pepperill said with another sigh. "It's in his blood, Brian, just as it is in yours. Don't tease him too much."

Pepper sat with the others until the sun sank below the glowing horizon and the evening shadows began to steal out over the Virginia hills. At last he rose and excused himself.

Hurrying upstairs to his room, Pepper quickly completed his carefully laid plans. While he was not sure that the Yankee troublemaker would return that night, he thought it best to be prepared.

All day Brian's description of Stuart's gallant Prussian dragoon, Heros von Borcke, had been running through Pepper's head. "He turned up in full hunting kit—so he'd be sure to catch the General's eye," Brian had said. Now what could Pepper do to catch the General's eye, too?

Thoughtfully Pepper opened the big clothes chest

and drew out his father's uniform. No, that would not do. His father had worn the Union blue of a colonel until a Comanche Indian arrow had cut him down on the Texas plains just two years before the outbreak of the Civil War. If his father had lived, Pepper was sure that he would have resigned his post and offered his sword to Virginia, as had Stuart, Lee, and most of the other southern generals.

Underneath his father's carefully folded uniform Pepper found the gorgeous doeskin hunting shirt that had been the gift of Chief Prairie Wolf. Dressed in this gaily beaded and fringed costume, Pepper was certain that he would "catch the General's eye."

Laying the hunting shirt, his father's long cavalry saber and heavy pistols on the bed, Pepper carefully replaced the worn blue uniform in the clothes chest and closed the heavy lid.

After pulling on his long riding boots, the boy took off his light coat and donned the gay doeskin jacket. It fit him perfectly. Pepper's heart swelled with delight when he remembered how much too big it had been for him when the Chief first gave it to his father. He was as big as a man now. Pepper smiled with satisfaction as he buckled on the great saber and one of the heavy pistols.

It was nearly dark by the time Pepper finished his preparations. Since there was still no news from Uncle Elijah, the boy lighted his candle and strutted up and down before the mirror, pleased with his warlike appearance.

"I'll have to get me a plume for this sometime soon," he told himself, picking up his broad-brimmed felt hat. "I want one like Jeb Stuart wears."

He was so busy admiring himself that he failed to notice the first light tapping on his door.

"Tap, tap, tap," came the sound again, and this time it was louder.

Pepper stepped eagerly to the door and opened it softly.

"Hit's me, Marse Pepper," whispered Uncle Elijah from the darkness of the hall. "Dere's two ob dem Yankees down at de quarters, jes' a-talkin' up trouble as hard as dey kin."

"Good," answered Pepper, stooping to blow out the candle. "I'll soon fix them."

Silently the old Negro and the boy crept down the dark stairway and out into the moonlit night.

"You say there are two Yankees this time?" Pepper asked as they moved toward the stables.

"Yessuh, de little ratty one wid de mustaches an' a strappin' big fella wid yaller whiskers. Dey's both got on long duster coats but I done see de blue uniforms under dem. When I snuck away, de little man was tellin' all de niggers to rise up an' he'd give 'em guns and swords to fight with."

"We'll stop that mighty quick. You hop into the stable and get some of that new rope that Uncle Buford just sent down from Richmond."

"Yessuh," said the old darky, darting off.

Pepper had just finished re-examining his pistol

when Uncle Elijah came back carrying a coil of light rope.

"You ain't figgerin' to hang dem Yankees, is you, Marse Pepper?" he asked in awe-struck tones.

Pepper chuckled.

"No, I'm just going to tie them up and take them for a little ride," he said. "Do those fellows have horses?"

"Yes, Marse Pepper," answered the Negro. "Dey's got 'em tied up jes' back ob de quarters."

"Good," said Pepper. "Now here's what I want you to do, Uncle 'Lije. Saddle Sunstar and then sneak out and get the Yankees' horses. Move them over into the orchard and wait until I call you. Mind now, don't let anyone see you. Do you understand?"

"Yessuh, Marse Pepper, I sho' does."

"All right, then, go get those horses."

As the old Negro disappeared in the dark, Pepper crept quietly toward the plantation's Negro quarters. With his hand clenched on the butt of his father's pistol, he wondered whether his heart was really pounding as loudly as it sounded to his excited ears. "Thump, thump, thump," it went—loud as a drum. Pepper hoped the Yankee agitators could not hear it.

He crept forward through the darkness of the tree-lined path toward the Negro quarters. When he reached the edge of the clearing, he paused and crouched in the shadow of a great oak tree to watch.

The slave quarters of Magnolia Hill plantation consisted of four long rows of neatly whitewashed cabins, each with its comfortable plank porch and mud-plastered chimney. A great bonfire had been kindled in the center of the main passageway between the cabins and, by the rosy light of the leaping flames, Pepper was able to see everything that went on.

The two Yankee agitators were mounted on one of the cabin porches and the Negro field hands were gathered in a great half-circle around them. The fire's glow was reflected sharply from the shiny black faces and rolling eyeballs of the crowd.

The big blond Yankee sat on a packing box, idly swinging his booted foot and smoking a battered corn-cob pipe. Meanwhile, his smaller companion was waving his arms and addressing the crowd of Negroes around the porch.

"You must rise, rise up in wrath and righteousness!" the little rat-faced Yankee was shouting. "Lift your heads and hear the trumpet call to glory! Join the holy cavalcade! Shout 'Hallelujah' and follow me. I know where there are guns and bullets, swords and knives and pistols. Come, arm yourselves and strike a blow for freedom!"

"Who is we gonna fight, white man?" called a gruff Negro voice from the crowd.

"Fight the southern rebels, the monsters who have enslaved you!" shouted rat-face. "Strike the fetters from your wrists! Wipe out your bondage in blood! Heed the call of the Lord and his angels. Rise now! Rise up and destroy your masters!"

"We ain't mad at our white folks," called a woman's

voice. "We's got plenty to eat and we is plum comfortable. Wha' for should we rise up agin' Marse Judge
and Miss Margaret?"

"Good for you, Aunt Lucy!" muttered Pepper under his breath.

The little Yankee swore in exasperation.

"I guess you'd better let me talk to 'em, Mac," the
big man said.

"Go to it, Ed," answered the smaller man. "I can't
pound any sense into their black skulls."

Rising from his seat, the man called Ed pocketed his
pipe and began to speak. Never in all his life had Pepper heard such oratory. The blond Yankee raved and
ranted and waved his arms, talking on and on while
the Negroes listened open-mouthed.

At last Pepper could stand it no longer. Moving
cautiously away from the oak tree he circled the crowd,
keeping out of sight in the shadows. There was little
danger that anyone would see him. The listening Negroes were fascinated by the big man's flow of words,
and both agitators had been swept away by the force
of their own eloquence.

Holding his father's pistol clenched in his right
hand, Pepper entered the back door of the cabin and
advanced silently through the dark interior. Then he
stepped boldly onto the porch and faced the crowd from
behind the shouting Yankees.

"That will be enough for tonight," said Pepper in a
stern voice. "Both of you put up your hands or I'll
shoot."

With smothered exclamations of surprise both Yankees swung around and stared at Pepper.

"I said put up your hands," repeated the boy, raising his big pistol.

Slowly and reluctantly the two obeyed. As the big man did so he glanced quickly over his shoulder as if hoping that the crowd of blacks would rescue him and his companion.

His hopes were groundless. Recovering from their surprise, the Negroes were gazing in rapt admiration at their young master.

"Look at Marse Pepper," said a voice. "Ain't he jes' de fines' lookin' sojer man?"

"He's de spittin' image of his pappy," agreed another voice.

"Hit done serve dem white trash right if'n Marse Pepper shoots 'em plum full er holes," chimed in a third.

"You folks go back to your quarters," Pepper told them, "and never let me catch you listening to such trash again. I'll take care of these varmints."

Obediently the crowd began to move away.

"Uncle 'Lije!" called the boy, catching sight of the old man on the outskirts of the crowd. "Bring up those horses."

"Yessuh, Marse Pepper, I'se a-comin'," replied the old darky, leading the two horses and shouldering his way through the crowd.

"Hitch the horses to the rail and then come here and help me," ordered Pepper.

While his young master kept the two Yankees covered with his pistol, old Elijah bound their hands tightly before them. Then their feet were securely tied together. After testing the bonds, Pepper called two of the slaves who still lingered.

"Here, Buck, you and Jonah help Uncle 'Lije sling these two face-down across their saddles and tie them there so they can't start any funny business."

"Yessuh," they chuckled. "You sho' is smart, Marse Pepper."

When the two agitators were securely fastened, in spite of their growls and curses, Pepper replaced his pistol in its holster and gathered up the reins.

"Is Sunstar saddled?"

"He sho' am," replied Uncle Elijah. "Sunstar am up in de stable all ready and a-waitin' fo' you. Lord-a-massy, Marse Pepper, if'n you don't look an' act jes' like yo' pappy. One peek at dat purty jacket ob yours and dese Yankees jes' fold up like busted sausage bladders."

When they reached the stable, Pepper handed the Yankees' reins to Uncle Elijah and prepared to mount Sunstar. As he turned, the boy saw a slender figure step out from the shadowy doorway.

"Pepper," his mother said. "Were you going away without telling me good-by?"

The boy swallowed hard and fumbled awkwardly with his bridle.

"Yes, Mother, I reckon so," he said miserably. "You see, I was afraid you might cry and ask me not to go."

His mother drew a deep breath that was half a sob.

"My little boy has grown up," she said. "You are so like your father."

"Then you don't care if I go?" Pepper asked eagerly. "Cousin Brian is here to look after you and Aunt Margaret until Uncle Buford comes home."

"I care a great deal, Pepper," answered his mother. "But I know what is expected of a soldier's wife and a soldier's mother. Where are you going?"

"I caught these Yankee agitators down at the quarters trying to stir up trouble," replied Pepper, pointing to his two captives. "I'm going to turn them over to General Stuart."

"I see," Mrs. Pepperill said. "It was a brave, rash thing for you to do, son. Stuart is a great soldier and a gentleman and I am proud to have you follow him. Your father was a cavalryman, too. I saw you leave the house, and I brought this for you."

She held out a beautiful brown ostrich plume which Pepper knew was one of her most prized possessions.

"Mother!" he exclaimed. "I can't take that!"

"Give me your hat," she said quietly.

Obediently Pepper handed her his felt hat. Taking a small gold pin from her dress, Mrs. Pepperill carefully looped up the brim and fastened the plume to it.

"There, son," she said. "And may God go with you."

"Thanks, Mother," was all Pepper could say.

His mother folded him in her arms for a minute and then stepped back to look at him with pride, even as her eyes filled with tears.

Pepper turned abruptly to Uncle Elijah.

"Take good care of the ladies, Uncle 'Lije, until Judge Cromartie gets back," he said hoarsely. "And don't let anything go wrong down in the quarters or I'll come home from the army and skin you clean down to the raw bones."

"You kin trust me, Marse Pepper," the old Negro answered earnestly. "I'll take good keer ob de mistisses and keep dem niggers a-walkin' de chalk line. Sho' will, Marse Pepper."

"All right, mind that you do," Pepper said. "Goodby, Mother! Good-by, Uncle 'Lije!"

Mounting the impatient Sunstar, Pepper stooped to give his mother a final kiss and then, gathering up the reins of the Yankees' horses, he spurred swiftly away through the moonlight.

CHAPTER THREE

Pepper and Salt

FIRMLY grasping the lead straps of his prisoners' horses, Pepper trotted Sunstar on through the bright night. Now that the ordeal was over, the boy's heart pounded jerkily under his gay hunting shirt. He had no definite plans. He simply headed toward Stuart's camp near Ashland and, once he got there, Pepper felt that events would take care of themselves.

Every few minutes the boy looked back at his captives to make sure that they could not escape. He had been careful to see that the ropes which bound them across their saddles were firmly tied. Just the same, he was not taking any chances.

The steady beat of the horses' hoofs echoed and re-echoed down the lonely road as the moonlit miles rolled behind. Pepper's chest swelled in expectation as Ashland came nearer.

"Halt!"

The sharp command shattered the silence as a mounted guard suddenly swung across the road from the shadows. A carbine muzzle was thrust unpleasantly close to Pepper's head.

"Who goes there?" demanded the picket.

"A friend," answered Pepper evenly. "A friend with prisoners for General Stuart."

"Well, singe my whiskers," rumbled the picket in surprise, blinking at the helpless figures of the two Yankees. "Where did you get them?"

"Who is it, Hagan?" a voice called from the darkness before Pepper had time to reply.

"A youngster with some prisoners, sir," answered the man who had stopped Pepper. "He looks like a wild Injun to me."

Before Pepper could object to the word youngster, a second horseman rode out from the shadows to stare at him. All the boy could see of the two pickets were great beards which seemed to sprout from under their low-pulled hat brims.

"I'm not an Indian," Pepper explained quickly. "You see, I found these two Yankees trying to stir up trouble among the slaves on my uncle's plantation, so I captured them. I put on this hunting shirt so General Stuart would be sure to notice me."

Both pickets laughed.

"Why are you so anxious to have Stuart notice you, son?" asked the second soldier.

"I want him to let me join the cavalry."

"Oh, I see," said the picket. "In that case we'll take you in to headquarters. Come along."

Riding between the two soldiers, Pepper's heart beat faster in anticipation of his second meeting with General Jeb Stuart.

"You're pretty young for the army, sonny," remarked the second picket after they had ridden for some time in silence.

"Oh, I'm past sixteen," replied Pepper. "And besides, Jeb Stuart's not so terribly old, himself. They say he's the youngest general in the army. That's why I hope he will take me on."

"The youngster's got the answers all ready, sir," laughed the man who had first stopped Pepper.

His companion chuckled softly.

As the three rode on, the second picket, who seemed to be an officer, questioned Pepper closely about his two captives. The boy explained how he had surprised the agitators in the Negro quarters and captured them.

"They have Yankee uniforms on under those long

coats," the boy concluded his story. "And besides, they had no business making trouble among my uncle's Negroes."

"Who is your uncle?" asked the soldier.

"He is Judge Buford Cromartie and he represents our county in the Virginia Legislature. My cousin, Brian Cromartie, was one of Stonewall Jackson's men until he got wounded at Seven Pines. He's home on sick leave now."

"What is your father's name?" the soldier wanted to know.

"My father is dead," answered the boy. "He was Colonel Lawrence Lee Pepperill of the Second U. S. Cavalry out in Texas until he was killed in a battle with the Comanches about three years ago."

"Hum," muttered the soldier. "I've heard of him. 'Fighting Colonel Pepper' they called him in the West. Served out there for eight years, myself, although I never met your father. So you're 'Fighting Pepper's' son and you want to join Stuart?"

"Yes sir," Pepper said eagerly. "Do you suppose I'll get to see General Stuart and ask him to let me stay?"

"Perhaps," was the reply. "We shall see."

The three rode on in silence. At intervals the two soldiers paused to answer the sharp challenges of watchful sentries. At last they pulled up on a little knoll close to a tent pitched under three tall pine trees. An orderly stepped out to greet them.

"Good evening, sir," he said.

" 'Evening, Sam," answered the man who had questioned Pepper. "You and Hagan untie these two prisoners. Then while Hagan brings them to headquarters, Sam, you make this young man comfortable for the night. Come back when that's done."

"Yes, sir," said the orderly, saluting as the officer moved off.

Pepper helped the two soldiers release his captives. Free to stand on their own feet once more, the two Yankees groaned and rubbed their cramped muscles.

"Rotten way to treat a man," remarked the big Yankee, "slinging him across a saddle like a meal bag."

The smaller captive swung toward Pepper, his thin face twisted with rage.

"I'll get you for this, you meddling young rebel," he snarled. "No young squirt can make a fool of me and get away with it!"

Hagan's ham-like hand descended on the captive's shoulder and the big cavalryman shook the agitator until his teeth rattled.

"That's enough outa you, Yankee," Hagan rumbled, reaching for the other prisoner and shoving them both toward the tent.

The man called Sam turned to Pepper.

"My name's Sweeney," he said. "How would you like to bunk with me and my buddy tonight?"

"Thanks," replied Pepper. "Are you the Sweeney who plays the banjo for General Stuart?"

"That's me," grinned the other, gathering up the reins of the two Yankee horses and leading them away.

"Then we must be pretty close to General Stuart's headquarters," exclaimed Pepper, following with Sunstar. "Do you reckon I'll get to see Stuart?"

Sweeney laughed.

"I reckon you already have seen him, son," he answered. "That was Jeb Stuart who brought you in."

Pepper gulped and followed Sweeney, stricken silent by what he had just heard. So it was Jeb Stuart who had stopped him. And here he had chattered away about Stuart's being the youngest general in the army! Pepper's cheeks burned red at the thought of his blunders.

"Well, here we are," Sweeney said suddenly, stopping before a small tent. "Hitch your horse and come in."

Pepper tied Sunstar to a small sapling and followed Sweeney into the tent.

By the glow of the candle that the banjoist had just lighted, Pepper saw a boy of about his own age stretched out across one of the cots, sound asleep.

"Hey, Salt, wake up!" called Sweeney. "We've got company."

The sleeper stirred, groaned once or twice, and then returned to dreamland.

"Come on, Napoleon!" Sweeney said, shaking the boy by the shoulder. "Wake up!"

This time his efforts were rewarded, for the boy sat up and rubbed his eyes drowsily.

"Whass'a matter, Sam?" he asked, yawning.

"Company's come," replied Sweeney. "Get up and make your manners."

"Oh, hello," said the other, catching sight of Pepper for the first time. "Where'd you come from?"

"He just brought in a couple of Yankees," Sweeney explained. "Stuart says he's to bunk with us tonight."

"That's fine," said the boy, straightening up and looking at Pepper with more respect and interest. "Two Yankees—let's shake on that. I'm Barry Salter, but my friends call me Salt."

"Thanks," said Pepper, grasping the outstretched hand. "My name's Potter Pepperill and everybody calls me Pepper."

"Well I'll be blowed," exclaimed Sweeney. "Salt and Pepper! You two ought to get along mighty well together. Just make yourself comfortable, Pepper. I've got to get back to headquarters."

"Sit down and tell me about your two Yankees," Salt invited as the tent flap dropped behind Sweeney's departing form. "Are you going to join up with Stuart?"

"I certainly am, if he'll only let me stay," replied Pepper, sitting down on Sweeney's cot. "What do you do in the cavalry?"

"Oh, I carry messages and do some scouting for the General," Salt replied. "My home's down in Georgia, but I came up here to join the cavalry as soon as my family would let me. I've been here about two months. Now tell me how you captured the Yankees."

Seated comfortably inside the army tent, Pepper related the adventures of the night.

"I never dreamed that I'd meet Stuart or I might not have talked so big," Pepper concluded his story. "I thought that the General and Hagan were just cavalry pickets."

"Stuart won't mind," Salt comforted him. "But you'll have to get used to finding him in queer places. He lives between the lines most of the time and he's not afraid of the whole Yankee army."

"Do you suppose he'll let me stay with the cavalry?" asked Pepper eagerly.

"Maybe," said Salt. "But he'll test you first and you'll have to make good."

"I'll do my best," Pepper resolved.

"That's the stuff," agreed Salt, settling back in his blanket. "Now let's turn in. I've had a hard day and I reckon you have too."

"I'll have to go look after Sunstar first," Pepper said. "I'll be back in a few minutes."

Rising, Pepper left the tent and made his way through the darkness to the place where he had tied Sunstar. A gentle whinny greeted him as the great black horse stretched out his soft muzzle toward his master.

"Well, old pal, we're here," Pepper whispered, laying his cheek against the steed's glossy head. "Let's hope we can stay."

Sunstar snorted softly as if he, too, hoped to remain with Jeb Stuart's famous cavalry.

Carefully, Pepper loosened the cinch strap, removed the saddle, and made his horse as comfortable as possible. The spring night was warm and there was no danger that Sunstar would be chilled. Tied loosely to the sapling, the horse could graze as much as he wished.

"Good night, Sunstar," the boy whispered, giving his horse a final pat before returning to the tent.

"Make yourself at home," invited Salt, yawning and pointing to the other cot. "Sweeney'll probably spend the rest of the night up at headquarters with Hagan."

Pepper pulled off his long boots and his hunting shirt before tumbling into Sweeney's blanket. Salt blew out the candle.

"G'night," he said sleepily.

"Good night, soldier," replied Pepper.

For a few minutes Pepper lay blinking up at the darkness. He could scarcely believe that so many things had happened to him in the few short hours that had elapsed since he first glimpsed the famous Jeb Stuart from the lawn of his uncle's plantation.

"I hope he lets me stay," the boy repeated over and over as he dropped off to sleep. . . .

It seemed to Pepper that he had scarcely closed his eyes before he felt someone shaking him. Pepper muttered indistinctly and tried to burrow deeper into the blankets, but the shaker persisted.

At last, opening a drowsy eye, he saw Salt standing over him.

"Get up, soldier, you're in the army now," said Salt, grinning at Pepper's flushed face and tousled head. "You slept right through bugle call. Come on out."

Pepper quickly tumbled into his boots and jacket before following Salt outside. The Georgia boy had already built a crackling fire, and the smell of sizzling bacon filled the morning air.

"Corn pone and bacon—army grub," Salt said. "The coffee's roasted corn meal—we can't get the real stuff through the Yankee blockade. It's not bad, though, once you get used to it."

The two boys were eating hungrily when Sweeney joined them.

"Son, you made a great haul last night," he told Pepper while helping himself to the bacon. "Do you know who those Yankees are?"

"Just a couple of agitators, I reckon."

"They are more than that," Sweeney told him. "Ed Buckett and Arch McGrigg are notorious Yankee spies."

"Whew!" Salt almost dropped his bacon. "I've heard of them. They're dangerous!"

"Tough customers," agreed Sweeney. "They carried papers that told about Yankee General McClellan's plans. I'll bet Stuart and Lee will have their heads together before long."

"What will become of the two Yankees?" Pepper asked.

"Oh, they'll be sent to Richmond for a court-martial," Sweeney answered with his mouth full.

The three were finishing the last of the bacon and corn pone when an orderly arrived from headquarters.

"General Stuart wants to see you right away," he told Pepper. "Bring your horse with you."

"Go to it," whispered Salt. "I hope he lets you stay."

CHAPTER FOUR
Stuart Tests Sunstar and Pepper

BRIGADIER GENERAL James Ewell Brown
Stuart, known to all the world by his nickname "Jeb"
Stuart, was seated before his tent breakfasting with
his "fighting Dutchman," Heros von Borcke.

In spite of a sleepless night spent in questioning the
two spies, Stuart was gay and full of energy. His keen
blue eyes twinkled and the morning sunlight brought
out the gold in his bronze beard and flaring mustaches.

Stuart wore a red rose on his jacket, and his glittering sword was belted on over a golden silk cavalry sash

with long tasseled ends. His gray riding cloak was lined with scarlet and his fawn-colored hat with its gold star and ostrich plume lay beside him on the grass. Pepper noticed that the General's spurs were golden, like those worn by the knights of old.

"Here's our young fire-eater," said the General, waving his cup in greeting. "Last night he brought in McClellan's two most dangerous spies, all tied up like meal bags. You see, Heros, we grow them young over here."

"I should like very much the young man's hand to shake," said the Prussian dragoon in his queer English, rising and holding out a large hand to Pepper. "I haf' for him a great admiration."

Stuart winked at Pepper while the dragoon shook the boy's hand vigorously.

"My friend usually gets things backward, but he always means what he says. What's your full name, youngster?"

"Potter Pepperill, sir," replied Pepper, saluting.

"Did Sweeney put you up all right last night?" Stuart inquired.

"Yes, sir. Salt—I mean Barry Salter—let me bunk with him," the boy replied.

Stuart laughed heartily.

"Salter and Pepperill," he said. "Salt and Pepper. I need seasoning like that in the cavalry. How would you like to stay on as my courier and scout?"

"Oh, sir," said Pepper eagerly. "That's just what I came for."

The General did not reply immediately. Instead, his

bright blue eyes looked searchingly at the boy and then wandered to Sunstar, carefully taking in all the horse's good points. He smiled approvingly as his eyes rested on the well-groomed mount and shining saddle.

"Come on," he said suddenly, rising from the table and picking up his hat. "You ride my horse, Skylark, and I'll ride yours. I want to try him. What's his name?"

"Sunstar, sir," replied Pepper handing the reins to Stuart and turning to the General's own spirited horse which was grazing near by.

Swinging gracefully into the saddle, Stuart cantered off, followed by Pepper on Skylark.

"*Mein* General, do not go too far beyond the picket lines," von Borcke called after them. "Haf' for yourself a care."

Stuart's only reply was a careless wave of his plumed hat.

On through the keen morning air rode the two horsemen, both forgetful of everything but the paces of their spirited animals. Trot, walk, canter—Stuart tried all of Sunstar's gaits and Pepper was proud as he saw the General nod in silent approval as he put the big black horse through his paces. Without seeming to do so, the General also watched Pepper, observing how well he handled Skylark, swaying easily in the saddle like a born horseman.

Farther and farther they rode. At intervals they passed watchful gray pickets and relief soldiers gathered around morning campfires.

"Good morning, General," said one sentinel, saluting. "I'm the last picket out. The enemy's lines begin just over the hill yonder."

"Good," said Stuart, swinging Sunstar off the road and into the rolling fields as if to try him over broken ground. Ditches and fences failed to daunt the riders. Their mounts cleared the obstacles with graceful ease.

After some time Stuart turned Sunstar into another road and started back toward camp.

Pepper, remembering all the tales he had heard about General Stuart's reckless daring, had been keeping a careful watch on the land. Suddenly he caught the gleam of a blue uniform and the flash of a bayonet through the trees some distance ahead. There were Yankee soldiers between them and the Confederate camp!

"General," the boy called in a low voice. "There's a Yankee picket yonder!"

"Oh, that's all right," replied Stuart. "They won't be expecting us from this direction. We're behind them. Come on—let's go!"

Gathering the reins, Stuart touched his golden spurs to Sunstar's flanks and, with Pepper close at his heels, the Confederate cavalryman dashed at a full gallop toward the unsuspecting blue soldiers.

The horses thundered swiftly down the road, stirring up great clouds of dust. The bewildered Yankees scattered before them, their startled yells ringing in Pepper's ears as the two Confederates tore through the picket lines.

They were a hundred yards away before the gaping blue pickets could gather their wits and fire after the racing horsemen. Musket balls whined harmlessly past the two riders as the distance increased behind them.

Neither Stuart nor Pepper spoke until they reached camp. Then the General swung to the ground, turned to the boy, and smiled.

"A fine horse you have," he said, handing the reins to Pepper. "Did you ever time him over the half-mile?"

"No, sir," Pepper replied. "Skylark's a mighty good horse, too."

"She is," agreed Stuart, stroking his mare's arching neck. "And, Pepper, I like the way you behave in a tight spot. Hereafter, you and Barry Salter are both my personal couriers."

"Thank you, sir!" Pepper was almost too delighted for speech.

"You have won the place and you must work to keep it," Stuart said. "Don't thank me, but live up to your record. The cavalry must be the eyes and ears of the army, and at the same time must keep the enemy guessing. As long as every man does his duty we will show the Yankees a thing or two. Now go over to the quartermaster and get yourself on the muster roll."

"Yes, sir," said Pepper and, saluting, he turned joyfully away.

The next few days were busy ones for young Potter Pepperill, but under the friendly guidance of Salt and Sweeney he quickly learned the routine of Stuart's camp. Soon he knew all the leading officers by sight, and many of them knew Pepper. His bright Indian jacket and curling ostrich plume attracted much attention. The hard-riding troopers of Stuart's cavalry called him "Jeb's Wild Indian" and "Big Chief Ostrich Feather," but all their jokes were friendly and Pepper soon became a great favorite at headquarters.

Even tall Infantry General Stonewall Jackson, usually solemn and thoughtful, had a smile and a kind word for the young courier, and one afternoon when the beloved gray-bearded General Robert E. Lee rode into Stuart's camp on his horse, Traveller, he stopped to praise Pepper for the capture of the two Yankee spies.

"As long as we have lads like you in the South, no northern invaders can take our homes," Lee said.

Pepper flushed with pleasure at the sincere praise, even though he was too embarrassed to say more than "Thank you, sir. I'll always do my best."

During this time there was little actual fighting. The great Confederate and Union armies lay facing one another, each commanding general waiting for his opponent to make the first move. The terrible battle of Seven Pines had nearly exhausted both forces and, for the time being, each was content to rest and recuperate while new supplies and equipment arrived to replace those which had been lost or destroyed in the struggle.

Every day brought rumors of skirmishes at the front where Confederate and Union pickets exchanged shots or rode at each other with drawn sabers along the wooded Virginia roads. In spite of the lull in the fighting, every man knew that something important was brewing at headquarters, where the leading generals met daily to scheme and plan campaigns.

Pepper's days were filled with hard work, for Stuart always found tasks to keep his couriers busy. Mile after mile Pepper and Sunstar traversed together, running errands for the cavalry General. The great black horse seemed to feel that his master was carrying important messages, for he arched his gleaming neck and pranced with pride, even though many miles lay behind his tireless hoofs.

When the day's duties were over and Sunstar made comfortable for the night, Pepper enjoyed the jolly times spent around the crackling campfire. Veterans of the year-old war refought former battles, recounting tales of Manassas, Dranesville, Seven Pines, and countless little skirmishes without names.

Then, when the tales were exhausted and the fire burned low, there was always Sweeney with his banjo to lead the songs. Evenings like this were the kind that Jeb Stuart loved, and often he added his rich baritone voice to the less musical ones of his troopers.

At these times the woods would ring with "Alabama Gals, Won't You Come Out Tonight," "Lorena," "Kathleen Mavourneen," and "The Old Gray Horse." But the final song of the evening, and the one that always filled the camp with joyous echoes was Stuart's favorite tune, which had thrilled Pepper on the June day when he first saw the General. This was the rollicking

> *"If you want to have a good time*
> *Jine the cavalry,*
> *Jine the cavalry,*
> *Jine the cavalry.*
> *Want to have a good time?*
> *Jine the cavalry. Bully boys, ho!"*

It was on such a night when the singers were gathered around the campfire that Salt, who had been absent on a long day's ride to Lee's camp, burst in on them.

"Something's up!" he told them excitedly, breaking in on one of the tunes. "Lee just sent Stuart a special dispatch and there'll be work for the cavalry before long!"

"What did I tell you?" exclaimed Sweeney, laying aside his banjo with a clatter. "Ever since Pepper brought in those spies something's been in the air."

"What do you suppose it is?" Pepper asked, eager for his first real action.

"There's no telling," replied Sweeney. "But if I know Jeb Stuart, it will be something that will scare the daylights out of the Yankees."

Next morning their suspicions were justified. Stuart called for a picked company and set off toward the west with his men riding four abreast behind him. He made no explanations to his troopers, but they followed him gladly down the turnpike road.

"We must be going to join Stonewall Jackson in the Shenandoah Valley," whispered Salt, urging his chestnut, Thunder, close to black Sunstar. "That's where this road leads."

CHAPTER FIVE
The Ride Around McClellan

ALL morning the column jingled over shady roads, swinging northwest as the sun rose higher. Finally the troop turned sharply east at Ashland Station. Mile after mile rolled behind the horses' hoofs as the column advanced.

"Say, this isn't the way to the Shenandoah Valley," remarked Pepper as he and Salt jogged along side by side, munching their noonday rations. "Where do you reckon we're going?"

"Search me," replied Salt. "But the General's got something up his sleeve. We've been in Yankee territory for the last hour."

When evening came the troopers bivouacked without campfires, making themselves as comfortable as possible in the brush-covered woodland. Horses and men were glad to rest; the column had made twenty-one miles since morning.

Pepper, Salt, and Sweeney were part of the advanced picket line that Stuart threw out to protect his sleeping column. The three rode carefully forward, keeping in touch with the other pickets, and took their position for the night along the edge of a pine thicket.

After making their horses comfortable among the trees, the three friends settled themselves on the thick pine needle carpet of the grove to talk.

"I'll bet my cap that we run into old Papa Cooke before this raid is over," said Sweeney chuckling softly. "And won't he be surprised."

"Who is he?" Pepper wanted to know.

"Papa Cooke? Oh, Sweeney means the Yankee cavalry commander, Brigadier General Philip St. George Cooke," Salt explained.

"But why do you call him Papa?"

Sweeney laughed softly.

"That's what Stuart calls him," he explained. "You see, Pepper, this is a funny war, and families got sort of mixed up when it came to choosing sides. General Cooke is Stuart's father-in-law. Jeb married Flora Cooke while he was serving in the cavalry out west."

"Fighting his own father-in-law!" Pepper gasped. "Say, that's hard to believe."

"The family's more mixed up than that," Sweeney continued. "Yankee General Cooke's own son is in the Confederate army, and one of his daughters is married to our surgeon general. The other daughter married a Yankee officer; so you can see what a mix-up it is."

"I reckon war's worse than I thought," said Pepper, shaking his head in perplexity.

"Oh, cheer up," laughed Sweeney. "You're fighting for what you think is right, aren't you? Well, so are they. A man's got to follow his own conscience. I reckon God will take care of the rest."

"I suppose you're right," agreed Pepper doubtfully.

"And now we've got to get busy," said Sweeney, rising and brushing the pine needles from his coat. "I'll take the first watch, Salt will take the second, and Pepper, you get to watch the sun rise. How's that?"

"Suits us," agreed the two boys.

"Good night, then, and just keep your eyes peeled for Yankees."

As the banjoist strolled off to take up his lonely vigil, the two boys curled up on the dry pine needles with their saddle blankets over them and went to sleep. Tired after the long day's ride, Pepper slept soundly until Salt shook him awake in the early morning hours.

"It's time for you to go on duty," Salt whispered as Pepper rubbed his sleepy eyes. "Be quiet and don't wake Sweeney."

"Did you see any Yankees?" asked Pepper as he rose to his feet and picked up his blanket.

"No," answered Salt. "Everything's quiet."

Leaving his two companions stretched out on the ground, Pepper quietly made his way to his post at the edge of the grove. Everything was deathly still and the woods were dark and ghostly. The moon had set, and the pale light of the stars did not penetrate through the dense thatch of pine branches far overhead.

The summer air was damp with early morning dew; Pepper pulled his blanket closer around his shoulders and shivered. Deeper in the woods an owl hooted and Pepper's heart thumped a little faster until he realized what it was. Then he laughed to himself, thinking,

"As Uncle 'Lije would say, 'Hit's a mighty skeerful mawnin' an' de debbil's rustlin' 'round!' I'm not scared, but I will admit that I'll be glad when the sun rises."

Choosing a comfortable spot at the foot of a tall pine tree, Pepper leaned his back against the sturdy trunk, folded his hands over his saber hilt, and settled himself to watch until dawn.

The minutes passed slowly and in spite of his determination to stay awake, Pepper's eyelids grew heavy and his head began to nod. Straightening up with a jerk, he shook his head to chase away the cobwebs from his brain.

"This won't do at all," he told himself.

For some time he marched up and down: ten steps forward, halt, pivot, ten steps more, and repeat. The dry pine needles rustled softly as he moved, and now and then a last year's cone crackled sharply underfoot.

Thoroughly awake at last, he resumed his post at the foot of the pine tree. Again the minutes dragged slowly by and the boy's head drooped lower and lower.

"Snap!"

The sharp noise jerked Pepper wide awake in an instant, muscles tensed and ears strained to catch the slightest sound. The little grove lay silent and dark. Pepper was just beginning to think that his nerves had played him false when he heard a steady rustle in the underbrush. Someone or something was creeping nearer. Pepper loosened his saber in its scabbard and reached for his pistol.

Nearer and nearer came the sounds. Pepper held his breath and waited. Visions of Yankee regiments rose before his eyes only to be chased away by the recollection that there were still bears and bobcats in the Virginia woods. What should he do? Pepper wondered miserably as he waited. A pistol shot would arouse the entire raiding party. It might also betray their presence within the Yankee lines. The thing was coming nearer, its breathing sounded clear and strong, but in the blackness Pepper could see nothing.

A soft snort sounded just behind the boy and then a warm, furry something rubbed against his shoulder, snuffing happily.

Pepper laughed with relief.

"Sunstar, you old rascal," he whispered, throwing an arm around his horse's neck. "What do you mean by scaring me out of a year's growth? Why, old fellow, I might have shot you for a Yankee."

The big horse snorted gustily, as if content at having found his master, and stretched out his head so that Pepper could scratch his ears.

"I sure am glad to see you, Sunstar," whispered Pepper as he stroked the glossy head. "Keeping watch alone is no fun and I'm pleased to have your company."

The rest of the night passed swiftly and soon the sky in the east was showing the first faint glimmering streaks of daylight. The horizon was just taking on a rosy hue when Salt and Sweeney joined Pepper, leading their horses.

"Everything all right?" inquired Sweeney.

"Everything's fine," replied the young sentinel.

"Good. Might as well fall in with the main company. They'll be moving soon."

The three scouts mounted their horses and rode back through the woods to the place where the raiding party had spent the night. The camp was filled with an orderly bustle as the men ate their cold breakfast rations and stood to horse, awaiting the command to mount and move on.

"Everything quiet at our post, sir," Sweeney reported, saluting the officer in charge.

"Good," was the answer. "These Yankees certainly keep poor guard. Get your rations and fall in."

Riding past the place where Jeb Stuart had assembled his field officers for a conference, Pepper and Salt heard the General's voice hailing them.

"Salt! Pepper! Come here, my well-seasoned scouts," Stuart called.

"Yes, sir," answered the two boys, dismounting and standing at attention.

"You are to ride eastward toward Hanover Court House," the General said. "Find out all you can about the enemy's activities and communications. Keep your eyes open for enemy cavalry. Rejoin the column when you have done that. Do you understand your duties?"

"Yes, sir, we do," replied the scouts, saluting and swinging joyfully into their saddles.

"Good luck, then," Stuart called after them, "and don't let the Yankees catch you."

The two boys cantered gaily out of the camp, following a winding forest track that led eastward. With eyes and ears alert for the first signs of blue-coated soldiers, the scouts rode on and on, their horses' hoofs making no sound on the soft grassy trail.

"Just think, Pepper," said Salt in a low voice. "We're miles inside the Yankee lines, and right behind McClellan's whole army. Won't 'Little Mac' be surprised when he hears about us?"

"Yes," agreed Pepper. "A raid like this has never been made before."

They rode in silence for some time, keeping a careful watch for the enemy. Then, faintly through the trees, they heard the sound of a bugle.

"Yankees," whispered Salt, as both boys checked their horses. "That was assembly call."

"I'll go ahead and find out how many there are," said

Pepper, dismounting. "I know this country better than you do. You stay here and hold the horses."

"Good luck, old timer," whispered Salt, also dismounting to lead the horses to cover behind a clump of trees.

Pepper stole forward, dodging from tree trunk to tree trunk, with all his senses alert. He had gone less than a hundred yards when the woods thinned and he caught sight of blue uniforms through the trees.

"I'll have to watch my step," he thought, dropping to the ground and worming his way silently from bush to bush, taking advantage of every bit of cover that the scrubby country afforded. At last he crouched watchfully behind a clump of choke cherry shrubs, scarcely fifty yards from a troop of blue-coated cavalrymen.

There was something familiar about one of the Yankee officers. Pepper's eyes widened in surprise as he recognized McGrigg, the spy he had brought in to Stuart.

"Now how did he get here?" Pepper muttered. "I thought he was a prisoner down in Richmond."

He was still puzzling over the spy's unexpected presence when the Yankee bugle sounded "Mount and Forward." The cavalry moved out of the clearing. When they had disappeared in a cloud of dust, the boy rose and hurried back to the place where he had left Salt and the horses.

"What did you find out?" his companion asked eagerly as they mounted.

"It was a troop of Yankee cavalry," replied Pepper.

"Must have been about a hundred of them and they headed northeast."

"Stuart will run into them if we don't warn him," exclaimed Salt.

"I know it," answered Pepper. "And Salt, that spy McGrigg was with them. He must have escaped from Richmond."

"Say, that's bad. He's dangerous," said Salt. "Sweeney told me how he threatened to get even with you. You'd better watch out for him."

"You bet I will. Come on, let's find Stuart and report."

The boys put their horses to a gallop and rejoined the raiding party not far from where they had spent the night. The scouts sought out their general and made their report.

"Fine work, boys," said Stuart. "Now fall in with the escort and wait for further orders."

It was not until nearly noon that the Yankees discovered Stuart's position far inside their lines. Then a scattering crackle of carbine fire told the main column that their advance guard had brushed with a company of enemy cavalry.

The "Stars and Bars," battle flag of the Confederacy, was released from its cover so that its diagonal blue and white starred cross on a red field floated free in the breeze. With sabers swinging, plumes waving, and horses' manes and tails streaming in the wind, the gray troops dashed toward the blue cavalry. Pistol balls spattered around them as the two forces drew together.

"Cut and thrust!" came the command from Stuart.

"Charge!" Pepper heard the Yankee officer shout.

Then, for the first time in his life, Pepper heard the famous wild "rebel yell" ring out from the galloping Confederates.

"Wahoo-ey!" the gray raiders screeched, and Pepper found himself yelling with them. "Wa-hooo-ee-ey!"

The cry rose shrill, then sank to a deep croak as the gray-clad men clashed with the bluecoats.

Pepper and Sunstar were swept forward with the rest of the troop and in a moment they were lost in the roaring tumult and dust-blanketed confusion that goes with a cavalry charge. All around Pepper saw, through the rolling dust clouds, horses plunging and rearing. Now a beam of sunlight would pierce the gloom and flash blindingly on a saber blade. Now everything was shrouded in dust. Occasionally a pistol barked sharply, but the fighting was too close for much gunfire.

Then came a ringing call, loud and clear as a trumpet.

"Wohl auf! Cameraden! Auf's Pferd! Auf's Pferd!" The Prussian dragoon had forgotten his English in the excitement of battle.

Peering around through the confusion Pepper saw the giant Prussian, his long dragoon sword flailing about like the blade of a crusader. Already the dust was thinning as the Yankees broke before the force of the Confederate rush.

Soon the Yankees were in full retreat, their broken ranks streaming away down the road or galloping across the rolling, brush-scattered fields.

"Com-pany, re-form!" came the sharp command.

Order came quickly out of chaos as the gray troops assembled in a column of fours along the road. Men and horses were panting from the brief struggle and here and there a wound showed bloody. But the light of victory burned in every eye.

"Com-pany, for-ward!" Stuart commanded.

Again the column moved on, penetrating ever deeper into enemy territory. Without being told, every trooper now understood that Stuart intended to ride completely around the giant Union army commanded by "Little Mac" McClellan.

Ever after, when Pepper tried to recall details of that famous ride, things seemed vague and confused. Events happened so quickly, skirmish following so closely on the heels of skirmish, that no one event stood out clearly in his memory.

There was an almost continuous clatter of shots from the advance guard. Vaguely he remembered dismounting to help tear up the tracks used by trains carrying McClellan's supplies. The squad had just begun to work when a locomotive, whistling its shrill warning, thundered through the barricade they had built and disappeared toward the east, followed by a hail of Confederate lead.

"That engineer's a brave man," commented Sweeney, staring through the smoke cloud that billowed in the wake of the wood-burning engine.

When a section of track was destroyed, the gray troops pounded on, gathering up blue prisoners as they went. Behind them stretched a path marked by upset supply wagons and by scattered, bewildered Yankees who had somehow escaped capture. The Union officers knew no way of stopping the daring raiders.

Afternoon faded into evening and the troopers began to droop in their saddles from weariness. Their horses, that had charged so spiritedly at noon, now moved with lowered heads and sagging ears.

At nine o'clock, after thirty-five miles of riding and fighting, Stuart granted his men a three and a half-hour rest on the grounds of the Federal hospital at Talleysville.

During the halt Pepper anxiously examined Sunstar, pleased to see how well the gallant horse was standing the long journey. True, Sunstar was tired, but his delicate ears still stood sharply erect and his nostrils quivered with pride and courage. Every inch of his glossy body showed the mark of the thoroughbred.

"I'm proud of you, old fellow," the boy spoke quietly, stroking Sunstar's head. "You're as good as any soldier in the army."

"Our horses carry a greater responsibility than we do, Pepper," said a voice behind him. "The life of every man in the column depends on his horse, not only tonight, but on every raid or scouting expedition we undertake."

Pepper turned to see General Stuart standing beside him, with Skylark's bridle in his hand. The General had just finished watering his horse in the little brook that flowed past the Union hospital.

"How is Sunstar standing the ride?" the General asked.

"Very well, thank you, sir," replied the young scout, saluting.

"That's good. And, Pepper, you are making an excellent record for yourself. I'm more than proud of you."

Stuart dropped a friendly hand on the boy's shoulder before moving on.

Pepper threw one arm over Sunstar's neck, unashamed of the tears of pride and happiness that rose in his eyes. Hadn't he won the praise of Jeb Stuart?

At midnight the Confederates started on the final dash back to their own territory. Eight miles of enemy country still lay between them and the Chickahominy river, which was the dividing line between the two armies. Gray scouts reported that Yankee cavalry was gathering to pursue and cut them off.

Thud, thud, thud, the trampling of many hoofs echoed and re-echoed through the darkness as the column moved ever nearer the safety of the Chickahominy.

"We've had a lot of rain this spring," Pepper heard Stuart remark to Lieutenant Christian, who was guiding the column. "Will we be able to cross the river?"

"There's a private ford on my farm at Sycamore Springs, sir," was the reply. "We can cross there if the stream is not too high."

Once again Pepper watched the eastern sky grow

light and saw his gray-clad companions take on a ghostly aspect as the first faint glimmer of day streamed through the clouds of dust and mist.

"We can't be far from the river now," remarked Salt as he and Pepper galloped side by side.

"Yes," agreed Pepper. "From the looks of this fog, we're almost there."

The boys were right. Soon the head of the column was halted on the muddy river bank.

"The water is a lot higher than I thought it would be, sir," said Christian. "The ford's gone."

"See if you can make it, Captain," said Stuart, turning to Rooney Lee.

The big trooper spurred his horse into the swirling water. Down they sank, down, down, until the horse was swimming, fighting valiantly against the current which almost swept his rider from his back. After a long struggle the gallant horse won through and Rooney Lee waved to his friends from the opposite shore.

"The column could never make it, tired as the men are. And we'd never get the prisoners through," decided Stuart. Turning to Christian he asked, "Lieutenant, where is the nearest place we can cross?"

"There used to be a bridge about a mile down the river, sir," replied Christian. "But it was burned early in the war and only the old pilings are left."

Stuart sat quietly thinking, stroking his golden beard, as he often did in crucial moments. At last he picked up his horse's reins and gave another order.

"Forward," he said. "We'll try that old bridge."

Once more the gray troopers pounded onward, following the river until they reached the blackened pilings of the ruined bridge. Stuart took in the situation with a glance.

"Tear down that old barn," he said, pointing to an abandoned building near by. "We'll use the lumber from it to build our own bridge."

In a few moments the gray troopers were working like a swarm of ants. The minute a board was torn from the barn, it was added to the rapidly growing structure spanning the river. By the time the barn was down, a crude bridge had been built.

"Company across," Stuart ordered. "The last man over will set fire to the bridge."

The troopers lost no time in mounting and soon they were clattering across the Chickahominy, reforming ranks on their own soil. Scarcely was the last man across than flint and steel were out and the pine boards of the bridge were ablaze. The column waited a moment, catching breath before resuming the ride back to camp.

The bridge was blazing fiercely when a shout from the opposite bank drew every man's attention. A company of almost exhausted blue-coated lancers had arrived just too late. A volley of pistol shots splashed harmlessly into the muddy river, but the majority of the bluecoats were too weary to do more than sit and stare at their escaping quarry.

Stuart waved his plumed hat at his helpless pursuers.

"I'll see you later, gentlemen," he called. "Forward, men!"

"That was a close shave," Salt remarked as he and Pepper trotted along behind Stuart. "If those Yankees had arrived just a half-hour sooner, the story would have been a lot different."

"Yes," Pepper agreed, "but they didn't. Just think, Salt, we've made a hundred miles and been inside the enemy lines for two days and two nights. We've come all the way around the Federal army. We've captured nearly two hundred prisoners and even more horses and mules. Why, we've done something that's never been done before."

"That's right," added Salt. "No one but Jeb Stuart could have done it. I can't—"

"Listen!" Pepper interrupted him.

The column was dirty, dusty and spattered with mud. The men were sunken-eyed and slump shouldered; the horses were worn and lathered with sweat. Yet a sound rolled up from the unconquered ranks, and the boys straightened proudly as they heard it. In spite of their aches and pains, forgetting their exhaustion, the horsemen were singing:

> *"We are the boys who went a-round Mc-Clell-i-an*
> *Went a-round Mc-Clell-i-an*
> *Went a-round Mc-Clell-i-an*
> *We are the boys who went a-round Mc-Clell-i-an*
> *Bul-ly boys, ho!*

Bul-ly boys, hey, Bul-ly boys, ho!
Bul-ly boys, hey, Bul-ly boys, ho!

"*If you want to have a good time*
Jine the cavalry,
Jine the cavalry,
Jine the cavalry,
Want to have a good time?
Jine the cavalry, Bul-ly boys, ho!"

CHAPTER SIX

Through the Lines with Mosby

STUART gave his men and horses a few days' rest before he returned them to active duty. During those days messages flew thick and fast between the cavalry general and Lee and Jackson. The hard-riding troopers knew that even greater adventures were in store for them.

The whole South rang with the story of Stuart's daring raid. In Richmond the ladies threw roses before the

General's horse when he rode in to report to Lee and to Jefferson Davis, the President of the Confederacy. Congratulations fairly filled the air.

"Whew," said Sweeney one evening while he and Pepper and Salt sat by the campfire toasting their shins. "I'll be glad when this love feast is over. A dance at headquarters last night and another one tomorrow— Wagh! What a life!"

"You're right for once, Sam," growled a voice behind him.

The three turned in surprise to see the black-whiskered Hagan standing near by.

"Hullo, Hagan," laughed Sweeney. "What are you fussing about? The General singled you out for special praise."

"The special praise business is all right, I reckon," Hagan drawled thoughtfully, sitting down beside the fire. "But it's these confounded women around the camp that I don't like. Dances and parties—young officers making sheep's eyes at the pretty girls. This is a war, not a costume ball!"

"Why, Hagan, don't you like the girls?" Salt grinned.

"Naw," growled the bewhiskered lieutenant. "Not in camp, anyway. They're always underfoot."

"I like the General's wife and little girl," Pepper remarked. "They don't get in the way."

"Mrs. Stuart is different," agreed Hagan. "She was brought up in the army and is a real honest-to-goodness regular fella—nice lookin', and smart, too. And Little

Flora is the best youngster I know. They're all right. It's these silly, fussy, 'Oh, you wonderful soldier' ones that make my whiskers curl!"

"You win, old trooper," Sweeney roared with laughter. "The only time you're happy is when you're smelling out Yankee supplies. How's everything up at headquarters?"

"Busy as a beehive tonight," was the answer. Then Hagan turned to Pepper. "Stuart wants you to report to his tent in half an hour."

"What for?"

"He's got a job for you, I reckon," Hagan answered. "Now don't look so scared. You haven't done anything wrong, soldier."

"I'm not scared about that," answered Pepper. "But it took me so long to get in the army that I'm always afraid I'm going to get sent home, or something."

"Don't worry, young fella," said Hagan, giving the boy a rough but kindly slap on the back. "Jeb Stuart's got some job he wants you to do."

"I wish he'd send for me, too," mourned Salt.

"Just keep your hair on, Salty old boy," said Sweeney. "Jeb'll have all of us busy 'fore long, or I'm a Chineyman."

"Well, I reckon I'd better ramble along," said Pepper rising. "Did the General say I was to bring my horse, Lieutenant Hagan?"

"No, just trot up to headquarters on your own hoofs, sonny," Hagan answered.

"Salt, will you take care of Sunstar for me?"

"Sure will. Good luck, ol' timer."

"Don't advise the General wrong, Napoleon," jibed Sweeney. "An' don't capture more'n a regiment of Yankees this time."

"Don't worry, chief. I'll let a few run loose for you," replied Pepper over his shoulder as he stepped briskly off toward headquarters on the hill.

Here he found everything humming with action. Messengers came and went at a gallop. Important looking dispatches were piled high on Stuart's small camp table. By the light of flickering lanterns staff officers pored over ponderous field maps spread out on the ground.

Pepper waited his turn, sitting on the grass in the shadows. The rush and bustle fascinated him, and the thought of adventure to come made his blood tingle. At last the flood of messengers slackened. General Stuart lifted a tired head and sighed as he folded the last of the papers on his table.

"Hello, Pepper," he said, his blue eyes lighting at the sight of the boy's gay Indian jacket. "Are you ready for a job?"

"Yes, sir," answered Pepper, standing before the General's table and saluting.

"Good," said Stuart. "I have a special assignment for you and John Mosby, here." Stuart motioned toward a small sandy-haired man who was seated inside the tent busy with maps and papers. When Stuart mentioned his name, the scout rose and stood beside Pepper.

"You two are to cross the lines and find out what effect our ride has had on McClellan's Grand Army of the

Potomac," the General continued. "There never was an
officer so sensitive about his lines of communication as
'Little Mac.' Since we cut in behind him so neatly, he
may make some changes. You must find out whether
our information is still accurate. Is that clear?"

"Yes, sir," said Mosby.

"When you find out all you can, John, send Pepper
back with the report. He'll stand a better chance of getting through the lines than a grown man would. You
may have to go on to Washington and find out how
things stand there."

Pepper's head was swimming. A scouting expedition
far inside the enemy lines—and the man beside him was
to penetrate into the very capital of the enemy. Here
was an adventure!

"This is a dangerous mission, Pepper," he heard
Stuart saying, "but I know that I can depend on you
to do your duty. The safety of Lee's entire army may
depend on the information you bring back."

"I'll do my best, sir," the boy said earnestly.

"I am sure you will," nodded Stuart. Then he turned
to Mosby.

"Well, John, you have your orders. You are my best
scout, and my friend as well. Good luck to you."

Stuart rose and the two men gripped hands in silence. Each knew the danger of the mission, and each
knew that the scout might never return.

"Good luck to you both," Stuart added as Pepper
followed Mosby out of the tent and down the hill.

A horse and buggy were waiting on the trail and

without a word the two scouts climbed in. Mosby picked up the reins, chirrupped to the horse, and they were off on their dangerous mission.

For a time they rode in silence. Pepper watched the dark outlines of the trees slipping past and tried to imagine what his mother and cousin would say if they knew he was going straight into the very heart of the Union army. Mosby, too, seemed lost in thought.

"Are you scared, Pepper?" he broke the silence at last.

"Scared?" Pepper repeated. "Well, no, I'm not just exactly scared—just sort of surprised, I reckon. I never did anything this important before."

"Good." Mosby nodded his head in approval. "I'm glad you're not afraid, and it's better not to be too cocky on a job like this. If we use our wits, we'll come out all right."

"I'll do everything I can to help, sir," said the boy earnestly.

"That's fine," replied his companion. "Let's shake on it. But don't 'sir' me," he added as their hands gripped in the darkness. "I'm just plain John Singleton Mosby, scout. So call me John."

"All right, John," said Pepper, feeling more a man than ever.

They rode in silence for a time, following a trail that Pepper knew led straight north toward the Confederate outposts and the Union lines. Every step the horse took carried them farther from safety and nearer to danger

—perhaps capture, prison, and even death. The boy's heart thumped a little faster at the thought.

At last Mosby checked the horse and their buggy stopped in front of a deserted, tumbled-down shed, nearly hidden in thick bushes and weeds.

"Here's where we begin to walk," Mosby said, looping the reins loosely around the upright whipstock and jumping lightly to the ground. Pepper followed and stood blinking, awed by the silence.

Mosby whistled softly three times, waited a moment and whistled twice more. A few moments later an answering whistle sounded faintly from somewhere in the darkness. The bushes rustled and a man appeared.

"Hello, John," he said. "You off again?"

"Yes, it's 'Little Mac' and Washington this time," replied Mosby. "Pepper, this is Thad Griffin who runs this station between the lines especially for scouts like us. A good many scouts owe their lives to Thad's help."

"How do you do, sir," said Pepper.

"Hi, youngster," the man grunted. "You're pretty young for this business."

"Sure he is, Thad," Mosby agreed, "but just the same he's the one who brought in McGrigg and Buckett a couple of weeks ago."

"Good work," said Griffin, looking at Pepper with more interest. "The Yankees won't love you for that, son. I hear McGrigg's escaped, and he's a mean customer. Don't let him catch you."

"Not if I can help it," Pepper answered.

"Heard anything suspicious over yonder, Thad?" inquired Mosby.

"Nope, everything's been quiet."

"Fine," said the scout. "I'll just get my special Yankee picket-passer, and then we'll be on our way."

Mosby fumbled for a moment under the buggy seat, taking out a small package which he slipped into his coat pocket.

"You take care of the horse, Thad. Come on, Pepper, let's go."

With the boy at his heels, Mosby turned and plunged into the darkness. The country was covered with timber and thickly overgrown with underbrush. Walking was difficult. Pepper stumbled blindly along through the dark, tripping over tree roots and scratched by bushes and brambles. It was hard work keeping his sure-footed companion in sight.

At last Mosby crouched suddenly and pulled Pepper down beside him.

"Careful," cautioned the man. "There are Yankee pickets right ahead. Look sharp and you can see their fires."

Sure enough, when Pepper strained his eyes through the darkness, he caught the faint glow of a watch fire. Off to the right was another one and to the left were three more. The boy's heart jumped alarmingly when he realized that he and Mosby were right in the midst of a line of Yankee outposts. One false move and the entire picket line would be drawn upon them.

"Here's where we use my special Yankee picket-passer," whispered Mosby, reaching in his pocket.

Pepper wondered vaguely what such an instrument might be. He visionized all sorts of ingenious devices.

"What is it?" he whispered.

"Here it is," Mosby answered, busily unwrapping a small object. "Do you want to feel it?"

Gingerly Pepper reached over and fingered a small metal object.

"Why," he gasped, "it feels like a cowbell."

"That's just what it is," his companion answered with a chuckle. "It's never yet failed to fool the Yankees. You see, we never could hope to creep through the darkness without making some sound. By hanging this bell around my neck and walking slowly through the underbrush, making a certain amount of noise, the Yankees think I'm just some Virginia cow out for an evening ramble."

The simple daring of the plan left Pepper speechless. He had never dreamed of walking directly through the Yankee lines, announcing his presence with a cowbell. But then, neither would the Yankees expect him to. The more he thought of the plan, the better he liked it.

"No wonder the Yankees call you 'Foxy John,' " he said in admiration.

Mosby slipped the bell around his neck and the two set off through the bushes, guiding themselves by the flickering beams of the Yankee watch fires to the right and left. Mosby's cowbell jangled merrily while bushes rustled and dry branches snapped under the feet of the Confederates. No Yankee took alarm.

Deeper and deeper they penetrated into the enemy's lines until the flickering watch fires disappeared in the darkness behind them.

"I'm glad that's over," sighed Pepper when he and Mosby sat down to rest at the edge of a thicket. "Every minute I expected a Yankee to get suspicious and start looking for the cow."

"At this time of night the pickets are much too sleepy to be very curious," answered Mosby, removing the bell from his neck, wrapping it and replacing it in his coat pocket. "That was the easiest part of the trip, Pepper, because we knew just where the pickets were. Now that we're behind the enemy's lines we've got to be careful."

Far off somewhere in the darkness a rooster crowed.

"What are we going to do when it gets light?" the boy asked.

"We'll have to hide. Some of the Yankee scouts know me and they may recognize that Indian jacket of yours. We can't take any chances yet."

Pepper could not control the involuntary question that rose to his lips. "Where are we going to hide?"

"I know a fine hiding place a little farther on. We'll have to move fast if we want to get there before daybreak."

The two scouts plunged on over plowed fields and bushy pastures. Now they threaded their way carefully between slender pine trunks in timbered woodlands, now they dashed swiftly across cleared plots. The hush that precedes the dawn gave way to a myriad of sounds. Birds began to chirp, roosters held crowing choruses, and cattle lowed at pasture gates. Dewy grass and bushes sparkled in the first rays of the rising sun.

"We're almost there," whispered Mosby as they scrambled down a rock-strewn hillside toward a stony little brook at the bottom.

Reaching the brook bank, the scout turned sharply to the left, following the rippling waters to a place where they had worn a miniature gorge through the valley.

Mosby walked carefully along the edge of the brook, feeling his way over the mossy stones and taking pains to leave no footprints on the soft bank. Suddenly he stooped, pushed aside a clump of alder bushes and disappeared. Pepper blinked in surprise.

A moment later Mosby's head appeared among the leaves. "Here's your hiding place, Pepper. Hop in quick!"

The boy pushed through the bushes and found himself in a snug little cave formed by an overhanging rock on the brook side. The smoothly rounded walls showed that the rushing waters of the stream had worn away the tight little hollow during flood times.

"I used to come here often when I was a youngster," said Mosby, sensing Pepper's question. "Found it myself and never told anyone about it."

"It certainly is the best hiding place I've ever seen," Pepper stated admiringly. "What shall we do now?"

"First of all, we'll get some sleep. We can't do any prowling until sundown, and we have a busy time ahead of us. Just curl up, Pepper, and make yourself comfortable."

Suiting his actions to his words, John Mosby was already stretching out on the smooth sand floor. Pepper was not slow in following his example.

"I wonder if Sunstar misses me?" Pepper whispered to himself as he was falling asleep. "I hope Salt takes good care of him."

CHAPTER SEVEN

In the Camp of the Enemy

A LONG thin streamer of sunlight pierced the screen of bushes that hid the little cave. The sunbeam crept slowly across the floor until it fell on Pepper's face. The boy awoke with a start, sat up and blinked his eyes in the effort to remember where he was.

"Have a nice nap?" asked a voice, and Pepper turned to see John Mosby grinning at him across the cave.

"Just fine." The boy grinned back. "Is it time to start?"

"Not yet," replied Mosby. "We'd better wait until sunset. How about a bite to eat while we're waiting?"

"Sounds good," Pepper said, rubbing his chin thoughtfully. "I didn't know we had any rations along."

"Take a look at this," the scout advised, pulling a bundle from one of the pockets of his old blue homespun coat. He spread out corn pone, bully beef, and dried apples. "It's not exactly a banquet, but fall to, Pepper."

They ate in silence for a time. Finally the boy had to voice the thoughts that had been running through his head.

"I never thought we could cross the Yankee lines so easily," he said as he turned a piece of corn pone in his hand and stared at it before he popped it into his mouth. "They didn't even suspect us."

"No, Pepper," replied Mosby. "Most people don't realize how easy it is to get through the lines. And remember, what two can do, a lot more can do, also."

"What do you mean, John?"

"Well, it has always been a theory of mine that a resolute band of men, like the ones who ride with Jeb Stuart, could dash across the lines at night and make a lot of trouble for the Union forces."

"How?"

"They could cut telegraph wires, tear up railroads, burn bridges, destroy supply trains, snatch prisoners and horses. Then they could ride away before the enemy could get together a force to stop them."

"That wouldn't be playing the game according to the rules, would it?" asked Pepper.

Mosby laughed.

"Pepper, there aren't any rules to the war game. It's just dog eat dog—and the strongest and meanest dog wins. You've never seen a real battle with artillery and explosive shells or you'd understand what I mean. The Yankees far outnumber us in men and supplies, but if the War Department would let me try my scheme their numbers would be a hindrance instead of a help."

"Tell me more about your plan," urged the boy.

"There isn't much more to it. Why, we could even break into Washington before 'Little Mac' could get under way to stop us. We'd keep the Yankees so upset they'd soon howl for peace."

"That certainly would be a queer kind of war," Pepper said.

"This is a queer kind of war we're fighting now. Brother against brother, father against son, families divided. And it's so senseless. Most of them haven't a ghost of an idea what they are fighting for."

"Oh, that can't be!" protested the boy. "We Southerners are all fighting for a great cause."

"Is that so?" smiled the scout. "Just what is this cause, Pepper? Why are you fighting?"

"Why, because—" Pepper began, then stopped in surprise. "I'm fighting because the Yankees have invaded the South, and some of them are trying to make our Negro slaves revolt."

"Hmmm," said Mosby. "And why was the South invaded? What started all the trouble?"

Pepper scratched his head.

"I'm not sure," he admitted slowly. "Something about secession and states' rights, but I never understood much about them."

"Neither do most people. Before the war I was a lawyer, and I tried to keep track of things that were going on. For a good many years the North and the South have been drifting apart. The North has turned its energies to manufacturing and business, while the South has continued to be a land of farms and plantations. The North wants a high tariff to protect its factories, and the South wants a low tariff so it can trade the cotton and raw material it raises for foreign goods. It's just a matter of dollars, after all."

"You mean we're fighting about things like that!" exclaimed Pepper. "Why, there's no glory in such a war!"

"No, I reckon not, but such prosy things are the true causes of the war, just the same. Of course, few people realize that. Most Southerners believe they are fighting to protect their homes from the cruel invader, and the Yankees have been led to think that they are fighting to save the Negro slaves from brutal and inhuman masters."

"But our slaves aren't mistreated. Every Negro I know is well cared for and happy," objected Pepper.

"Sure, most of them are. But just try to make the Yankees believe that. Well, it's quite dark now so I think we'd better be moving."

Quickly the scouts gathered their few belongings.

Mosby replaced the rest of the food in his pocket and crept outside, with Pepper close at his heels.

"We'll keep on until we find a camp where we can learn something," said Mosby. "We're far enough inside the lines so the Yankees won't be suspicious. Just act as if you belong here and no one will dream that you are not a native. Fortunately this is border country and your Virginia drawl is not broadly southern. Lots of Yankees talk like you do."

Mosby led the way across the valley until he came to a well-traveled road leading northeast. Darkness had already closed in and the country seemed deserted.

"This is the Mechanicsville pike that leads straight into 'Little Mac's' headquarters," Mosby explained. "We'll follow it and see what we can find out."

"Is there anything special you want me to do?"

"No, just pick up all the information that you can. Pretend you live around here and are thinking of joining the army. Here's some Yankee money in case you need it."

Pepper pocketed the silver coins and the two scouts trudged onward. Out of the silence behind them came the sound of galloping hoofs, coming nearer and nearer on the hard-packed bed of the road.

"Watch this now, Pepper," whispered Mosby, pulling the boy to the edge of the road, and then taking a stand toward the center of the trail.

"Halt! Who goes there?" he demanded in a loud voice as the horseman bore down on him.

The rider swerved and pulled his panting horse to a standstill. In the darkness Mosby's blue homespun looked very much like a Federal uniform and the rider suspected nothing.

"A messenger with papers for General Porter," panted the courier. "It's urgent."

"Give the password," commanded Mosby.

"The Union forever," answered the rider.

"Pass on," said Mosby, stepping aside as the Yankee messenger spurred his horse away and disappeared in the darkness.

"There now, we have the Yankee password," said the scout triumphantly as he rejoined Pepper. "I thought we could get it that way, and it's a handy thing to have when you're wandering around the enemy's lines in the dark."

"Whew!" marveled Pepper. "I thought that man would be sure to recognize you."

"It's bluff that counts most of the time," explained Mosby as they tramped down the road. "Have you ever heard the story about the time Jeb Stuart fooled a squad of Yankees?"

"No, how did he do it?"

"It was last fall, just after the battle of Manassas. Stuart was out riding alone when he came upon a squad of bluecoats in a grove. The day was chilly and Jeb had his old blue army overcoat thrown over his gray uniform. When he spied those Yankees he did a bit of fast thinking."

"He'd have to," observed Pepper.

"Quick as a wink Jeb called, 'Squad! Atten—shun! Tear down that fence so my cavalry can get through.' "

"What did the Yankees do?"

Mosby laughed.

"What could they do but salute and start to work on the fence? While they were busy, Stuart rode calmly away and got back to his own lines. The squad never knew anything was wrong, and that very night Jeb led a raid right through the place where they had torn down the fence for him."

Pepper laughed softly.

"You were right, John. This is a queer kind of a war. I wonder whether I could think that fast if I got caught in a tight place."

"You'll have to if you want to be a real scout," Mosby replied.

After walking an hour or so, they saw the lights of Mechanicsville twinkling ahead. Pepper gulped and his heart sank down to his toes when he thought of walking into a town that was filled with Federal soldiers. He was getting accustomed to roaming through enemy territory, but the thought of meeting so many Yankees face to face made his scalp prickle and little cold chills chased one another up and down his spine.

"Remember now," he heard Mosby saying, "just act natural and no one will suspect you."

Pepper nodded wordlessly, unable to trust his voice for fear it would reveal how scared he was.

By this time they had passed the dim outskirts and were strolling unconcernedly down the main street of

Mechanicsville. Union troops roamed through the streets and loafed at the corners. Smartly uniformed Federal officers sat on the broad front porches and visited with the townspeople. Everything seemed bright and gay. Except that the uniforms were blue instead of gray, Pepper could easily have imagined himself behind Confederate lines. Never before had he realized how truly brother was fighting brother in this war.

"I'm going to stop and visit a while with them," whispered Mosby, nodding toward a group of soldiers loafing around the general store. "You stroll on and keep you eyes open. If we get separated, I'll meet you here before noon tomorrow."

Pepper nodded and walked slowly on, wishing that his heart would stop thumping so madly under his doeskin jacket.

"Hullo, Indian, where's the powwow?" called a jovial Yankee private.

"Down the road a ways," answered Pepper, hoping his voice sounded natural.

"Looks like he fell out of a medicine show," laughed a red-bearded soldier who reminded Pepper of Lieutenant Hagan back in Stuart's camp, even to the slow drawl of the Southerner.

"Maybe I did," retorted the boy, surprised to find how easy it was to bandy words with the enemy. "Would you like to buy a bottle of liniment?"

The Yankees burst into roars of laughter.

"Sonny, you'd better take your liniment over to the rebel line," said one of the bluecoats. "They'll need it more than we will after we get through with them this time."

Pepper pricked up his ears. Here was news! The Yankees were planning an attack and he must find out more about it.

"Tell me where to find the rebels, and I'll try to drum up some business," he said jokingly.

Before the soldiers could reply, the high, clear notes of a bugle came echoing through the town.

"Call to quarters," grumbled the red-beard. "And the night's scarcely begun."

"Stay out of the army, sonny," advised another soldier as the group moved away. "Keep on sellin' your liniment. You can be your own boss and won't have to go to bed when Pappy McClellan tells you to."

Pepper stood and watched the Yankees disappear. The streets were filled with blue-coated soldiers returning to quarters for the night.

"If that bugler had only waited a couple more minutes, I'd have picked up some valuable information," he mourned. "Something's being planned, but now I'll have to start all over again to find out what it is."

The boy looked around him. Most of the soldiers had already disappeared and the streets were nearly deserted. Lights in homes were blinking out, one by one, and the town was soon lost in darkness. Mosby was nowhere in sight. Pepper scratched his head.

"I can't stay out here in the dark," he told himself. "I might make the Yankee guard suspicious. Now where shall I spend the night?"

He followed the street to the edge of town. Through the gloom his eyes could just make out the rounded outlines of a haystack standing just beyond the snake fence that edged the road.

"There's just the place for me," the boy thought as he climbed over the bars and crawled into the warm, fragrant hay. In a few minutes he was fast asleep.

CHAPTER EIGHT
Pepper Finds a Yankee Friend

A HORSE snorted suddenly.

"Come on now, Cricket, old boy. Why don't you help yourself to the hay?" a voice asked.

Pepper opened sleepy eyes, blinked, and then popped a tousled head out of the haystack to see what was going on. The sun was shining brightly and Pepper squinted owlishly in the glare. He saw a blue-uniformed boy of about his own age standing near by, holding the reins of a great bay horse.

Pepper's heart did a flip-flop of surprise before he

remembered where he was, and what he was supposed to be doing.

The other boy grinned. He had a round pleasant face, topped by a mop of fiery red hair. His snub nose was thickly sprinkled with freckles.

"Hullo," he said. "Sorry if I woke you up. I was trying to persuade Cricket to have some breakfast, but I guess he smelled you and was nervous."

Pepper smiled back, relieved that the boy was not suspicious.

"Glad you woke me," he said. "And I'm sorry if I frightened your horse. Does this hay belong to you? I had to sleep somewhere last night and this stack looked mighty comfortable and inviting."

"It's a stack of forage for Major Rush's Pennsylvania Lancers," replied the Yankee boy. "I guess sleeping in it didn't hurt it any. Who are you, and why did you have to sleep out here?"

Pepper crawled out of the haystack and brushed the bits of dry grass from his clothing. Vaguely he wondered how much truth he could put into his tale without giving himself away. He had little confidence in his ability to tell a convincing lie.

"My name's Potter Pepperill," he answered, "but most folks call me Pepper. I live over in the next county and I came here to see the soldiers. I've heard a lot about McClellan's Army of the Potomac, so I decided to take a look at it myself. Stayed longer than I expected to, and I had to sleep somewhere."

"McClellan's army is worth looking at," agreed the other boy, "no wonder you stayed longer than you figured on."

"Nice horse you have there," remarked Pepper. "He looks like a thoroughbred. I've got a black horse named Sunstar."

The Yankee boy smiled and stroked the bay's glossy flank.

"Cricket is a mighty fine horse and a real thorough-bred. Took two blue ribbons at the Crawford County Fair last year. My captain says he's the best horse in the company."

"He sure looks it," said Pepper. "What's your name, and is your company camped around here?"

"My name is Stephen Reynolds, and I'm at loose ends just now waiting for my outfit to come back from chasing that crazy rebel Jeb Stuart. I was off on courier duty when they were ordered out after him."

Pepper could scarcely repress a smile at that. He had an idea that the chasing was the other way around.

"What do you do in the army?" he asked. "Do they keep you very busy? I was sort of thinking of joining up."

"Say, that would be fine," Stephen said, unbuckling his wallet from the saddle and sitting down on the grass. "Come on, have some breakfast with me and we can talk. I wish you would join my company because I'm the youngest man in it and it's hard to make friends with the older men."

With a queer feeling of guilt in his heart, Pepper sat down. For some reason he hated to take advantage of this boy. Yankee though he was, Pepper felt that Stephen and he could be friends just as he and Salt were. But, on account of the war, they had to be bitter enemies.

Meanwhile the Yankee was spreading out his breakfast rations and Pepper's eyes fairly bulged at the sight. Stuart's riders never had such food as that.

But Stephen apologized. "Sorry this is all I've got. I left in a hurry and didn't have time to go around to the quartermaster to get my proper rations."

"Looks mighty good to me," answered Pepper. "Sleeping in that haystack has given me an appetite. Where do you come from, Stephen?"

"My home is in western Pennsylvania, over near the Ohio border. I joined the Lancers a couple of months ago—as soon as they'd take me. I'm only sixteen, but I told them I was eighteen. You can do that, too, if you decide to enlist."

"What made you want to join?" Pepper asked curiously, remembering what Mosby had told him the evening before.

"I want to do my part in freeing the slaves," the Yankee boy said earnestly. "I can't enjoy American liberty and justice myself while black men are being held in slavery."

"That sounds like something out of a book," exclaimed Pepper scornfully. "Where did you read such trash?"

"I read it in Harriet Beecher Stowe's book called *Uncle Tom's Cabin.*"

"I thought so," Pepper snorted. "Slaves aren't mistreated in the South."

"Oh, yes, they are," the Yankee boy broke in. "I went to New Orleans once with my father and I saw slaves sold on the auction block, just like cattle. One old Negro woman was being separated from her daughter and I'll never forget how she cried and carried on."

This was a new thought for Pepper and he didn't know just how to answer. The dark side of slavery had never occurred to him. He knew that Uncle 'Lije and all the other Negroes on the Magnolia Hill plantation were happy, contented and carefree. Judge Cromartie never sold his slaves.

"The overseers carry big whips and beat the poor Negroes," Stephen continued. "They abuse 'em something awful."

"No, they don't," Pepper contradicted. "They'd be crazy to do that. Even if a master wasn't friends with his slaves, he wouldn't mistreat 'em any more than he'd mistreat a valuable horse or any other piece of property. Any slave's worth a couple hundred dollars and a good one represents at least a thousand-dollar investment."

"That's a funny way to talk about human beings," Stephen retorted. "I think every man has a right to freedom and happiness. Slavery is a terrible thing."

Pepper drew a deep breath.

"It's all too mixed up for my poor brain. Don't you

reckon people in the South have something to say? After all, the Union army has invaded Virginia."

"Say, you seem to know a lot about the rebels," remarked Stephen.

Pepper's heart skipped a beat.

"Living between the lines like I do, I hear a lot from both sides," he said calmly enough. "And I've spent a lot of time on my uncle's plantation down in lower Virginia. Just yesterday a man told me that the North and South are really fighting about business and industry. He said that the thing narrows down to whether there is a high tariff to protect factories in the North, or a low tariff so the South can trade its cotton and tobacco for foreign goods. Really a matter of dollars."

"Tariff!" snorted Stephen. "That's crazy. Who would fight about a thing like that? It's ideals we're fighting for, and freedom for all people."

While they were talking the boys finished breakfast and Stephen stowed the remains away in his knapsack. The horse, Cricket, had also eaten his fill of the hay.

"I've got to go now," Stephen said. "McClellan's whole army is on the move and I have to report to headquarters. Want to come along?"

Pepper pricked up his ears. Here was news that Stuart should know as soon as possible.

"No, thanks," he answered as Stephen swung into his saddle. "I'll have to go back home and tell my folks. I'll join you later, maybe, if you'll tell me where to look for you."

"You can inquire for Major Rush's Pennsylvania Lancers, and I'll be looking for you. I want you in my company. We can have grand times together. Good-by!"

Pepper stood waving his hat to Stephen as the Yankee boy rode away.

"Yes," he said to himself, "Stephen and I probably could have grand times together, but we're on different sides. It sure is a funny war."

Slowly and thoughtfully Pepper made his way back into town. If McClellan was on the move Stuart and Lee should hear of it. But first he must find Mosby and ask for further instructions.

There was a strange stir in the air as Pepper walked down the main street of the little town. The blue soldiers seemed more alert and the very houses wore a tense air of expectant waiting.

"I wonder what's the matter," thought Pepper as he strolled slowly along, hoping to catch sight of Mosby.

The morning passed slowly for the anxious boy. Loafing is one of the hardest jobs in the world, especially when one knows that the lives and safety of others depend upon him. For a long time Pepper forced himself to sit calmly on the steps of the Mechanicsville general store. To the casual observer, the boy seemed half asleep. His whole attitude was one of relaxed detachment. Little that went on, however, escaped Pepper's watchful, half-closed gray eyes.

The warm June sun rose higher and higher, bathing the country in golden light. A soft breeze sprang up, blowing gently from the west. On that gentle breeze was carried a sound that made Pepper's scalp prickle. Faintly, but surely, that breeze brought the sound of guns, of cannon roaring in battle. Where? Who? Pepper nearly forgot himself in his eagerness to know what was happening.

The Mechanicsville citizens and the Yankee soldiers heard the sounds, too. Civilians gathered on the steps of the general store to talk, and Union orderlies hurried past with worried looks. The soldiers in blue had learned to have great respect for rebel guns during the first year of the war.

Someone sat down beside him and Pepper glanced up with a start to find John Mosby grinning at him.

"Hello, son," said the scout, loud enough for the people around to hear him. "Sounds like the rebels are starting monkey business again."

"It sure does," replied the boy. "I wonder what the trouble is."

"Oh, just some more rebel foolishness. Looks like they won't be satisfied until McClellan gives them a real good licking."

The two scouts sat side by side on the steps, talking idly and listening to the faint, far-off sound of gunfire. Gradually Mosby lowered his voice. The people around were too busy to notice the shabbily dressed man and the boy in the Indian jacket who sat talking quietly on the steps.

"Those must be Stonewall Jackson's guns," Mosby whispered. "His camp lies off in that direction. They sound pretty far away, though."

"Did you hear about McClellan moving his army?" Pepper asked anxiously. "Won't that make some change in Lee's plans?"

"Yes, I heard about it last night. Our army must know as soon as possible. 'Little Mac' has already changed his base and moved his headquarters away from this town."

"Where is our nearest post?" Pepper wanted to know.

"Well, if these guns mean that Lee is advancing, A. P. Hill's men should be just across the Chickahominy. They were to attack the Yankee headquarters. You see, Stuart outlined the plan for me before I left. But I didn't think it would come so soon."

"What shall we do?"

"I've got some special information for Stuart," Mosby answered, tossing a crumpled tobacco wrapper on the ground. "Pick that up after I'm gone—my report is written inside. I'll go on to Washington. You stick with the Yankees as long as you can and then join Stuart at White House Landing. He should be there tomorrow."

"All right," Pepper nodded. "Good luck."

"Thanks, sonny," Mosby raised his voice again. "Give my regards to your pappy and come to see us when you can."

The scout rose and slouched away while Pepper remained on the steps, wondering how he was going to follow Mosby's instructions.

He did not have to wonder long.

Suddenly a great burst of sound roared up from

across the river. Cannon balls whistled in the distance
and Federal bugles blew the alarm. A. P. Hill's troops
were attacking.

The crowd in front of the general store disappeared
as if by magic. Stopping only to snatch Mosby's tobacco
wrapper, Pepper followed the rush of blue-coated men
as they ran back to their earthworks east of Mechanicsville.

Scarcely ten minutes behind them A. P. Hill's bat-
teries galloped through the empty street, unlimbered in
the fields east of town and opened the attack on the
strongly intrenched Union lines.

Pepper, who was well behind the Federal lines by this
time, looked around in bewilderment. He had no idea
what to do next.

"Where are headquarters?" he called to a courier
who cantered past.

The man waved his arm vaguely toward the east.

Musket balls and shell fragments were beginning to
spatter overhead and suddenly Pepper saw the Yankee
courier sway limply in his saddle. Feeling the reins go
slack, the courier's horse slowed to a walk. Heedless of
his own danger, Pepper ran forward, caught the dragging bridle, and led the horse behind the shelter of some
trees. Gently he aided the wounded man to dismount.

A dark stain was gathering on the courier's blue
jacket. Blood ran down his sleeve and trickled in great
scarlet drops from the fingers of his right hand.

As well as he could, the boy staunched the flow of

blood, tearing strips from the courier's shirt to bind up
the bleeding wound in his shoulder.

"You'll be all right until the hospital squad comes,"
Pepper said, shouting so that his voice could be heard
over the roar of the battle.

Feebly the soldier raised his head and Pepper bent to
catch his whispered words. With his ear almost at the
wounded man's lips, Pepper heard him gasp, "Dispatches . . . take . . . General Porter." The Yankee
dragged a packet of neatly wrapped papers from his
pocket. Then he fainted.

Pepper made the unconscious courier as comfortable
as possible before taking the dispatches. Swinging himself into the saddle, the boy rode east, keeping watch for
some one who could help the injured man. Not far away
he saw a stretcher squad, already busy. The boy shouted
directions to them, pointing the way to the wounded
courier. The squad leader nodded and Pepper galloped
away.

The crash and roar of battle were left farther behind.
Only now and then a spent ball tore its way through the
underbrush, coming to rest with a dull thud against a
tree. Pepper slowed his horse to a canter along the woodland trail while he decided what to do next.

"I certainly am not going to deliver these dispatches
to General Porter," he told himself. "I'll deliver them to
General Lee instead. In the meantime they will be a
good excuse to get me through the Yankee lines."

As the boy rode on through the afternoon he met long

files of blue-clad troops marching to reinforce the Federal lines. To all their challenges Pepper called, "Special dispatches for General Porter," and waved the papers importantly. Not a single Union soldier suspected him or tried to stop him. As afternoon grew into evening the noise of battle died out in the distance.

Night was closing in when gnawing pangs in Pepper's stomach reminded the boy that he had not eaten anything since early morning. Enemy territory stretched all around him and although he had been lucky so far, he dared not risk turning up at a Yankee camp for rations.

"Let's see," he said to himself, "Stephen carried his rations strapped to his saddle. Maybe this courier did the same."

A careful search of the saddlebags did not reveal a single thing to eat. Pepper grew hungrier and hungrier.

"This will never do," he said, pulling his belt a notch tighter. "I'll have to feed and rest the horse, anyway."

He rode slowly on through the darkness. Suddenly, as he rounded a bend in the trail, he saw a fire flickering ahead.

"Halt!" ordered a sharp voice. "Who goes there?"

"A friend," Pepper answered. "I have dispatches for General Porter, but I've lost my way in the dark."

"What's the password?"

Pepper racked his brains trying to remember the password that Mosby had learned the night before. Ha, he had it! "The Union forever," he said, hoping that it had not been changed in the meantime.

"Come over to the light where I can see you," ordered the voice, and a hand reached out from the darkness and took hold of his horse's bridle.

"You're a funny looking courier," remarked the picket as the firelight fell on Pepper's jacket. "What do you mean by giving last night's password? Don't you know it's been changed?"

"I was afraid of that," said Pepper quite honestly. " 'The Union forever' was the password when I started out. I've been lost and I had to make a detour to get around the battle at Mechanicsville. That's the reason I'm wandering around trying to find headquarters."

"Sure, and it must be truth that the b'y is speakin'," said a big red-faced soldier who was sitting on the other side of the fire. "Don't ye go bein' too hard wi' him, buddy."

"All right, Pat," growled the sentry. "But it looks queer to-me."

"Can you tell me where I am and how I can find General Porter?" Pepper asked, looking over at the big, kindly Irishman. "I'm tired and I haven't had a bite to eat since morning."

"Ye're five mile' northwest of White House Landing," replied the gruff sentry. "General Porter's headquarters are on the Williamsburg pike."

"Sure and ye can light down long enough to take a bite wi' us, can't you, me b'y?" asked Pat. "Ye can tell us how the battle went."

"All right," said Pepper, dismounting. And while he shared their rations, the Confederate scout told the

Union sentries all he knew about the battle at Mechanics-ville.

It was well past midnight when Pepper again mounted his horse and said good-by to the Yankee sentries.

"Follow the trail for half a mile and then take the right-hand fork for the Williamsburg pike. The left fork goes to White House Landing," the blue-coated sentries told him.

The boy cantered slowly on, grinning to himself when he took the left-hand fork. General Porter would never receive his dispatches if Pepper got free of the Union lines.

The little used trail was dark and deserted and Pepper rode slowly, sparing his tired horse as much as possible. Awed by the stillness, he strained eyes and ears to pierce the darkness.

Suddenly the deep silence was shattered by a thunder-ous roar. Pepper could feel the ground tremble under him and red flames licked up into the sky ahead. He checked his horse in alarm and waited. A few minutes later a second explosion rumbled through the stillness. The deep silence that followed each burst of sound was breath-taking.

"That can't be cannon," Pepper told himself. "No cannon in the world ever made such a noise."

Spurred on by this thought the boy rode rapidly for-ward again. At gradually lengthening intervals the night silence was split asunder by tremendous roars which grew louder as Pepper neared White House Landing.

At last he paused on a hilltop and looked down over the open country toward the place where White House Landing stood on the banks of the winding York River. A dull red glow from burning buildings illuminated the night sky. In this terrible radiance Pepper could see blue-clad soldiers scurrying about. As he watched, a tremendous sheet of white flame shot into the air, to be followed a second or two later by another ground-shaking roar.

"An ammunition dump explosion," Pepper thought. "The Yankees are destroying their supplies before they retreat."

All the rest of the night Pepper remained on the hilltop watching the Union soldiers at work. Just before daylight he saw the last of the blue column ride northward, leaving behind nearly two miles of smoldering dumps and charred Federal supplies.

As soon as the Yankees had disappeared in the distance, Pepper mounted his horse and trotted cautiously toward the deserted town. The sun was just rising as he rode along a smoke-filled street and came face to face with a gray cavalry troop advancing from the south.

"Halt!" shouted the gray riders.

"Don't shoot!" Pepper called, urging his horse forward. "I'm a friend."

"Well, comb my whiskers, if it isn't the wild Indian again," exclaimed a well-known voice as Lieutenant Hagan recognized the boy's gay jacket. "Where did you pop up from, youngster?"

"I've come from Mechanicsville and I have some dispatches for General Stuart," Pepper retorted. "Where is he?"

"Over yonder."

Hagan waved to where Stuart sat on Skylark, stroking his beard and gazing reflectively at the smoldering ruins.

Pepper spurred toward the General.

"Good morning, sir," he said, dismounting and saluting. "I just came through the Union lines from Mechanicsville with a report from Mosby. I also have some Yankee dispatches that were intended for General Porter."

"Good work." Stuart opened the papers and glanced through them with a twinkle in his eye. "I'll see that these reach General Lee as soon as possible. Mosby has sent some valuable information and I congratulate you both on the good work you have done."

"Thank you, sir." Pepper saluted again and turned away.

"Pepper! Hi, how are you?" Salt's welcoming shout rang out in the still morning air. "When did you get back, you old buzzard?"

Even Stuart smiled as the two boys greeted each other noisily and then rode off together.

"Say, Pepper," Salt said, after hearing all about his friend's adventures, "you've been inside the Yankee lines so long you must feel like one yourself. Any danger of your going over?"

"Not a chance," laughed Pepper. "I'm still a rebel."

He was silent for a minute, then he continued.

"You know, Salt, some of those Yankees seem like mighty fine folks, just the same."

"I reckon so," was the answer. "Too bad they have to be fightin' us. Say, where did you get that horse?"

"I borrowed him from a Yankee courier who was wounded at Mechanicsville. How's Sunstar?"

"Fine, but I think he misses you. We left him in camp when we started on this raid."

"I can scarcely wait to ride Sunstar again," Pepper told Salt as they dismounted to explore a half-burned Federal storehouse. "This Yankee horse is just a nag compared to him. How much longer do you think this raid will last?"

"There's no telling," answered Salt.

The Seven Days' Battle around Richmond was on, and the cavalry was kept on constant duty. For nearly a week the gray-clad raiders galloped from place to place on the York and Chickahominy rivers, snatching surprised Union soldiers, raiding supply trains, and throwing out screens of sabers and carbine fire to protect the advancing Confederate infantry.

All this time the spirited black Sunstar pawed the floor of his stable with impatient hoofs, while his young master followed Jeb Stuart's plume on a captured Yankee horse.

CHAPTER NINE
Jeb Stuart Loses His Plumed Hat

JULY was full of activity for Stuart's hardy troopers. Union Major General John Pope had been appointed chief of staff for the army in blue and his energetic pushes kept the gray cavalry busy. Blue raiders appeared in parts of Virginia where they had never been seen before. Stuart galloped to meet them and the rattle of carbine fire and the clash of sabers sounded from many a peaceful Virginia highway.

"It is wonderful the way men admire the General," Pepper said one night to John Mosby. The two scouts sat looking across the starlit camp toward the bright bonfire where General Stuart was playing with his two children, Flora and Jemmie, while his wife watched them with a tender smile on her lips. It was during one of his family's rare visits to camp and Stuart was making the most of the brief hours he could spend with his loved ones.

"When are you starting for Washington, John?" continued Pepper.

"Pretty soon, now, but first I'm going down to Richmond. That's why I stopped in tonight, Pepper. I came to say good-by. Wish you were coming along again."

"So do I. But you know, John, the more I see of the Yankees, the harder it is for me to hate them—even if they are our enemies."

"Yes, I've found it that way, too," agreed the scout, "and I hope the feeling will continue. Up to this time both sides have shown a lot of chivalry and kindness to people who are not connected with the war. Now Pope is beginning to seize hostages. He mistreats civilians and takes his supplies from farmers without paying for them. That's the way savages carry on warfare. It's bound to bring more bitterness into this war, and I'm frank to say that I don't like the looks of it."

"What do you mean, John?"

"Well, of course, fighting men are expected to take certain risks. They make the war and they stop the lead.

But women and children, and old men and people who are not active in the fighting should all be respected and cared for by both sides."

Pepper nodded slowly, without saying anything. The two scouts sat in silence for some minutes, then Mosby rose.

"Time to say good-by, Pepper," he said, holding out his hand.

"Good-by, John, and good luck." Pepper stood up and grasped his friend's hand. "How long will you be gone?"

"Not more than a couple of weeks. I'll be back before the middle of August."

The sandy-haired scout turned abruptly away. Pepper watched him until the slim figure disappeared in the shadows.

"He's a soldier and a gentleman, and I believe he really hates this war," the boy told himself.

After a time Pepper turned toward the tent he shared with Salt. His young companion was already sleeping, tired out by a long day in the saddle. Pepper pulled off his jacket and boots and tumbled into his blankets.

A bull-like roar snatched Pepper out of dreamland. Breathless he sat up and listened. Bellow after bellow sounded from the darkness close by.

"What's wrong?" demanded Salt, who also had been awakened by the tumult.

"Listen!" replied Pepper.

Strange guttural foreign words were intermingled with the bellows. "*Vas ist das? Eine Schlange! Gott in Himmel!*" roared the voice.

"It's von Borcke! Let's go see what's wrong."

The boys yanked on their boots and ran outside where a crowd was gathering. Laughter and delighted applause from the spectators mingled with the yells of the big Prussian.

Pushing their way to the front, Salt and Pepper saw a ludicrous sight. Someone had tossed fresh wood on the campfire and its eerie glow fell on the gigantic Prussian dragoon. Shirtless and barefooted, he was capering wildly around his rumpled blankets. He swung his great sword in flashing circles and continued to bellow at the top of his voice.

"Get him, Major," urged one aide.

"Chop him up," advised another.

While Salt and Pepper were craning their necks to discover the cause of all the disturbance, Stuart joined the group.

"What's the trouble, Major?" the General asked, his eyes twinkling at the Prussian's quaint appearance.

"Matter!" gasped the dragoon, continuing to caper and wave his sword. "*Himmel Gott!* Serpents! Monsters! Look vat I haff in bett schleeping mit me found!"

Poking gingerly among the blankets with his sword, the Prussian uncovered a large Virginia diamond-back rattler. The snake was coiled snugly, apparently enjoying the warmth of the blankets. When the cover was removed it raised its wedge-shaped head and hissed angrily. At the same time the rattles on its tail whirred a sharp warning.

The sight seemed to send von Borcke into a towering rage.

"You vill mit me schleep, *hein?*" he shouted. "Whedder I ask you or not, you sneak into *mein* blankets and maybe try to bite me. I fix dot!"

The heavy sword fell with a crash on the snake. Again and again it flashed through the air, accompanied by the delighted applause of Stuart and his aides. Not until the big snake was literally chopped to mincemeat would the dragoon stop.

At last, still snorting angrily, von Borcke went off to bunk with Captain Farley and quiet again fell on the camp.

"Whew," remarked Pepper as he and Salt returned to their blankets. "The Major looked mighty funny, but I'd sure hate to get in the way of that sword of his."

"Me, too," agreed Salt. "Say, Pepper, do you reckon that snake has a brother or a relative around here?"

"Nice time of night to think of that," grunted Pepper. "Go back to sleep before you think up something else."

Toward the end of the month Stuart was called to Richmond. When he returned to camp he wore the brand new jacket of a major general. Jeb Stuart now commanded all the cavalry in the Army of Northern Virginia.

July faded into August and Stuart kept his troopers busy. Lee and Jackson were on the march, ready to strike Pope and McClellan before the two Yankee generals could join forces. The thunder of cannon rolled up from Northern Virginia as Jackson and Pope clashed at Cedar Mountain.

It was the job of Stuart's men to cover the advance of the gray-clad soldiers, keeping the bluecoats puzzled as to "what that rebel Lee is up to now." Pepper and Sunstar galloped mile after mile over the Virginia hills, carrying messages that helped keep the Confederate advance in perfect timing.

The great black horse had greeted his master's return from the Union lines with delighted snorts and many nuzzlings. To the captured Yankee horse, the Confederate steed had bared his teeth and laid back his ears, ready for combat.

"I think he's jealous," marveled Sweeney. "I never saw anything to beat it."

"Sure he's jealous," replied Pepper, rewarding his pet with a stalk of sugar cane. "I'd be just as jealous if he let someone else ride him."

During the second week in August, John Mosby joined Stuart's staff and told a marvelous tale of how he had been captured by Yankee raiders while he was waiting for a train at Beaver Dam station.

"How did you manage to get away?" asked Pepper.

Mosby smiled.

"I was exchanged, but I learned a few things while I was gone. I'll tell you sometime, son," he answered. "I know this country too well to let the Yankees hold me very long."

On August sixteenth a courier dashed into camp, bearing special orders from Lee to Stuart. Jeb Stuart read them carefully, refolded them and returned them to their oilskin envelope. Then he handed them to his adjutant, Major Fitzhugh.

"Take care of these papers, Major," he said. "They give the details of Lee's newest plan of attack."

"Yes, sir," said the Major.

Turning to Pepper, who stood near by, the General continued. "Tell Major von Borcke, Captain Mosby, the Lieutenants Dabney and Gibson I want them ready to ride with me early tomorrow. Fitzhugh, you are to go, too."

"Yes, sir," said Pepper, "and may—?"

"Certainly, both you and Salt will come along."

"Thank you, sir. We'll be ready." Pepper saluted and hurried away to deliver his messages.

Next morning the little party set off eastward down the Orange Plank Road toward Raccoon Ford where they were to meet Fitz Lee and his brigade. Off to the west, beyond Clarke Mountain, lay John Pope's army; but none of the party gave it a thought. They felt as much at home between the lines as they did inside their own picket fires.

The little troop rode slowly, expecting any minute to contact Fitz Lee's brigade. All day they kept on but still they met no gray troopers. Stuart was both annoyed and worried. Robert E. Lee's plan demanded perfect timing for success. The cavalry dared not delay too long.

The day passed slowly. Morning grew into afternoon and afternoon faded into evening. At dusk Stuart and his staff reached Verdiersville, a tiny village on the Orange Plank Road.

"Good evening, gentlemen," the General said, touching his hat to a group of men in front of the general store. "Has a body of Confederate cavalry passed through here today?"

"No, sir," replied a gray-bearded farmer. "We ain't seen nary a soldier 'round here for 'most a week."

"Thank you." Stuart rode off with his staff at his heels.

At the edge of town he checked his horse in front of a deserted house set back some distance from the road and surrounded by a fence and a weed-filled garden.

"We will billet here for the night," the General said, reining Skylark through the rickety gate. "Major Fitzhugh, ride on and see if you can locate Fitz Lee."

The Major saluted and rode onward while the rest of the party settled themselves on the wide porch of the old house. The stars twinkled brightly in the August night sky as the five rationed themselves from their haversacks.

"Just listen to those cicadas," Salt remarked as the

shrill piping of the insects sounded out of the darkness nearby. A bullfrog in a distant marsh added his deep croak to the chorus and then, somewhere in the weedy garden, a mocking-bird sang its night song.

"It's beautiful," sighed Pepper. "It reminds me of the nights at Magnolia Hill, my uncle's plantation."

"Yes, it is beautiful," agreed General Stuart. "It's a real rest from the roar of cannon and the rattle of sabers."

The company sat silent for a time, listening. The soft, monotonous noises gradually lulled Pepper to sleep, his head nodding lower and lower. With an effort he jerked himself erect.

Stuart laughed and glanced around at his drowsy followers.

"Time to turn in," he said, removing his haversack and side arms.

"Is it not best with our weapons to sleep, here between the lines?" von Borcke asked anxiously.

"No, you'll sleep much easier without them," answered Lieutenant Gibson. "No Yankees have been seen around here for a week."

The big Prussian made no reply, but Pepper noticed that he did not remove his sword belt and equipment before rolling up in his cloak. With the others, Pepper stretched out on the edge of the porch, listening drowsily to the soft footsteps of the horses which had been left saddled but free to graze in the yard. Sunstar came quietly to the porch and rubbed his master's arm with a soft nose. In the darkness Sunstar was all but in-

visible, but Pepper stroked the glossy head for a time
before the horse moved away.

"Good night, old fellow," the boy whispered. "Just
make yourself comfortable until morning."

Early dawn brought the distant sound of cavalry approaching from the southeast. The little party shook
itself awake and listened.

"That probably is Fitz Lee at last," Stuart said.
"Mosby, take Salt and Pepper and ride out to make
sure."

The three quickly buckled on their side arms and
walked out in the yard to catch their horses. Bareheaded,
leaving his scarlet-lined riding cloak and his haversack
on the porch, Stuart strolled to the gate to watch. The
rest of the party remained on the porch.

Pepper swung himself into the saddle and, giving
Sunstar's shoulder a soft pat of greeting, rode out of
the yard. The Georgia boy and Mosby followed.

The road curved sharply just beyond the house and
the scouts soon lost sight of their companions. Side by
side they rode through the keen morning air. The thud
of approaching hoofs came nearer but the riders were
hidden behind another curve in the road.

"Be careful," advised Mosby. "Let's not take any
chances."

The words scarcely had been spoken when the first of
the riders came into sight around the bend. Blue uniforms shone in the early morning sunshine.

"Yankees!" Salt and Pepper exclaimed together.

"Come on!" Mosby yelled, wheeling his horse.

Followed by a hail of pistol shots and the yells of their pursuers, the three Confederates galloped back toward Verdiersville.

"Keep down," Mosby warned, shouting over his shoulder.

Bending low over their horses' necks, the scouts rounded the bend with the Yankees hard at their heels.

"Yankee cavalry!" they shouted to Stuart and his companions.

One look was enough. Stuart vaulted into Skylark's saddle, jumped the rickety fence and, leaving his plumed hat and his equipment on the porch, made off toward the woods. Von Borcke and Dabney scrambled to horse and followed, with Gibson close behind.

After warning the staff, the three scouts scattered. All made for the woods, each taking the route which seemed best and quickest. The Yankees were hot on their heels for a few yards, but soon the fleet southern thoroughbred steeds left the panting northern horses far behind. A Yankee bugle sounded "Recall" and the bluecoats assembled at the porch to view their prizes.

Stuart's party gathered in the woods, out of breath but safe. The General made a wry face as he watched the Yankees loot the gear he had abandoned. They waved his red-lined cloak triumphantly in the morning air and rifled his leather haversack. One Yankee tried on Stuart's famous plumed hat. To Stuart's chagrin, the soldier wore it away. Soon the bluecoats reformed and pounded away to the north.

"Look!" exclaimed Pepper, pointing to one gray rider in their midst. "Isn't that Major Fitzhugh?"

"Sure is," agreed Salt. "They've captured him."

"Lee's dispatches," mourned Stuart. "I gave them to the Major yesterday and he is still carrying them. Now the Yankees will know how to escape us. We've got to get back and report."

Bareheaded, and without his cloak, the General led his staff away.

"You are now very comfortable without your side arms, Lieutenant Gibson, eh?" von Borcke teased the young officer wickedly, patting his own sword and pistol significantly.

Gibson looked sheepishly at the place where his side arms should be swinging. He flushed and said nothing.

Stuart, too, was strangely silent. Tying a handkerchief around his head as a protection from the hot August sun, he led his staff westward. The loss of the dispatches weighed heavily on his mind.

Toward noon they met long files of infantry in gray, and Stuart stopped long enough to buy a plain wool hat from a well-stocked sutler. The tale of the lost hat ran like wildfire through the gray ranks. The soldiers thought it a fine joke.

All day the cavalry leader was greeted with joyous shouts from the men in the gray infantry.

"Lookee, boys—Jeb's got him a new hat!"

"Hi, cavalry, where's the big feather?"

"Reckon I'll get me a fancy hat some day."

Once Stuart swung around in the saddle and grinned ruefully at his staff.

"Gentlemen," he said, "I intend to make the Yankees pay dearly for that hat."

"He'll do it, too," Mosby whispered to Salt and Pepper, "just mark my words. Old John Pope had better watch his knitting."

CHAPTER TEN

Jeb Stuart Gets Pope's Coat in Exchange

"Yankee Doodle had a mind
To whip the Southern traitors,
Because they did not choose to live
On cod fish and po-ta-ters.
Yankee Doodle, ha, ha, ha,
Yankee Doodle dan-dy,
And so to keep his courage up
He kept his rifle han-dy!"

SWEENEY sang the rollicking words as he thumped gaily on his banjo. Salt and Pepper lay stretched on the ground beside him, and as many troopers as could squeeze into the crowded circle were huddled about the campfire. The day was gray and cloudy, and, though it was August, the damp air made the warmth of the fire very welcome to the thinly clad cavalrymen. The South was feeling the pinch of the Federal blockade and uniforms were scarce.

"Sing some more," urged a lean gray rider when the minstrel came to the end of his song.

"Sure, come on," added the others.

Sweeney was just tightening a banjo string before striking up another ditty when Jeb Stuart joined the crowd.

"At ease!" he commanded. "Boys, we've been around McClellan, and we had some fun with him. How would you like to try the same thing on Pope?"

"Yipee!" yelled the lean rider. "That's better than any song!"

A chorus of enthusiastic exclamations told Stuart what he wanted to know. His troops were eager for action.

"All right, men. Mount and assemble."

With joyous shouts the group broke up. They acted more like a gang of schoolboys off for a lark than like soldiers about to start on the grim work of a dangerous raid.

"I'll bet here's where the Yankees pay for Jeb's hat," Salt told Pepper as they swung into their saddles and found places in the rapidly forming column. Soon the ranks were full and the bugles blared.

"Forward, men!" Stuart called, taking his place in the lead.

Sweeney slung his banjo across his saddlebow, struck a few well-known chords and, as the column swung off down the road, every trooper was singing at the top of his voice:

> *"If you want to have a good time*
> *Jine the cavalry. . . ."*

Twelve miles eastward they rode, first to Warrenton, then seven miles more to Auburn, and by the time evening came they were well behind Pope's army. All day the leaden gray clouds had hung threateningly above them and, when it grew dark, great splashes of rain began to fall. Lightning flashed and the god of thunder fought an artillery battle in the skies.

"This is the darkest night I've ever seen," Pepper shouted to Salt above the roar of the thunder and the steady hum of the driving rain.

"Ye-ow! I'm soaked already," was Salt's ready answer.

The boys caught only occasional glimpses of the dripping countryside in the blinding glare of lightning flashes. Men and horses alike were soaked. Little cascades of rain ran off hat brims and trickled from soggy plumes. The troopers pulled their rain-heavy cloaks closer around them and pounded doggedly onward.

The gray advance guard rounded up a few surprised Yankees at Catlett's Station, and the main body rode compactly into the little town with Stuart's felt hat flapping disconsolately in the lead.

"Lawd bless me, if it ain't Marse Stuart!" cried a voice from among the Yankee prisoners, as a brilliant flash revealed the General.

"Who's that?" demanded Stuart. His quick ear had caught the voice over the noise of the storm and the yells of the raiders.

"Hit's me, Marse Stuart." A very wet Negro broke away from his captors and ran to the General's stirrup. "Don' you remember me? I's 'Mericus Jenkins what used to live on yo' pappy's plantation, back in Patrick County."

"Hello, Americus," answered Stuart. "What are you doing here?"

"De Yankees done cotched me an' made me a mule driver. But I'se powerful glad to see some home folks, an' Marse Stuart, I'se got som'pen to tell you." An ivory grin split the wet shiny face.

"Speak up, boy," ordered the General.

"De Yankee Gin'ral Pope done got his headquarters jest down de road a piece, please suh. You kin cotch de Gin'ral if you rides quick. I'd be proud to show de sojers de way."

"Good," said Stuart. "Climb on this horse, and lead on."

In no time at all the gray column was splashing confidently after its black guide. The dashing rain and the roll of thunder covered up all sounds of approach.

"Right dere 'tis," said Americus, checking his horse

and pointing to a few lantern lights flickering dimly through the rain.

"Ready, boys! Forward!" ordered Stuart, and away dashed the raiders, charging into the camp, yelling and shooting.

"You, Salt and Pepper, cut the telegraph wires," Stuart called, as the column swept forward.

The two boys swung off, shouting gaily and slashing at tent ropes with their sabers as they passed. Aided by the lightning they soon located a telegraph pole.

"Hold Sunstar, Salt," shouted Pepper, tossing the reins to his chum and, with saber clattering about his heels, the boy swarmed up the wet pole, his boots slipping dangerously on the dripping footholds. The wind whistled through the taut wires above his head and the cold rain blinded him.

Pepper braced himself with one leg over the cross-arm and drew his blade, slashing and sawing at the wires. The quicker the wires were down, the less chance there would be for the surprised Federals to call for help.

"Whack! Wham!" The blade bounced off and away from the singing wires. The unexpected resistance almost cost Pepper his balance. Swinging his saber high, he brought it down with a mighty blow. This time one wire parted and hissed away into the darkness. Another blow and the remaining wire joined the first in a writhing coil.

Returning his saber to its scabbard, Pepper took a look around in the blackness. Far, far off, to the east, he saw a signal lantern flash momentarily against the black sky. Again and again it glittered, striking a halo of light from the rain about it.

Pepper slid to the ground.

"Salt!" he shouted. "Where are you?"

"Right here, on your left," came the answer.

A lightning flash revealed Salt with Sunstar, waiting. Pepper ran, climbed into the saddle and called his friend to follow.

"The Yankees are on the ridge signaling for help. We've got to tell Stuart."

The camp was in an uproar. The gray troopers were yelling and shooting as they tossed burning brands into wet tents and looted overturned supply wagons. Dazed Yankees were still running aimlessly around in the darkness until captured.

"Say there, where's Stuart?" Pepper called to a boisterous gray raider.

"Right over yonder! See him? There by the big tent," the man answered, his hands full of Yankee rations.

By the dull glow of the sluggishly blazing tents, Pepper caught sight of the General. Stuart stood stroking his wet beard and superintending a squad of men chopping away at the wooden piers of a railroad trestle.

"The Yankees are signaling for help, sir," said Pepper, reining up and touching his sodden hat in salute. "I saw a lantern from the top of the telegraph pole."

Stuart nodded. Another courier dashed up.

"Cedar Run is rising with this rain, sir," he reported. "It's swimming-deep already."

The General nodded again, his eyes still on the laboring axes.

"Sound 'Recall,' " he said quietly to the bugler beside him. "Come on, boys, we won't have time to cut the trestle."

The bugle blared through the rain-filled darkness, calling the scattered raiders back to ranks. The troopers rounded up their prisoners and captured horses, herding them out of the wrecked camp and off to safety in the dark.

In good order the column pounded on through the night, keeping a sharp lookout for pursuers and driving their captives before them. By daylight they were in Warrenton, where the delighted citizens turned out of their beds to give them a hearty welcome.

The still bewildered prisoners were rounded up in the town square, and Stuart sat down in the lobby of the little hotel to take stock of his prizes. Pepper and Salt tied their tired horses to the hitching rack and sprawled out on the hotel porch to wait and rest.

"Looks like we've caught everything from privates to colonels," said Pepper, yawning and casting a lazy eye over the prisoners.

"Too bad old Pope had to be away from his headquarters," mourned Salt. "It's just our luck to make a raid while he was away."

Sweeney came out of the hotel and joined them, hearing Salt's words.

"Talk about luck," he chuckled, "ours isn't so bad. We got Pope's official papers, telling all about his plans and reinforcements. They pay for the ones the Yankees got from Major Fitzhugh. Better still, we got Pope's best dress uniform. That makes up for Jeb's hat. They're even now, even though we did miss Pope himself."

"A full-dress uniform for a hat," grinned Pepper. "I'll say they're even now."

"Look, here comes the General," added Salt. "He certainly does look pleased."

A few minutes later the bugles blew and the column jingled out of Warrenton. By noon the boys were cooking lunch over their home campfire. Yankee General John Pope was minus his best uniform, all his headquarters equipment and papers, as well as several of his highest staff officers. The gray cavalry had had a glorious time.

Next morning while the two boys were idling around the campfire, waiting for assignments to duty, they heard the General's voice hailing them.

"Salt! Pepper! Come here. I want to give General Pope's coat the best seasoning possible."

"What do you suppose he means?" Pepper asked, as the two scrambled to their feet.

"There's no telling. Let's go see."

The General grinned widely at them as they pulled up, panting, just inside his tent.

"General Pope's coat is entirely too good for the

cavalry to keep to itself," he told them. "A courier has already gone ahead with Pope's papers, but I want you two boys to conduct his fine coat to Richmond and present it to the War Department with my compliments."

"May we show it to people on the way, sir?" inquired Salt.

"Yes, it's too good to keep secret. Just handle it with care."

He handed them the Yankee general's gorgeous blue coat, richly decorated with gold braid and glittering with buttons spaced in threes down the front.

"I hope we will be able to catch General Pope himself next time we take a trip around his army," Stuart added. "And, boys, by the way, while you are in Richmond tell Mrs. Stuart that I need a new hat with a plume."

The boys scampered away to get their horses. Long practice had taught them to fit bridle and saddle quickly. Soon they were ready to start for Richmond.

"Say," Pepper said, pausing with his foot in the stirrup, "we ought to fix that coat so everybody can see it."

"Great," agreed Salt. "But how?"

"Easy enough. Give it here."

Pepper cut some small branches from a nearby tree and lashed them together in a light framework.

"I catch on," chuckled Salt, lending a hand.

In a few minutes the boys had General Pope's gorgeous coat mounted on the framework, with its fresh

blue and its glittering gold and brass carried like a
banner. With this held aloft they rode gaily through
each Confederate camp, beginning with that of Stuart's
cavalry.

As they rode, they chanted an improvised song.

> "Old John Pope has lost his coat
> And soon he'll lose his army.
> Stuart, Lee, and Jackson, too,
> Will chase him out of Dixie.
> Yankee Doodle, ha, ha, ha,
> Yankee Doodle dan-dy.
> You'd better throw your guns away
> And with your heels be han-dy!"

By noon the next day, the coat was attracting great
crowds of spectators in Richmond where it was placed
on display in a main street show window. With a dress
coat for a plumed hat, Jeb Stuart had evened up the
score.

CHAPTER ELEVEN
The Second Battle of Manassas

FRESH activity was brewing even before the two couriers could get back to Stuart and the cavalry. Lee was out to crush his blue opponents before another winter set in. The late August sun shone golden on the dusty Confederate columns as they advanced for the struggle.

As usual, Stuart's men were ordered ahead to clear

the way. The boys arrived in camp late for evening mess to find their comrades busy with preparations for another jaunt.

"Hi, boys! Light down and get some rest," Sweeney called as they rode in. "We're off before morning."

"Hoo-ray!" both answered at once as they tumbled off their horses.

Carefully they removed the saddles, rubbed down their dusty horses, and turned them out to graze. A good cavalryman always looks after his horse before he thinks of his own comfort.

"Rest all you can, Sunstar, old boy," whispered Pepper, giving him an affectionate pat. "Looks like more work ahead."

The horse snorted softly, tossed his head and trotted away as if to prove that he was ready for any activity.

"I think our horses enjoy this as much as you and I do," Pepper said as he and Salt strolled back to headquarters. "They seem to know when something big is in the wind."

"Sure they do," answered Salt. "They make fine soldiers. Say, am I hungry!"

"Me, too! Sweeney, is there anything left to eat around here?"

"Corn pone and bacon," Sweeney answered. "Same as you've been eating all summer."

"Lord, but I'd like a change," groaned Salt. "My stomach begins to grunt every time I see a pig."

"And I expect to have corn tassels sprout out of my ears any day now," agreed Pepper.

But, in spite of their grumbling, the boys fell to with a right good will. Hunger was always the best sauce in the cavalry and every crumb of corn pone and every strip of bacon disappeared like magic. With full stomachs, the boys stretched out luxuriously on the soft grass.

"Here, you young loafers," Sweeney called. "Last ones through wash the mess kits."

Groaning mightily, Salt and Pepper scrambled up and gathered the dirty dishes.

"Army life," grumbled the boy from Georgia. "Washing dishes is no kind of a job for a soldier."

But washing dishes in the cavalry was not a hard task, for Stuart's men had reduced their mess kits to the barest of essentials. A single frying pan and coffee pot served an entire squad. Each man had his own canteen, plates were a luxury, and sheath knives took the place of spoons and forks. In a short time the frying pan was scrubbed clean of grease and the coffee pot was rinsed in the little stream that trickled near by.

At two o'clock the next morning cavalry bugles sounded the assembly and the troopers climbed into their saddles. By sunset the same day Stuart's leading squadrons dashed into Bristoe Station, scattering the blue pickets and taking charge of the huge Federal depot that stretched to the eastward.

The Yankees had not anticipated a raid in this direction and the great depot was lightly guarded. With captured picks and crowbars some of the raiders set about tearing up the railroad tracks while their comrades foraged through the depot or rounded up prisoners and equipment.

"Well, we're right back where we were a year ago," remarked Sweeney, as he and the boys rummaged gleefully through the Yankee supplies.

"What do you mean?" Pepper demanded, reaching for a choice bit of Vermont summer sausage.

"Manassas Junction is just five miles southwest of us. That's where the first big battle of the war was fought. The Yankees call it the battle of Bull Run." The banjoist had his mouth full of Yankee grub.

"That'll be all right. We can chase the bluecoats just as well this year as we did in the spring of '61," Salt mumbled, talking around a sizable chunk of Pennsylvania cheese.

Before midnight Stonewall Jackson's dusty infantry began to pour into the Station. Throughout the night and all during the next day the "foot cavalry" joined Stuart's riders in reveling in the Federals' choicest stores. The ragged gray soldiers fitted themselves out with brand new Yankee equipment and stuffed themselves with supplies. Like a bunch of schoolboys, they frolicked through the great depot.

When the troops moved on at last, each gray soldier had a bag of Yankee coffee slung over his saddle—they had not enjoyed this beverage since the blockade closed in. Jackson's infantry marched with their haversacks bulging. Many a soldier had a big northern ham skewered on his bayonet. Pepper's own pockets were stuffed with sugar lumps, snatched from the bluecoat

officers' supplies. In the unexpected prosperity, the boy
had not forgotten Sunstar's sweet tooth.

Stonewall Jackson's troops swung out of sight down
the road toward the fighting position their leader had
selected. Stuart rode west toward Gainesville, sending
Salt ahead to open communications with General Longstreet who was coming east.

Pepper looked longingly after him as his friend disappeared in a cloud of dust. Even Sunstar seemed to
sense his master's disappointment for he pranced and
pawed the ground restlessly.

Stuart took an amused look at the boy's downcast
face.

"Cheer up, Pepper," he comforted, beckoning the boy
to his side. "I'll have a job for you soon."

"Thank you, sir," Pepper said, his face brighten-
ing.

The sharp rattle of carbines sounded from ahead and
a messenger came galloping back from the advance
guard.

"There's enemy infantry and a few squads of cavalry
drawn up at Gainesville, sir," he reported. "It will take
us a little time to dislodge them."

Stuart nodded, and then turned to Pepper.

"Ride to General Lee at headquarters," he said, "and
tell him that Jackson is in position in the woods southeast
of Aldie. I will chase the Federals out of Gainesville and
hold the town. It is most important that General Lee
know exactly where we are and that we are ready to
crush Pope on the Manassas plain. I won't write the

message for fear the Yankees may get you. But ride far to the north and you have a good chance to get through."

"Yes, sir." Pepper saluted and swung Sunstar away from the road as the rest of the column surged on toward Gainesville. The sharp rattle of musketry and the yells of Stuart's men faded in Pepper's ears as he and Sunstar started off to find General Lee.

The region was thick with blue columns marching up from the place where Pope had been concentrated on the Rappahannock. Pepper kept to the back trails and thickets, galloping swiftly across open fields from one place of cover to the next. Looking down from the crest of a ridge, he saw long dusty columns of troops tramping toward Manassas.

"I've got to get through! I've got to get through! General Lee must know where Stuart and Jackson are. Pope must not escape us." Pepper repeated the words over and over.

He reached forward and patted Sunstar's glossy shoulder.

"A lot depends on us, old fellow. On your hoofs and my eyes and wits—yes, and on your wits, too," he whispered.

The great horse jerked his head gracefully up and down at the sound of his master's voice, as if to show that he understood. With one ear pricked sharply forward to catch the slightest hostile sound, and with the other one back, ready for any command from Pepper, Sunstar galloped onward.

All afternoon cannon rumbled faintly in the distance, now here, now there, as the blue and the gray armies maneuvered for fighting positions.

Three times Pepper and Sunstar hid in the underbrush of woodland tangles while marching blue-coated soldiers filed past.

At last, just as the sun was setting far in the distance ahead, Pepper pulled up on the crest of a hill and saw the golden rays gleaming on the roofs and church steeple of the little town where General Lee had established temporary headquarters.

"We're almost there, pal," he whispered, putting Sunstar into a final gallop.

"Special message for General Lee from General Stuart," he called to the lone sentry who challenged him.

"General Lee has already left to join Longstreet," the sentry answered. "Say, boy, you look worn out. Get down and rest. I'll send your message on by a fresh courier."

Pepper shook his head.

"I'm not tired," he declared, although his haggard face and wind-reddened eyes told a different story. "I've got to deliver the message in person. Which way did the General go?"

"He went north toward Manassas."

"Thanks." With a steady hand Pepper pulled Sunstar around and horse and rider were soon lost in the dusk and the evening shadows.

Again, on and on, past woods and bridges, lighted

farm houses and shadowy barns, Pepper rode. He had been in the saddle since early morning.

He lost all track of time and was conscious only of the steady "tap, tap, tap" of Sunstar's tireless feet. On and on, over hill and through valley, past thicket and brook until it seemed as though he had been riding since the beginning of time. Darkness and dust, "tap, tap, tap."

At last he saw a fire twinkling ahead and heard a voice call "Halt!"

"I have a special message for General Lee," Pepper said mechanically.

"Good." A friendly hand reached out and took hold of Sunstar's foam-flecked bridle. The great horse was too tired to do more than toss his head as the guard led him quickly through the sleeping camp to a small tent where a light still burned.

" 'Marse Robert' is in there with General Longstreet," the sentry said, helping Pepper to dismount.

"Thank you, sir," the boy said, walking wearily forward.

Timidly lifting the tent flap, Pepper stepped inside and stood at attention. General Robert E. Lee's gray-bearded, kindly face smiled inquiringly at him, and General Longstreet's steady blue eyes looked at him from that officer's ruddy, brown-bearded face.

"General Stuart's compliments to General Lee, sir. General Stuart reports that General Jackson is in position in the woods southeast of Aldie. General Stuart is holding Gainesville. They are ready to advance on Ma-

nassas when ordered. General Stuart was chasing the
Yankees out of Gainesville when I left." Pepper's report
became less formal.

The two generals listened carefully, questioning the
young messenger closely about their comrades, and
about the positions of the cavalry and infantry. They
checked his answers on a large military field map that
lay spread out on the table before them.

"Pepper, my boy, you've done a good job," kindly
General Lee smiled at last, laying a friendly hand on
the boy's shoulder. "You look mighty tired, lad. Go rest
while you can. We march at dawn."

"Thank you, sir," said Pepper, saluting and leaving
the tent. The two officers had already turned back to
the map and their plans.

Waiting only long enough to loosen Sunstar's saddle
and bridle, leaving him free to graze, Pepper rolled up
in his riding cloak. In an instant he was asleep.

The sharp tattoo of a bugle broke into Pepper's
dreams. Something soft and warm touched his cheek and
the boy opened his eyes to see Sunstar standing over
him, watching him with bright eyes.

"Hello, old boy," Pepper said, sitting up and yawning. "Were you afraid I was going to sleep through
reveille?"

"Well, you usually do, lazy bones," said a familiar
voice.

Pepper swung around in surprise.

"Salt!" he exclaimed. "Where did you come from?"

"From over there by the fire," was the answer. "Stuart sent me through to Longstreet yesterday. The question is, how did you get here?"

"Simple enough, Stuart sent me to Lee. Say, do you suppose there's anything to eat around here?"

"Sure, come over by the fire."

The boys were munching the last of their morning rations when the bugles called the troops into line. Mounting their horses, the two couriers fell in with Lee and Longstreet and their staffs, while the long gray infantry columns streamed out behind.

With Jackson in position along the Groveton woods, and with Lee, Longstreet, and Stuart united at Gainesville, the Confederates swept on to conquer the bewildered Federal General Pope on the plain of Manassas. From the heights on both sides flame-red cannon blasts roared forth, tearing long gaps in the opposing ranks.

At last Lee sent couriers galloping to his generals. Stuart's men got to horse. Jackson's infantry was tense with expectancy. Longstreet's bugles sounded the charge. The "Stars and Bars" led the way and the gray battle line, nearly three miles long, surged forward. Shrill above the roar of the cannon rose the "rebel yell."

Pepper and Sunstar swept on with the rest, lost in the maelstrom of battle. The great horse lashed out with flying hoofs and Pepper's heavy saber glittered. Bullets ripped past. Shells burst around them. The

Confederate line was enveloped in a raging, artillery-blasted chaos, and the charge thundered onward against the Union guns. Blue uniforms and gray were mixed and enemy battle flags flew side by side as hand-to-hand fighting became the order of the day. Pepper lost all track of time while the thick yellow smoke and dust gathered in a great cloud over the battlefield, blotting out the sun.

The Union troops could not resist the fierce southern charge. The Yankee lines wavered, broke, and melted away. For the second time the men in blue suffered defeat on the field of Manassas.

The hush that fell on the battlefield was painful to the ears after the terrific roar of combat. But this silence was broken by the even more terrible cries of the wounded, screaming in agony, begging for water, pleading for aid. Pepper shuddered as he looked upon the torn shapes in gray and blue, lying so thickly on the blood-reddened, shell-blasted plain.

Sick and reeling, he let Sunstar pick his way gingerly across the field and the boy breathed a sigh of thankfulness as they turned at last into the still, clean coolness of untouched woodland.

Hoofbeats sounded ahead and Pepper lifted tired eyes to see Jeb Stuart and his staff making their way carefully through the forest. Riding forward quickly, he joined them, heartily glad for human companionship after the horrors of the battlefield.

"Hello, Pepper," General Stuart greeted him. "You did good work in getting through with your message.

And I'm glad to see that my staff's seasoning is still complete."

"Thank you, sir," Pepper answered, saluting as he fell into line beside Salt and Sweeney.

"What became of you?" Salt wanted to know. "I missed you when the attack started."

"Oh, I got caught in the charge and rode with it," Pepper answered. "I can't remember much about it, but what I do remember is awful."

Sweeney laid a hand on his shoulder.

"It was pretty bad," he agreed. "I like our quick raids where not many are hurt. That's real fun. But artillery battles where the ranks are shot to pieces—no, thanks."

So ended the Second Battle of Manassas or, as the Northerners called it, the Second Battle of Bull Run.

Pope's troops retreated hurriedly to the shelter of their forts along the Potomac. Pepper and Salt, riding with a party of Stuart's advance scouts, saw the last of the blue soldiers file into the Washington fortifications.

General Lee had defeated an army which outnumbered his, had driven the blue-clad troops sixty miles, and had relieved the pressure on Richmond, the Confederate capital. The entire South rang with praises for his triumph.

CHAPTER TWELVE
The Lost Orders

"YOU know, Salt, Maryland is almost as nice a state as Virginia," Pepper told his companion. "I like it here."

The two boys were riding leisurely through the pleasant Maryland country, sniffing the bracing mountain air which came to their nostrils from the tree-clad ridges to the west. Much had happened during the week that had elapsed since the second battle on Manassas plain. Lee's army had crossed into western Maryland, invading territory heretofore held by the enemy.

As usual, Stuart's gray riders were stretched out across the front of the army, ready to brush aside any blue attackers thrown against them. The cavalry was strung out for twenty miles, from Poolesville to New Market, and the lean, war-hardened troops were being much admired by the Marylanders.

Jeb Stuart's headquarters at the little town of Urbana were crowded daily by throngs of visitors, gentlemen and ladies of the section, who rode or walked in, hoping to catch a glimpse of the famous cavalry leader. Although the state of Maryland had never formally seceded from the Union, many of its inhabitants threw open their homes to make the Confederates welcome.

"Yes, it is a pretty state," agreed Salt, after long and thoughtful consideration of his friend's remark. "Just the same, I like Georgia better."

Pepper laughed.

"I know you, Salty Salter," he said. "You wouldn't admit liking it, even if you thought it was pretty close to heaven. What have your red clay Georgia hills and grim cypress swamps got that will compare with that?"

He pointed to a pine- and maple-covered ridge that rolled away to the southwest, its deep green crest already turning rosy in the biting air of early autumn. Ridge after ridge rolled behind it, each one just a little higher than its neighbor, until they faded away into the misty heights of Catoctin Mountain on the eastern edge of the Blue Ridge.

"Just the same, old Georgia's home," retorted Salt. "That makes all the difference in the world."

Pepper nodded silently, his thoughts flying southward to the pleasant hills of his own plantation home. A swelling wave of homesickness swept over him when he thought of his mother and the friends he had left behind. He had been away three months now. His mother wrote regularly, long, loving letters full of clever little accounts of the Negroes in the quarters, and entertaining stories about the activities of the plantation. He received an occasional letter from his uncle and aunt, and once Cousin Brian took time to scrawl a note. "I'll be back in the 'foot cavalry' before the end of September," he promised, "and then you'll see some regular soldiering."

"Salt! Pepper! Hi there! Wait for us!" A distant shout broke in on the boys' thoughts. Turning, they saw Sweeney and Hagan galloping toward them from a side trail.

As the two riders came closer the boys observed that their arms were loaded with gaily colored autumn leaves, red and gold and brown, riches gathered from the gloriously flaming ridges.

"Oh, girls, let's go pick violets," taunted Salt when the two soldiers checked their galloping horses and pulled up alongside.

"Thank you so much, boys," cooed Pepper coyly,

reaching his arms for the bouquets. "I think you're just too, too sweet to pick these for me."

"Aw, go fry your ears," growled Hagan. "If you think I enjoy playing flower girl for a bunch of goggling civilians you're just plain crazy. Makin' us just a bunch of play-boy tin soldiers!"

"The Dutchman sent us out to get decorations for the Urbana academy hall," Sweeney told the boys. "The staff's giving a dance tonight."

"Yeah, this is turning out to be one fine war!" growled Hagan. "We invade the enemy's territory, and then what do we do? Fight? No! We all get together and dance—it's a wonder they don't ask McClellan over to lead the grand march."

By the time he had finished his tirade, Hagan's fierce black whiskers were fairly bristling with indignation, and his audience was nearly paralyzed with laughter. Pepper laughed till his sides ached and tears were rolling down Salt's cheeks. Sweeney roared.

"Come on, you two," Sweeney managed to say after a time. "Help us get some more decorations. That hall's as big as a barn and as bare as a 'possum's tail. It's going to take a powerful lot of leaves and things to fix it up."

Still speechless from laughter, the boys nodded agreement and followed Sweeney and the still sputtering Hagan along the woodland trail. Two hours later the four troopers rode into Urbana loaded down with autumn leaves and greenery.

Other heavily laden squads, also, were riding in with small pine trees, autumn leaves, branches, and all manner of colorful decorations. A dozen soldiers were busy hanging up the regimental battle flags and covering the bare walls of the hall with festoons of leaves and branches.

Big von Borcke was everywhere at once, giving directions and supervising the work.

"*Das ist sehr schön!*" he exclaimed, forgetting his English in the excitement. "*Sehr gut.* Ver' much I like dot."

"To look at him now you'd never think he'd be much of a fighter," Hagan grumbled. "If I hadn't seen that Dutchman swing his big sword in battle, I'd say he was just an overgrown dancing master."

"Yes, and just look at all the tough cavalrymen running around with pretty leaves in their hands. They look like a bunch of boys from the village academy. I'll bet old John Pope and McClellan wouldn't believe their eyes if they could see Jeb Stuart's men right now."

Under the combined efforts of many hands the bare walls soon took on a festive air. Before the sun sank behind the western ridges everything was ready. At dusk the colonel and staff officers from a near-by infantry regiment arrived, bringing with them their regimental band to play for the dance.

Before long the ladies of the neighborhood began to gather, escorted by Stuart's personal staff. The band struck up a lively quadrille, and the dance was under way.

Salt and Pepper stood in a corner and watched. Sweeney was already dancing with a dark-eyed Maryland lady, but Hagan had snorted his indignation and disapproval before stalking away to the company of a strictly masculine campfire group.

For a time the two boys stood silent, watching the gay throng and listening to the music. The infantry band was blasting out polkas, waltzes, and quadrilles with more sound than art. The candlelight gleamed softly on brass buttons, gray uniforms, and the colorful gowns of the Maryland belles.

"Say, I'd like to dance, too," Salt said, his eyes following Sweeney's smiling partner. "I'm going to make Sam Sweeney introduce me. Come on!"

"Thanks, I reckon I'll stay here and just watch." Pepper felt shy in the presence of the glittering company that whirled and swayed in time to the music.

"Aw, don't be scared—come on!" Salt's hand fell compellingly on his friend's shoulder, but Pepper shook him off.

"No—I'd rather not—" he was stammering when the hall door was thrown open and a dust-covered orderly clanked across the dance floor. Saluting General Stuart, the man reported. His voice jarred harshly with the music.

"Our pickets are having a brush with enemy cavalry, sir. Perhaps you'd better come."

Stuart nodded and made a sign to the band leader. The musicians broke off in the middle of a bar, and the dancers heard in the sudden silence the sharp firecracker report of gunfire in the distance.

Stuart's officers filed out, buckling on their swords as they went.

"We regret the interruption, ladies," the General explained, as he stood bowing at the door. "We'll be back shortly. It's just a little disagreement, but it is quite rude of the Yankees to choose this moment for it."

With the others, Salt and Pepper scrambled into their saddles and pounded away after Stuart. The fighting swelled along the Washington pike, sabers rattled and pistols spat viciously in the darkness. Pelham's horse artillery moved into action, throwing shells into the enemy, and slashing the darkness with streaks of fire.

The blue patrol broke and scattered before the fury of the gray attack. The rattle of the engagement thinned out and finally died away with the thud of the Yankees' fleeing horses.

"Serves 'em right," grumbled Sweeney. "They had no business butting in just when we were beginning to have a good time."

"How about introducing me to your partner," suggested Salt as he and Pepper cantered back to town beside the banjoist. "I was just coming over to ask you when we were interrupted."

"Sure," grinned Sweeney. "Always ready to help a

friend. But mind now, only one dance for you. I want
the rest of 'em myself."

It was well past midnight when they rode in to finish
the dance. The ladies were tremulously admiring, and
even Pepper's chest swelled under their praises. He
quite forgot his bashfulness when the music began
again and was only too sorry when it stopped.

Two days later General Lee completed his military
plans and the infantry began to move into fighting positions. Stuart's cavalry rode into Frederick, the troopers singing their own special version of "Maryland, My
Maryland":

> *"Oh, Bob Lee's heel is on thy shore,*
> *Maryland, my Maryland—*
> *You won't see your old horse no more,*
> *Maryland, my Maryland.*
> *We'll sneak him out the stable door*
> *And ride him till his back is sore,*
> *Then we'll come back and get some more,*
> *Maryland, my Maryland."*

Brushes with the Yankee cavalry became more and
more frequent as McClellan dashed his regiments
against the gray cavalry's line of outposts. Nearer and
nearer the Federals came to Frederick until, on the
twelfth of September, the smoke and roar of battle
rolled up from the eastern edge of the little town and
echoes rumbled from ridge to ridge along the foothills.

As he sat on his horse watching the progress of the battle, Stuart beckoned Salt and Pepper to his side.

"Salt," he said. "You ride to General Lee and tell him that I am withdrawing from Frederick to take up a stronger position along Catoctin Mountain. I can hold McClellan for another five days until the plan outlined in Special Orders 191 gets under way."

"Yes, sir," said Salt, and saluting he spurred his horse, Thunder, away toward the west.

"Pepper," continued the General. "I've got a harder job for you. Are you game?"

"Yes, sir." The boy's eyes were shining.

"Good. When the cavalry rides out of Frederick, I want you to stay behind. Keep out of sight and wait until the Yankees move in. Try, if you can, to find out their strength, and learn what their plans are. This is a dangerous task, but I know I can depend on you."

Pepper's heart thumped with a mixture of delight and terror as he watched the gray troops ride through town and disappear behind the western ridges. Stuart was the last man to leave, waving his plumed hat to the young scout as he rode away.

"Sunstar, old fellow," Pepper whispered to the black horse which stood fretting restlessly, eager to be gone with the others, "we've got the hardest job we've ever had ahead of us. It's going to take all the wits we have to keep the Yankees from getting us."

Purple shadows were stealing out from the western hills as Pepper rode cautiously out of Frederick, circling back a few minutes later to keep under cover of the trees along the hills that crowded closely into the town.

A tumbled-down, abandoned barn loomed up before them and Pepper guided Sunstar toward it.

"Here's a fine hide-out, pal," he whispered, dismounting inside the ruined structure and leading Sunstar deeper into the shadows of one corner. "I certainly don't want the Yankees to catch sight of you."

Pepper made the black horse comfortable, tying him securely in the corner and feeding him some hay from a stack in the barnyard. Then he sat down to ration himself from the contents of his haversack.

Twilight deepened and night drew on, filling the old barn with dense shadows. Black Sunstar was completely invisible in the darkness.

"Be quiet, old fellow," Pepper whispered, reaching up to stroke the horse's ears with loving fingers. "I'll be back as soon as I can find out about the Yankees."

Sunstar snorted lonesomely as the boy's footsteps died away in the darkness. Then the great horse settled down resignedly to await the return of his young master.

Meanwhile Pepper made his way carefully back into Frederick, taking pains to keep in the shadows. The night seemed breathlessly silent, as if waiting for something to happen.

Then, from the east came a steady rumbling, growing louder and clearer. Pepper dropped flat on his stomach and pressed his ear to the ground. In this way he heard the rumbling even plainer, and recognized the sound for what it was—the steady tramp, tramp, tramp, of thousands of marching feet. McClellan was on the move.

The Confederate scout looked around in the darkness, his eyes searching for a hiding place that would permit him to watch the Yankee approach. A door creaked nearby and Pepper crouched silent, waiting. No sound broke the stillness, then the door creaked mournfully again and a soft, cold breeze fanned Pepper's cheek.

Stealing cautiously forward, the boy found that the noisy door belonged to an empty store building, opening onto the main street of Frederick. The door was swinging loosely in the slight breeze. Inside, a stairway led up into the blackness of a loft above the storeroom.

Stepping inside, Pepper carefully secured the door so that its creaking would not attract anyone to his hiding place. Then he crept up the stairs where he lay down on the floor of the loft and prepared to await further developments.

The next thing Pepper knew, a warm rosy light was shining on his face. Opening his eyes in alarm, he saw that the beams of the rising sun were streaming in through a tiny window in the store loft. He was stiff from his bed on the dusty floor, but he crept over to the window and looked down on the main street of Frederick.

The sight that met his eyes made his heart pound fearfully. There were Yankees in the street, Yankees on the porches—Yankees everywhere. While Pepper slept, the army in blue had entered the town and established headquarters.

Voices drifted up to him through the shattered pane of glass in the window. Pepper kept his ear close to the opening while he munched at the rations remaining in his haversack.

"I hope Sunstar is safe," he said to himself, as his eyes were roving from group to group of bluecoats in the street below.

The Federals were totally unaware that hostile eyes were watching them. In twos and threes, soldiers in blue strolled up and down the street, calling jokes to each other. Once, while Pepper watched, a regimental band came swinging down the street, blaring forth a Yankee marching song, their brass instruments glittering in the sun. Pepper found it hard to realize that less than twenty-four hours before gray troopers had been filling the places now occupied by blue ones.

For more than an hour the scout lay in the store loft, watching and listening to everything that went on. After some time he began to tire of the inactivity and his eyes wandered idly up and down the street.

A bit of white paper held Pepper's attention. It fluttered on the ground just opposite his window. He watched it indifferently for a moment as it moved in the breeze. Evidently the paper was wrapped around something heavy enough to keep it down, for the breeze did not dislodge it from its position on the grass.

For some reason that bit of paper fascinated Pepper. At the same time it filled him with a vague uneasiness.

He wanted to rush downstairs and snatch up that paper before any Yankee noticed it. Of course that was impossible, for the street was full of lounging soldiers.

Pepper shook his head, trying to drive off the uneasy feeling.

"Don't be silly," he told himself. "That's just a worthless scrap of paper. What's the matter with your nerves, Potter Pepperill?"

But other eyes also had been attracted by the fluttering piece of paper. Even as Pepper scolded himself, a Union private strolled across the street and idly bent down to examine the paper. Pepper watched him curiously, puzzled by the feeling of dread that had crept over him. The Yankee carelessly unwrapped the paper and his face broke into a pleased smile as he noted its contents.

"Well, lookee here!" Pepper heard the soldier exclaim as he held up three cigars. "Talk about luck."

He put one cigar in his mouth and carefully stowed the other two in his jacket pocket. Then, as he was about to toss the paper away, something on it seemed to catch the Yankee's eye. The cigar drooped forgotten from the corner of his mouth while the Yankee studied the paper.

"Now I wonder—" Pepper whispered to himself, the feeling of dread sweeping over him again.

"Hey, boys," the Yankee called, beckoning to two companions across the street. "Come here!"

"What's eatin' you, Mitchell?" the pair wanted to know, crossing curiously to his side.

"Just listen to this," the man called Mitchell answered. Holding the paper with both hands, he began to read.

" 'Special Orders 191, Headquarters Army of Northern Virginia, C. S. A. . . .' Say!" the Yankee broke off. "That sounds like something important!"

"Go on, read some more," his friends urged.

"Gosh, it's all about where each rebel general is to take his command. It mentions Jackson and Longstreet and a bunch of other rebel officers."

"Who's it signed by?" demanded one of the Yankees, making an eager snatch at the paper.

"Hold your horses," retorted Mitchell. "Let's see, where's the end of it?" Then he gasped. "My gosh! It says 'Robert E. Lee, General Commanding, C. S. A.' "

"That *is* something. We'd better take it to headquarters."

As the three moved off Pepper's eyes followed them in despair. There was no way of stopping them. Soon McClellan would know all of Lee's carefully laid plan. Someone at the Confederate headquarters had made a careless mistake and fate had played into the hands of the Yankees.

"Now I've got to get back to Stuart and report," Pepper told himself. "Our whole army is in danger. How am I ever going to get out of here without the Yankees catching me?"

Although he knew that every moment was precious, Pepper saw that he could not risk escape while the streets were filled with bluecoats. Forcing himself to be patient, the boy kept his place in the store loft until the bugles blared mess call at noon. A few minutes later, when the street was nearly deserted, the boy left his hiding place and crept quietly down the stairs. He slipped carefully outside and dropped out of sight behind a clump of bushes in the overgrown yard of the old store. A searching look around showed that no one had seen him.

Selecting his next hiding place carefully, Pepper slipped from the bushes and dashed across the open space, diving gratefully into the shelter of an open shed. In this cautious and jerky fashion, the boy made his way through town toward the place where Sunstar waited.

He was just ready to enter the weed-grown grove that hid the deserted barn when Pepper heard a voice hailing him.

"Hey, you," the voice demanded. "Where do you think you're going?"

Casting a frightened look over his shoulder, Pepper saw a blue-coated officer standing some distance down the road. There was something familiar about the man's slouching figure and Pepper gulped as he recognized Arch McGrigg, the Yankee spy.

At the same moment McGrigg recognized Pepper and drew his pistol.

"I've got you, you meddling rebel," he snarled. "And here's where I put a bullet in you."

Before the spy could aim, Pepper flung himself to

one side and dived headfirst into the thicket. A bullet whined through the leaves as the boy scrambled to his feet and pushed farther into the grove's shelter.

As he raced toward the old stable, Pepper could hear the spy shouting angrily. Heedless, the boy ran on, paying no attention to briars that snatched at his clothing and tore his hands and face.

He reached the old barn and heard Sunstar's welcoming snort just as McGrigg began beating his way through the weeds and underbrush.

"Old pal," gasped Pepper, fumbling with hasty fingers at the rope that tied his mount, "we've got to fly faster than ever before, and this time the Yankees are going to be hot after us."

The hitching rope loose at last, Pepper swung into the saddle and guided his horse out into the sunflecked grove.

"Stop, or I'll fire!" panted McGrigg, halting in the underbrush to raise his pistol as he again caught sight of his escaping quarry.

Pepper dug his heels into Sunstar's flanks and the great horse bounded forward like a thunderbolt. A bullet from the Yankee's gun clipped the bark from a limb close by as the boy bent low over his horse's neck and urged him forward.

In a moment they were out of the woods and thundering down the dusty road toward the west. Pepper knew that he must pass the Yankee outposts before word could be sent ahead to stop him.

"There's no time to take to the woods now, Sunstar," he whispered into the horse's ear. "The safety of Lee's army depends on us."

The great hoofs cut into the ground, sending clods of earth rattling into the weedy roadside and raising great clouds of dust behind them. Sunstar fairly flew through the bright Maryland countryside. Uphill and down, clattering over plank bridges and swaying around curves, the courageous horse sped on.

At last his rider checked him to a canter.

"There's no use wearing yourself out, old pal," Pepper said, patting the glossy neck. "We've got a long way to go and the Yankees will have to ride fast to catch us."

The sun passed the zenith and started its long slide down toward the western horizon. Once Pepper heard hoofs approaching from ahead. Pulling into the woods, the Confederate scout watched while a dusty blue courier dashed past, headed for Frederick.

A little farther down the road Pepper and Sunstar came to a little brook that rippled merrily over its stony bed. The horse sniffed thirstily and Pepper discovered that his own throat was parched and dry.

"I reckon I'd better stop a minute," he said, sliding out of the saddle and leading Sunstar toward the water. Throwing himself on his stomach, the boy drank as thirstily as his horse. The cool, sweet water put new life and courage in both of them.

Standing up at last, Pepper stretched his arms and

looked around. Sunstar shook his head and eyed his master. Then he sniffed anxiously over his shoulder.

"What's the matter, boy?" Pepper asked. "Do you hear something?"

Sunstar snorted nervously and Pepper dropped to the ground, listening with his ear close to the earth. Once again he heard the rumbling "thud, thud," and this time he knew it meant approaching horses.

"They're after us," he said, springing to his feet and leaping for the saddle. "Now we've got to run for it."

Sunstar shot forward in a long, tireless gallop. The wind whistled past Pepper's ears and the country whizzed by in a meaningless blur. Glancing over his shoulder the boy caught sight of his pursuers topping a rise far, far behind. Then they were hidden from sight as Sunstar swept around a bend.

"We can keep ahead of them," Pepper whispered joyously to Sunstar. "You can outrun any Yankee horse."

Then a new menace choked the words back into Pepper's throat. Ahead of him a blue picket line stretched across the road. Already the soldiers had heard him coming. With rifles half raised, they stood watching his approach.

In the crisis Pepper's mind worked like lightning. Checking Sunstar slightly and waving his arm, as if in greeting, the boy bore down on the pickets. They watched him curiously.

"Hold on there, you," one of them called.

Closer and closer the boy rode, keeping to the middle of the track. When he was almost upon them he swerved suddenly to the left and, digging his heels into Sunstar's sides, Pepper tore through an opening in the picket line.

Away dashed Sunstar, faster than the wind, as the startled yells of the Yankees sounded behind him. Shot whistled past horse and rider, raising little puffs of earth as they plowed into the dirt road around them. But dust and surprise disturbed the Yankees' aim, and before they could reload the Confederate scout had thundered out of range.

"Whew, that was a close call," said Pepper, bending close to Sunstar's neck as they raced along.

As evening came the hills grew sharper and the road wound upward between rocky outcroppings and then dipped steeply down into stony valleys. Pepper and Sunstar pushed their way ever onward, climbing deeper and deeper into the Blue Ridge Mountains.

Twilight was fading into darkness as they topped a stony rise and paused a moment to draw breath. A stir in the underbrush beside a huge boulder reached Pepper's ear. As he urged Sunstar nearer to investigate, a deep voice called sharply.

"Stay where you are, I've got you covered!"

Pepper's heart sank. Had he come this far on his way, only to be stopped on the very threshold of his destination? His eyes searched the underbrush for a sign of the man who had spoken. His mind sought madly for some means of escape.

"Up with your hands or I'll put a bullet in you," the hidden guard said again, his voice sounding deep and harsh.

"Where are you?" Pepper demanded, playing for time as he slowly raised one hand. The other crept stealthily toward his pistol.

Expecting the worst, Pepper was totally unprepared for the reply. A roar of laughter came from the roadside as the hidden guard tumbled out of the bushes. Pepper found himself staring into Salt's laughing face.

"I got the drop on you that time, Napoleon." The Georgia boy was almost doubled up with laughter.

"It's lucky for you I didn't send a pistol ball into those bushes," Pepper retorted, half angry at the trick his friend had played. "What are you doing, anyway, perching behind rocks like a setting hen?"

"I'm on picket duty," Salt replied indignantly. "Stuart's camp is down yonder by the brook. I'll be relieved in an hour. Better come and wait with me."

"Sorry, I can't," Pepper answered. "I've got some important news for Stuart."

"All right, run along. I'll see you later." Salt turned and crawled back into his hiding place while Pepper urged Sunstar down the hill.

Dismounting before the General's tent, the scout stood at attention.

"Special news for General Stuart," he told the orderly who lounged outside.

The man nodded and entered the tent to report. A moment later the boy heard Stuart's voice calling him.

"Come in, Pepper. I've been expecting you."

Entering the tent, Pepper saluted, took a deep breath and began.

"I remained in Frederick until noon, sir. McClellan has made it his headquarters. While I watched from a store window, I saw a Yankee private pick up a copy of our Special Orders 191. He read them out loud so I knew what they were."

"Special Orders 191!" exclaimed Stuart. "Where were they?"

"Lying on the grass wrapped around three cigars, sir. Someone from General Lee's headquarters must have dropped them by mistake."

Stuart stroked his beard thoughtfully, and the fingers of his left hand drummed sharply on the table. The deep wrinkles of worry across his usually smooth forehead showed how serious he thought the loss was.

At last, turning his sharp blue eyes on Pepper, Stuart said, "Now Pepper, tell me carefully everything that you learned about the Yankee army. How strong are they, did they look tired, how well are they equipped? Then tell me again how the Special Orders were found."

Carefully and in detail, the boy related all that he had seen in Frederick. Stuart listened intently, his blue eyes never leaving the scout's face. As Pepper talked, the wrinkles in Stuart's forehead deepened.

At last the General stood up and placed his hands on Pepper's shoulders. "Boy, you've done a good piece of work. Lee must have this information at once. Even now it may be too late to recall all the troops he has sent out. I'll go and tell him personally."

"Shall I go along?" Pepper asked.

"No, you look nearly worn out. Go and rest while you can. There's heavy work in store for the army soon."

Stuart clapped on his plumed hat, pulled his red-lined cloak about him and strode out, shouting for his horse.

Pepper watched him ride away before turning back to Sunstar.

"I reckon we brought bad news this time, old pal. The General looked mighty worried."

The tired horse sighed gustily as he rubbed his head against the boy's shoulder. Pepper threw an arm across Sunstar's neck and buried his haggard face in the long mane. Then he gathered up the reins and walked slowly away, the horse tramping wearily at his heels.

CHAPTER THIRTEEN
A New Coat for Stonewall Jackson

FIVE days later the great guns that had flamed across peaceful Antietam Creek and through the town of Sharpsburg were stilled. The battle smoke drifted like a yellow pall across the shell-shattered ridges and cornfields.

Thousands of soldiers in blue and gray lay silent on the field or were sleeping forever along the little farm road known thereafter as the "Bloody Lane." The

Union and Confederate armies had met and pounded each other mercilessly. Now both were exhausted. During the final hours of the terrific battle, men had walked like ghosts through the smoky haze.

Outnumbered, red-eyed from lack of sleep, and drooping with weariness, the gray ranks held firm during the fierce cannonading on the seventeenth of September. Next day they grimly awaited a second Yankee attack.

But McClellan, overcautious as always, failed to follow up his advantage. Except for occasional sharp bickerings along the picket lines, the two armies were motionless.

In the evening General Lee led his army across the Potomac into Virginia and the men gratefully lay down to rest on their own southern soil once more. The Maryland campaign was over.

The battle had been a jumbled nightmare to Pepper. It was strictly a clash between infantry and artillery. The cavalry could do little against the flame-belching cannon of the Union army. Dismounted, Stuart's troopers had given what help they could to their weary comrades.

Salt and Pepper, with other gray raiders, had served a Parrott gun. Ramrods in hand, blackened by the smoke and grime, the boys had rammed, swabbed, and felt the earth tremble from the concussion so often that they lost all track of time. The unceasing roar had deafened them.

When the gray troops began to withdraw across the

Potomac, Stuart's bugles rang out. His men climbed into their saddles and galloped off to act as a screen for the southern army.

"This is more like it," Pepper called to Salt as they followed Stuart's waving plume. "It sure feels good to have Sunstar between my knees again."

"You bet," agreed Salt, reaching forward to stroke Thunder's neck. "No more feeding iron balls to cannon for mine. Give me a live horse every time—there's darned little that's affectionate about a steel gun. Reckon I wasn't cut out to be an artilleryman."

The troopers followed the bank of the Potomac for several miles. At Shepherdstown they missed the ford and went splashing through the cold water of the river, swimming their horses over the deeper parts of the channel.

"We all need a bath after that battle," Pepper shouted to his Georgia friend, "but somebody forgot to heat the water."

"Burrrrr!" shivered Salt. "I'd rather wait and take mine next summer."

Up stream they galloped, chasing the Federal pickets. For two days the gray troopers tormented the fringes of McClellan's army, now here, now there, acting as the eyes and ears of Lee's forces, keeping the Yankees worried, and making sure that the Confederate escape was unchallenged.

Then, their work done, Stuart led his men back across the river to rejoin the main wing of the southern army.

A well-earned rest, food, shelter and relief from the roar
of battle awaited men and horses in Virginia.

The last days of September and the opening days of
October were happy ones for the cavalry. Their white
tents were pitched in the shade of oak trees near the
Dandridge estate, which reminded Pepper sharply of
the Magnolia Hill plantation he had left behind.

Autumn followed the troops back from Maryland
and the green Virginia hills were taking on a golden
tint. Oak and sumac flamed red on the ridges. Golden
sunlight filled the days and the scent of ripening apples ·
was heavy in the air.

Salt and Pepper took long rides through the countryside, feeling like schoolboys on a holiday. Sunstar
and Thunder pranced proudly, fretting at their bits
and teasing their riders to let them run. Laughing, the
boys would give in, enjoying the headlong races as they
galloped neck and neck, the bracing air whistling past
their ears and stinging against their eyeballs.

The cavalrymen were in high spirits. New boots and
uniforms were issued by the quartermaster to those who
needed them. Rations were more plentiful with the har-
vest, and everybody was rested. The Dandridge family
held open house every evening for the staff, and there
was singing and laughing around the campfires.

One bright day, early in October, a messenger arrived from Richmond carrying a large flat box. Pepper
and Salt, sitting idly outside cavalry headquarters,

watched him curiously as he disappeared into Stuart's tent. In a moment he returned empty-handed, mounted his horse, and cantered back toward Richmond.

"Now what do you reckon he brought in that box?" Pepper asked lazily.

Salt shook his head and tossed an acorn at a saucy gray squirrel scolding him from a near-by tree trunk.

"Pepper!" Stuart called, popping his head through the tent flap. "Ask Major von Borcke to come here. The two of you come back with him."

"Yes, sir," and Pepper scrambled to his feet and made off toward the Dutchman's quarters while Salt and the squirrel stared after him.

In a few minutes the huge Prussian dragoon clanked into sight with Pepper trotting at his heels. Salt got up, brushed the leaves from his uniform and fell into step behind them. Indian file they entered Stuart's tent, where von Borcke had to keep his shoulders hunched so that his head would not bump the ridgepole.

Stuart sat at his camp table, the large flat box lying before him.

"Gentlemen," he said, smiling and stroking his beard, "for a long time the condition of General Stonewall Jackson's coat has been worrying me. It may have been fine when it was first tailored, but after two years of hard campaigning it has become something that no respectable officer would be caught dead in. I have sent to Richmond for a new one, and here it is."

Stuart indicated the large box with a graceful wave of his hand.

"I want you three to ride over to Stonewall's camp and present it to him with Jeb Stuart's compliments and all due ceremony. And—see that the General wears it."

A short time later the three envoys were riding merrily toward Jackson's headquarters at Bunker Hill. The day was filled with golden sunlight and the breeze rustled through the vari-colored leaves, while puffy little autumn clouds sailed across the sky, casting soft shadows that glided gently along the hillsides.

"The day, *sehr schön*, so beautiful," said von Borcke, all the sentimentality of his Teutonic soul bubbling to the surface. "Almost I could quote poetry. It makes me think of *mein Vaterland*."

"Does Prussia look like this, Major?" Pepper asked.

"*Ja und nein*, yes and no," replied the Major pulling his long mustaches thoughtfully. "In Prussia it is all hills and rocks, rugged and beautiful—a man's country. Now this is a man's country, too, but here one can look far, far away and see in the distance miles and miles of country. In *mein Preuszen* the crags and mountains cut off the view. Here it is very different. You understand?"

"I think so," answered Pepper.

"Which country do you like best, Major?" asked Salt.

"I love your Southland—I come here to fight for it— *aber das Preuszen ist mein Vaterland*. Some day I return there."

Stonewall Jackson's tents were pitched in another

oak grove along the crest of Bunker Hill. Riding into camp, the three envoys turned their horses over to orderlies and von Borcke handed the box to Salt. Then the three filed into Jackson's tent where von Borcke proceeded to pay his compliments to the General. Very formal and proper the Major was, clicking his heels and bowing from the waist, in the approved Prussian military style, his quaint English giving an odd touch to the occasion. Even Jackson's solemn eyes twinkled and his firm mouth twitched with amusement.

At last the formalities were over, but General Jackson was still puzzled about the visit. Formal military courtesies were not common among Confederate officers.

"I'm glad you came over, Major," said Jackson. "Now let's have some dinner."

"Von moment, General!" exclaimed the Prussian. "But first I bring a liddle gift from *Herr* General Stuart with his respects. May I haff permission to open it?"

Jackson nodded, looking mildly curious.

Salt stepped smartly forward, holding the big box that was all wrapped up like a gigantic Christmas present.

Von Borcke took the box, broke the string with a flourish and, while Jackson and his staff crowded closer to see, lifted a new general's coat out of its nest of wrapping paper. A murmur of awe arose as they saw the rich gray garment with its facings of blue silk, its gilt buttons, and its gold embroidery. A golden silk sash and white gauntlets completed its glory.

Much moved, Jackson looked from the gorgeous creation to his old coat, weathered to a queer shade of greenish-gray after two years of rain, powder smoke, campfires, and hard usage.

"Please convey my deepest thanks to General Stuart," he said at last. "I'll keep the coat for a souvenir because it is much too fine for the hard usage I must give it."

"Oh, *nein, nein, mein* General," objected the Prussian. "You must wear it."

"By all means, General," his staff officers insisted. "You should try it on."

Smiling, but embarrassed, Stonewall Jackson at last consented to take off his battered old coat and substitute the gorgeous new one. It fit him to perfection, making him a dashing martial figure. All the officers spoke their admiration. Self-conscious, the General wore his new coat through dinner, while his men, as the rumor of the coat spread through camp, pressed close to marvel and admire.

While the officers were chatting, Salt and Pepper strolled off to look over the infantry camp. The tents stretched for several miles along the ridge and the smoke of countless campfires filled the air. Returning at last to the clump of trees where their horses were tied, Pepper saw a tall infantryman stroking Sunstar's head and talking gently while the great horse rubbed against his shoulder in a friendly fashion.

"Say, that's funny," he said to Salt. "I never knew Sunstar to take up with a stranger like that."

The infantryman's shoulders looked very familiar, Pepper thought. Then the soldier heard him coming and turned.

"Cousin Brian!" Pepper shouted. "When did you come back to the army?"

"Pepper!" Brian answered. "Doggone! You've grown so much I didn't know you at first."

In a few minutes the three boys were comfortably settled under a tree with both Pepper and his cousin talking at once.

"I was pretty sore when I heard how you'd rounded up those spies all by yourself back home," Brian said. "Why didn't you tell me about 'em?"

"Didn't have time," answered Pepper. "Anyway, I was sure I could handle 'em myself."

"Well, you'd better watch out for that McGrigg. He sounds like bad business to me."

"I will," Pepper promised. "Now tell me about yourself."

Brian had been back in the army only two days and he was full of news about Magnolia Hill plantation and its people. He was also anxious to learn about Pepper's adventures, especially about the Special Orders 191.

"Who do you reckon lost those orders?" he asked.

"Nobody knows," Pepper replied. "Couldn't have been a spy because no spy would risk throwing away an important paper like that. I know the Yankee private found it by accident. Made a lot of trouble for us, though—'Little Mac' wouldn't have caught us at Sharpsburg if he hadn't known Lee's plans."

"Yes, I've heard that Sharpsburg was the bloodiest battle of the war," Brian agreed. "I wonder who did lose those orders."

"I've heard one explanation," Salt broke in. "One of General Lee's headquarters orderlies got thrown off his horse when the army was leaving Frederick. The orders may have slipped out of his pocket when he fell."

"Why doesn't somebody ask him about it?" Pepper wanted to know.

"They can't very well," was the answer. "He got killed at Sharpsburg."

"Then I reckon we never will know for sure," Pepper sighed. "It was a terrible loss for us. We had some hard fighting and some mighty anxious moments because of it."

The boys sat in thoughtful silence for a moment. Then Brian punched his cousin.

"Say, Big Chief, what's happened to your Indian jacket?" he asked. "There's scarcely a bead or a bit of fringe left on it."

Pepper looked ruefully at his once gorgeous jacket. Long exposure to rain and weather had stained and spotted it, while nights around the smoky campfire and bivouacs in the woods had turned it dark and dingy. Briars had ripped away most of the beads and fringe.

"I reckon it is pretty much the worse for wear," he

admitted, "but it still keeps me warm and dry. After all, there are a lot of soldiers with worse uniforms than mine in the Confederate army."

"Just wear it as long as Stonewall Jackson wore his," laughed Brian, "then maybe Jeb Stuart will give you a new coat, too."

"Maybe he will," grinned Pepper. "Do you reckon he'd put a general's star on the collar?"

"Here come the Dutchman and Stonewall," Salt interrupted the cousins' conversation and scrambled to his feet. "It must be time for us to start back."

The two cousins rose also. After unhitching their horses and von Borcke's, they walked toward the crest of the hill where the Major and General Jackson stood talking. The infantry commander still wore his new coat, looking very smart and handsome in it.

"Try to get permission to come over and see us, Brian," Pepper urged.

"All right, I will. But remember that I belong to the 'foot cavalry' and it's a long walk to Stuart's camp. Both of you come back when you can."

"We will," the couriers answered.

Brian remained a short distance down the hill, watching while the cavalrymen mounted. Waving gaily, they soon disappeared over the hilltop.

On the following evening, while Stuart and some of his staff officers were away for a conference with Lee, the gray troopers gathered around the campfire for a session of yarns and tall stories.

This was the kind of an evening that Pepper and his friend Barry Salter loved, with the firelight glinting on bronzed faces, and the scent of pine smoke in the air. Two weeks had blotted out some of the stark horrors of Sharpsburg, and now the troopers were living over daring deeds and adventures.

" 'Little Mac' had three times as many troops and guns as 'Marse Robert,' " boasted one rider. "But we held him back, anyway."

"You bet, and we've chased him back sixty miles since June," agreed another.

"Won't Lee feel the terrible losses at Sharpsburg?" Pepper asked, remembering how the Confederate dead had lain in silent heaps along the "Bloody Lane" and in the cornfield below.

"Naw, we can get more men—stragglers and replacements are coming in every day," the trooper retorted. "We'll lick 'em yet."

"Sure we will," agreed Hagan. "The Yankees caught us in a bad way between Antietam Creek and the Potomac, and they did their worst. But here we are, in pretty good shape and getting better every day."

"Don't you worry about us, son," advised Sweeney joining the group just in time to hear the final remarks. "As long as 'Marse Robert's' got officers like Jeb Stuart and Stonewall Jackson to back him up, no Yankees can lick us."

"Hullo, Sam," called Hagan. "Where have you been all evening?"

"Up at the Dutchman's tent helping him rehearse

his part in a skit, 'The Pennsylvania Farmer's Wife.'
He and Colonel Brien are going to put it on for the
Dandridge's party tomorrow night," Sweeney replied
as he sat down on a log in front of the fire.

"A play!" snorted Hagan. "Well of all the—!"
Sweeney laughed.

"Sure, a play. We actors have to help each other out.
You should see von Borcke all dressed up like a farmer's wife—gingham dress, bonnet, corset stays and all!"
Sweeney laughed until the tears ran down his face at
the recollection.

"Aw, come on and sing for us," urged a trooper.

"Yeah, and make it funny," growled Hagan.

Sweeney fingered his banjo and strummed a few
chords.

"Here's one you all like," he said, "but I'm playing
it especially for Barry Salter from Georgia. He looks
kind of homesick tonight."

With that he burst into a song that had long been a
favorite of all the men in gray.

> "*Sitting by the road side on a summer day,*
>   *Chatting with my messmates, passing time away,*
>   *Lying in the shadow underneath the trees,*
>   *Goodness, how delightful, eating goober peas!*"

The banjoist paused for a moment at the end of the
stanza and looked at the men around him.

"Come on," he commanded. "Sing!"

The banjo thumped again and every man joined in
the chorus.

"Peas! Peas! Peas! Peas!
Eating goober peas.
Goodness, how delicious,
Eating goober peas!"

Carried away by their enthusiasm, they sang the chorus three times, their voices ringing out through the night. Pepper looked around and marveled that these same faces, so friendly and full of fun, could turn harsh and grim in battle.

"Thanks, Sweeney," Salt said after the laughter and applause had died down. "Do you know any new ones?"

Sweeney scratched his head and looked reflectively at his banjo.

"Let's see. I reckon so. Have you heard this one?"

He struck up a lively tune that Pepper recognized as an old song his father used to sing. But Sweeney's words were vastly different.

"The Yankees are cute; they've managed, somehow,
Their business and ours to settle;
They make all we want, from a pin to a plough.
Now we'll show them some real Southern mettle.

"We've had just enough of their old Northern law,
That robbed us so long of our rights, men,
And too much of their cursed abolitionist jaw—
Now we'll see what they'll do in a fight, men."

"You bet we will," Hagan agreed. "We'll be ready and waiting for them."

"What do you have against the Yankees that makes you hate them so?" Pepper asked curiously.

The black-whiskered lieutenant blinked at him, started to answer, blinked again and then abruptly subsided, muttering indistinctly into his beard.

Sweeney laughed and winked at Pepper.

"Hagan is the ideal soldier, son," he said. "He fights first and then looks around for a reason."

"Oh," said Pepper. But he looked puzzled.

"You see, son," the banjo player continued, "war is a good excuse, that's all. Why the Yankees and the Southerners should hate each other is hard to understand—we all have the same history and we speak the same language. War just makes people lose their heads, I reckon."

"Why did you join, Sweeney?" the boy asked.

"Me? Well, you see, my vaudeville show had gone on the rocks and soldiering looked easier than starving. The bands were playing and everybody in Richmond was all excited, so I just joined up."

A new thought struck Pepper.

"Sweeney, if your show had gone broke in Washington instead of in Richmond, would you have joined the Yankee army?" he asked.

The ex-actor scratched his head thoughtfully.

"You've got me there," he admitted. "Maybe I would have—I don't know. I was born in the South. When I began to get hungry I just fell in step with the Confederate recruits and marched toward the mess kitchen. Never gave the war much thought."

"Hey, cut out the jaw and sing some more," a
trooper called.

Sweeney picked up his banjo in relief. The boy's
questions had made him strangely uncomfortable.

Pepper lay back in the grass, staring up at the stars
that twinkled merrily in the black void above. Scarcely
hearing the songs and jokes of the troopers, he was
wondering over and over just why were the North and
South fighting—and he kept thinking about those
tangled piles of dead at Sharpsburg.

Next morning Pepper popped his head outside his
tent to see a crowd of troopers gathered around a tree
trunk near by. The ones in back were craning their
necks in an effort to see over the heads of the others.

"What do you reckon is going on?" Pepper asked
Salt when his tent mate joined him.

"Search me! Let's go out and see."

"What's the matter?" Pepper asked one of the crowd
as he and Salt elbowed their way toward the front.

"That's what we're tryin' to figger out," was the
answer. "There's a piece of paper posted on the tree,
but none of us can read it very good. We ain't so strong
on book learnin'."

"I'll read it for you if you'll let me through," volun-
teered Pepper.

"Gangway, boys," a giant trooper bellowed, picking
the boy up by the scruff of his neck, like a kitten.
"Here's somebody what can read."

The crowd gave way and soon Pepper found himself

staring at a neat proclamation tacked to the oak tree.

"What's it say?"

"Read it loud."

"Quiet, so's we can hear."

Pepper took a deep breath and began to read.

" 'Soldiers: You are about to engage in an enterprise which, to insure success, imperatively demands at your hands coolness, decision and bravery: implicit obedience to orders without question or cavil, and the strictest order and sobriety on the march and in bivouac. The destination and extent of this had better be kept to myself than known to you. Suffice it to say that, with the hearty cooperation of officers and men, I have no doubt of its success—a success which will reflect credit in the highest degree upon your arms. The orders herewith published for your government are absolutely necessary and must be rigidly enforced.

(Signed)   J. E. B. Stuart,
Major General Commanding.' "

"Well, what do you think of that?"

"What does it mean?"

"Them big words is hard to understand."

"There's some more, men," Pepper had to shout to make himself heard over the noise of the crowd.

"Be quiet, let's hear the rest," bellowed the man who had first spoken to Pepper.

"All right, but don't use such high-falutin' language. Let's have it easy like," remarked a lanky cavalryman.

"We're to make another raid," Pepper explained,

staring at the proclamation. "It'll take us into Pennsylvania and we're to collect all the horses we can, but we're not to bother private property or molest citizens."

"Yippie!" yelled the lanky rider. "That's the stuff!"

"So it's horses he wants this time. Well, we'll get 'em," agreed another.

"When do we start?"

"We'll start tonight at midnight, men," said a voice behind the crowd, and the troopers turned to see General Stuart leaning on his saber and watching them.

CHAPTER FOURTEEN
Jeb Stuart's Ruse

EVERY member of the headquarters staff turned up at the Dandridge mansion that night to witness von Borcke's triumph in the play, "The Pennsylvania Farmer's Wife." Jeb Stuart laughed till the tears ran down his whiskers. Even Hagan condescended to chuckle when the big Dutchman took the center of the stage, dressed in a huge gingham Mother Hubbard dress and a bright pink sunbonnet.

After the play Sweeney's banjo became the center of attraction, and the staff officers led the Dandridge ladies in to dance on the shining ballroom floor. At eleven o'clock Jeb Stuart raised his hand and the music stopped. The officers gathered around Sweeney for one final serenade before leaving. Their voices rang clear and mellow in the brightly lighted hall.

For some reason their mood was mournful and somewhat sentimental so with one accord they chose the well-loved "Lorena":

> *"The years creep slowly by, Lorena;*
> *The snow is on the grass again;*
> *The sun's low down the sky, Lorena;*
> *The frost gleams where the flowers have been.*
> *But the heart throbs on as warmly now*
> *As when the summer days were nigh;*
> *Oh! the sun can never dip so low*
> *Adown affection's cloudless sky. . . ."*

Their serenade over, the officers said good night and filed out, mounting their horses in the driveway. Stuart swung his hat in a wide arc and away they trotted, their sabers jingling against stirrup irons, and the gleaming shoes of their horses striking sparks from the hard stone road. As they disappeared in the distance, a rollicking song went floating back to the group on the Dandridge veranda. Listening carefully, the ladies caught the words

> *"If you want to have a good time*
> *Jine the cavalry. . . ."*

Back at the cavalry camp bugles rang out through the sharp night air; waiting troopers climbed into their saddles, and the gray riders were off for another raid. Northward they rode, under stars that twinkled like tiny points of fire in the cold October sky.

"Whereabouts are we headed this time, I wonder," Salt said to Pepper as they rode, knee to knee, behind the General.

"Somewhere in Pennsylvania," Pepper answered. "That's what the general orders to the troops said. Of course, there's Maryland between us and Pennsylvania. Both states are crowded with Yankee soldiers, but Stuart never lets a little thing like that bother him."

"Why should he?" shouted Sweeney over his shoulder. "We can outride and outfight any Yankee outfit that ever took the field against us."

"As long as we feel that way, no Yankees can ever lick us," Pepper told Salt. "The rule books call it 'morale,' but I reckon self-confidence is another name for that feeling. Stuart's men are just bristling with self-confidence."

"Why shouldn't they be?" Salt wanted to know. "Haven't we been clear around McClellan, didn't we get Pope's coat, and haven't we got the best record for service in the whole army?"

Stuart's chuckle interrupted the boys' discussion and they subsided into an embarrassed silence.

"Keep it up, boys," the General told them, swinging around in his saddle to smile at their embarrassment. "When soldiers feel that way, nothing can beat them."

Hour after hour they pounded northward until the gray October dawn chased away the stars. A heavy mist rolled up from the Potomac river as the column splashed across the shallows at McCoy's Ford. When the advance column set foot on the Maryland shore a sudden spatter of pistol shots rang out through the mist, and a blue picket force scattered before the gray raiders. A Yankee prisoner and several captured horses were forced to join the Confederate band.

Friendly fog shrouded the column for several miles up the Potomac valley and the surprised blue forces fell back before the gray riders who suddenly materialized like ghosts out of the mist. A few detachments of Yankee cavalry clung to Stuart's flank, but the horsemen in blue could not screw up courage enough to risk a head-on clash with the reckless-riding, hard-fighting Confederates.

By noon Stuart's men rode into Mercersburg, ten miles inside the Pennsylvania border. Details of gray troopers were sent out to the right and left of the column with instructions to sweep up every horse they could find. All animals were carefully receipted in the name of the Confederate States of America so that their owners could ask payment from the government.

"Impress all horses you find in Pennsylvania," the General ordered, as he sent out the detachments. Then, on second thought, he added, "Don't take the ones ridden by ladies; this is a man's war, we're not fighting women. And don't harm private property."

"Yes, sir," agreed the raiders, galloping off on their missions.

Salt and Pepper elected to remain with the main body until the afternoon, halting in Mercersburg long enough to have Sunstar and Thunder shod with Yankee iron. They gave Confederate bills in payment. Details came in every hour with captured horses and fresh men went out to get more. The Confederate army was in dire need of horses, and Stuart was determined to end that need.

"Salt," Stuart said, as the column galloped out of Mercersburg, "you ride with Captain Farley out to the right and keep your eye open for horses. Pepper, you and Hagan do the same to the left. Rejoin us at Chambersburg this evening."

Obeying, the four saluted and wheeled away in opposite directions from the main body of troops.

The Pennsylvania countryside was brown and dreary looking in contrast to the still glowing Virginia hills which had not yet felt the freezing breath of winter. Crisp dead grass rustled under the horses' feet and tree limbs hung gaunt and bare against the cloudy gray sky. Only the dead, yellow stubble of summer corn and wheat stood in scraggly rows on the rolling hillsides.

"Say, son, I'm hungry," Hagan remarked to Pepper as they rode along in early afternoon, six captured horses clattering close behind them.

"So am I," replied Pepper, "but how are we going to get anything to eat in enemy country?"

"Easy," the black-whiskered lieutenant smiled mysteriously. "Didn't anybody ever tell you that I'm the best forager in the army?"

"Y-es," said Pepper doubtfully, "but still I don't see how you're going to do it without disobeying the General's order about not harming private property."

"See that house over there? That's where we're going to get our dinner. Just you string along with old man Hagan and you'll eat hearty. They'll be glad to give it to us—in fact, they'll beg us to take it."

The boy still looked unconvinced but he made no further objection. Instead he swung around in his saddle and surveyed the hills that rolled endlessly all about them. The sky was growing more overcast as the afternoon advanced, and the Pennsylvania countryside looked bleak and cold.

"What's that?" Pepper asked suddenly, pointing to a cloud of dust that was just disappearing over a hill crest in the distance behind the farmhouse they were approaching.

"Looks like the men folks have taken their livestock and scooted," the lieutenant replied, tugging at his whiskers. "Since they're so unneighborly, son, we don't need to feel so bad about getting something to eat. Serves 'em right for running away."

Silently Pepper followed Hagan as they rode into the farmyard and dismounted beside the house. They tied their horses to a hitching rack and proceeded to the front porch. Hagan brushed his hand upward through his whiskers so that they bristled more fiercely than ever and hitched his sword and pistols into sight.

"Now watch me," he commanded.

Hagan clumped up the steps and pounded on the door with the butt of one of his heavy horse pistols. There was no answer. He waited a moment and then pounded again, louder than before.

This time the door opened cautiously and a round Pennsylvania Dutch face peered out at him. Inside the room the two raiders could see three other plump women who sat and stolidly rocked fat, rosy Pennsylvania babies.

"Good afternoon, Ma'am," said Hagan, touching his cap. "My young friend and I belong to Stuart's Confederate cavalry and we just stopped in for a bite to eat."

The fat expressionless face did not change.

"Dere is *kein steck* food in diss house," the woman said with a heavy accent. "Go avay. *'Raus mit!*"

Hagan drew himself together, clattered his saber against the step, clapped his hand on his pistols. Sniffing hungrily, he placed his foot so that the woman could not slam the door in his face. Then he looked with wolfish eyes toward the fat babies.

"Wa-al, Ma'am," he drawled, "I'm mighty hungry and I'm going to eat. Up to now I've never tasted any baby meat, but I reckon I can try right now." He drew his saber and tested the shining blade gingerly with a heavy thumb.

The woman's eyes popped wide in terror, and her fat face paled.

"*Lieber Gott!* Vait!" she said, waving to the others with trembling hands. "Don't do dot. Come in und I get you somedings. Shust a minute. I feed you."

While the four women rushed around laying out great pies, jars of preserves, ham, sausage, milk and cheese, Hagan turned and winked slyly at Pepper.

"See how it's done," he rumbled.

"I see, all right. But I couldn't get away with it. I don't have a set of whiskers like a Barbary pirate."

Toward evening, bountifully fed, Hagan and Pepper cantered into Chambersburg just as great cold drops of rain began to fall. The threatening skies were at last making good on their promise of a general downpour. The men in Stuart's main column were already busy removing stores from the Chambersburg Federal depot and long lines of captured horses were plodding through the mud into town.

All night the rain continued to fall, soaking quickly through the thin gray uniforms and turning the streets of Chambersburg into ankle-deep streaks of soupy mud. No fire would burn in the dampness and the troopers huddled under what shelter they could find, or scurried about in the effort to keep warm.

Salt and Pepper splashed through the night, carrying messages from Stuart to his subordinates. Their horses' hoofs sloshed in the slimy mud at every step. It was no easy matter to keep the party in hand and the officers had to be in constant touch with their chief.

At four o'clock in the morning Stuart's bugles sounded "Assembly" and the rain-soaked column formed

in the marketplace, a great herd of captured horses in
their center. Dawn was gleaming feebly through the
rain when the troop moved eastward out of town. The
dull boom of an explosion thundered after them as the
rear guard blew up the supplies that were left in the
Yankee army depot.

The homeward journey carried them far around the
fringe of the Union army zone, between Frederick and
Washington. Stuart, daring as ever, was determined
to outwit the enemy and to surprise him by choosing
the longest way out. All day they cantered onward, the
troopers remounting themselves on captured horses
when their own steeds showed signs of giving out. Mile
after mile the column thundered on, leaving Pennsylvania behind and entering Maryland again.

Small detachments of Federal horsemen were hard
at his heels all during the wild ride, but Stuart's ruse
in taking the least likely, as well as the longest, way out
had bewildered the blue pursuit. They did not know
just where to look for Stuart and every minute they
spent in aimless search saw the gray cavalry drawing
nearer to the Potomac and safety. The rain thinned out
toward noon but banks of heavy clouds still hid the sun.

Onward the troopers pounded. Emmitsburg, Rocky
Ridge, Woodsborough, Liberty, New Market, Mon-
rovia, Hyattstown, Barnesville, and Beallsville—town,
village, and hamlet rushed by in an endless succession
as the riders urged their horses forward. At last the
Potomac, already swollen by the rain, came into sight

before them. A feeling of thanksgiving and relief filled Pepper's heart. Safety lay just ahead.

A faint roar from behind turned his delight into horror as the boy swung around to see a Federal detachment massing on a hilltop a mile or so behind them and swarming down in eager pursuit. Then a wood hid the advancing Yankees.

"General, look yonder, sir!" Salt's voice broke the tense silence.

Pepper turned to see Stuart and his staff gazing across the right flank of the column. There a swarm of infantry in blue was already drawn up on the high ground commanding the ford across the Potomac. It looked like certain disaster.

"Caught between two fires," muttered Hagan. "They'll pound us to pieces while we're crossing over."

The other staff officers looked grim and worried. But Stuart had already seen a loophole. Snatching a scrap of paper and a pencil from his pocket, he scribbled hastily for a moment. Then he read his note aloud.

"Commanding officer, U. S. troops: General J. E. B. Stuart with all his cavalry is on your front; the hopelessness of your situation is apparent to you. To avoid unnecessary bloodshed you are called on to surrender; if you do not, we will charge you in ten minutes. Your situation is hopeless."

Stuart handed the note to Hagan.

"Lieutenant, tie a handkerchief to your saber and deliver this to the Yankee commander. It's our only chance. The troops ahead won't be able to see the ones behind us for several minutes—we may be able to bluff the Yankees and make them move back."

Hagan saluted, drew his saber, and fixing a white square of cloth to the gleaming blade, he galloped toward the menacing blue lines on the right.

Anxious eyes followed him as the tired troopers prepared for a fight to the death. No one had much hope that the ruse would work. The minutes ticked by on Stuart's big watch as Hagan topped the rise and disappeared in a swarm of blue-clad soldiers. Ten minutes passed and the General closed his watch with a sharp click that sounded like the snap of a trigger in the tense silence.

"Captain Pelham! Ad-vance the artillery!" came the command in the ringing tones of Stuart's battle voice.

The young gunnery officer raised his arm for the signal; then Sweeney's voice broke in.

"Look," he said, pointing.

Hagan was galloping back down the slope toward them, and from the hilltop came the sound of a Yankee drum beating the long roll. Hagan waved his arm wildly toward the Potomac and the blue ranks retired from sight behind the hill.

"It worked!" gasped Sweeney.

"Forward, men! Let's get across the river," Stuart ordered, setting spurs to his horse's flanks.

The column hurried forward, anxious to get across the river before other pursuing troops came in sight, and before the Yankees realized how they had been tricked. Pelham's horse artillery splashed across the Potomac ford in the lead, pulling up in battery formation on the southern bank to cover the crossing of the troopers.

The main body, with the led horses and prisoners, galloped over the ford to safety. Finally came the rear guard, shooting back at the first of the Yankee infantry who were just now breaking through the woods that had hidden them from their comrades. Pelham's guns began to bark from the river bank as the last of the gray troopers came splashing through the ford. One of the most audacious ruses of the whole war had succeeded.

Raindrops were splattering down again as the last Confederate raider rode up the south bank of the Potomac. The Union soldiers halted on the north bank and panted, too exhausted to push across into enemy territory. With a last laughing look at his now harmless pursuers, Stuart gave the marching command and his jubilant column, with prisoners and captured horses in its midst, rode forward through the rain toward camp, rest, and food.

CHAPTER FIFTEEN

Pepper Meets a Bullet

"I STILL don't see how we did it," Pepper insisted the next night when he and Salt, with Hagan and Sweeney as visitors, were lounging in the boys' tent, taking shelter from the rain and discussing the recent raid.

"You don't see how we did what?" his Georgia friend inquired lazily.

"I don't see how we fooled those Yankees back there

on the river bank. The General's note sounded fierce enough, but even so, it just doesn't seem possible."

"Son, you'd have to see the Yankee officer's face to understand that," Hagan explained. "When I rode up under the flag of truce and handed him Jeb Stuart's note, I thought he was going to faint. I tell you Jeb's almost like the Devil, himself, to the Yankees; they want to cut and run when they know he's near."

Sweeney winked at the boys.

"Even allowing the lieutenant fifty per cent off for imagination, it's surprising the effect Stuart's name has on the Yankees," he said.

"It's not surprising at all when you remember what he's done," Salt chimed in. "Why, just think, on this raid we made eighty miles in a day and a night, rode clear around the Yankee army a second time, and brought home a bunch of prisoners and twelve hundred captured horses. Match that if you can."

"I know," said Pepper, "but it's hard to believe, now that it's over."

"Yes, and we had plenty of anxious moments," Sweeney remarked. "I thought we were goners for sure when that blue line showed up above the river. It would have been 'good night' if those fellas had been a mile nearer."

"Aw, we just wore 'em out and then walked away from them," Salt scoffed. "They never had a chance."

"I wonder what will happen next," said Pepper.

"There's no telling," Sweeney answered, "but there's to be a celebration ball up at the Dandridges' tomorrow night, and Jeb's going to send out the captured horses to bring in the guests."

"That's good—sending Yankee horses to bring Virginians to a ball celebrating a Confederate victory," Hagan chuckled. "For once I think the joke's good enough to excuse the dance and folderol. I may go and swing a foot myself."

"Whee-ew!" whistled the banjoist. "Jeb Stuart ought to include that in his regular report. 'Lieutenant "Pirate Whiskers" Hagan so overcome by victory that he breaks the rule of a lifetime to play with the ladies.' "

"Go on and laugh," growled Hagan. "I'll bet that I can step a polka and kiss a lady's hand just as well as you can."

Salt nudged Pepper.

"Ouch! If he kissed a lady's hand, those whiskers of his would tickle her to death," he snickered.

Pepper's gray eyes twinkled as he nodded agreement.

Sweeney reached for his banjo.

"I know a nice little tune that will just fit you, Hagan. I'll dedicate it to you tomorrow night at the dance."

"Play it now," suggested Salt.

"Yes, you'd better," threatened the bewhiskered lieutenant. "If I don't like it and you try to play it tomorrow night, I'll smash that banjo over your head. I'm inclined to get rough when things rile me."

"Just you try it, little feller," Sweeney answered

sweetly. "I'll come out with both fists full of whiskers and yelling for more."

"Come on, Sam, let's hear the song," Pepper broke in on the friendly wrangling.

"Yes, go on and play it," Salt begged.

After the proper amount of coaxing, the banjo player condescended to strum a few chords before he burst into the jolly song.

"As they rode through the town with their banners so gay,
 I ran to the window to hear the band play;
 I peeped through the blinds very cautiously then,
 Lest the neighbors should catch me watching the men.
 Oh! I heard the drums beat, and the music so sweet,
 But my eyes at the time caught a much greater treat;
 The troop was the finest I ever did see
 And the lieutenant blew kisses through his whiskers at me.

"When we met at the ball, I of course thought 'twas right
 To pretend that we'd never met ere that night,
 But he knew me at once, I perceived by his glance,
 And he twisted his beard when he asked me to dance.
 Oh! He sat by my side at the end of the set,
 And the sweet words he spoke I shall never forget;
 And my heart was enlisted and could not get free,
 Now the lieutenant and his whiskers are married to me."

"That sounds pretty good, Sam," a new voice broke in as the song ended. "You always could pick a mean banjo string."

"Why, hullo, John Mosby," Sweeney exclaimed as the other three rolled over to see the famous scout standing just outside their tent with the rain drops trickling from his hat brim.

"Come in and make yourself at home, John," Pepper invited, moving over to make room on the cot for his friend. "Where have you been? We missed you on the last raid."

"I've been in Washington for the past couple of weeks," the sandy-haired scout answered, taking off his dripping oilskin cape and making himself comfortable on the cot. "You fellows certainly did have the Yankee capital up in arms this time."

Hagan laughed harshly. It always pleased the big lieutenant to give the Northerners a scare.

"Did they evacuate the city again when they heard that Jeb Stuart was loose?" Sweeney asked.

"They almost did. I tell you all the Yankee politicians and officers were mighty worried. You'd have thought Jeb Stuart was getting ready to ride straight up Pennsylvania Avenue to the White House. President Lincoln took it best, I think."

"What did old 'Father Abraham' have to say?"

"Well, he was standing on the portico, with his big top hat on his head and his plaid muffler around his neck, when they told him that Stuart was out again. He just sort of smiled and drew two circles on the floor with the point of his umbrella. 'When I was a boy we used to play a game called three times and out.' he said. 'Stuart's been around McClellan twice now. The third time and McClellan's out!' "

" 'Three times and out,' " repeated Sweeney. " 'Little Mac' had better watch his knitting. First thing he knows he'll be doing duty as a recruiting sergeant back east somewhere."

"You bet," grunted Hagan. "Hope we can get the third crack at him before winter sets in."

"Say, John, there's going to be a big celebration dance up at the mansion house tomorrow night. Better get out your best uniform and your other shirt and come along. Hagan, here, has promised to give us some pointers on ballroom tactics." Sweeney reverted to their former talk.

"Sorry, can't make it," the scout replied. "As a matter of fact I came in to see if some of you boys didn't want to go on a little scouting party with me. Jeb told me to pick my men."

"Jeb's detailed me to the music stand," Sweeney answered. "I'm stuck."

"I'll go along, Mosby," Hagan grunted. "I'd rather fight than dance any day."

"Count me in with you," Salt said, yawning. "Dances are all right if you don't have anything else to do, but scouting suits me a lot better."

"I'd like to go along too," Pepper added. "My feet don't track right at a dance."

"Good," smiled Mosby, rising and reaching for his

cape. "I knew I could count on you fellows. I'll meet you here in the morning. Be ready as soon as you finish first mess. We'll be out for some time so you'd better get rations for a couple of days from the quartermaster. After they're gone we'll have to live off the country."

"All right," the three answered. "We'll be ready."

"Good night, John," Pepper added as the scout disappeared into the rain and darkness outside.

"That sure gives my plans a black eye," Sweeney mourned. "And just when I was all set to get a few pointers from Hagan's ballroom manner."

"You and your dances," growled the lieutenant. "What kind of a war do you think this is? A tea-guzzlin' picnic?

"I'm going to turn in," he added, rising and stretching himself as much as the limits of the small tent would permit. "If we're off on another trip we need some sleep."

"Want me to stick around and sing you to sleep, boys?" suggested Sweeney, grinning, as he rose and prepared to follow Hagan. "I know some very excellent lullabies."

"No, thanks," Pepper laughed. "We can manage without being tucked in, I reckon. So long."

"Good night," Salt called as the two guests stepped outside and dashed across the wet darkness toward the shelter of their own tent. Then turning to his tentmate, he added, "Can't say we're not doing our part. Just one day in camp between raids. Maybe we should transfer to the infantry and take a rest."

"Haw, haw," jeered Pepper. "They couldn't pry you out of the cavalry with a bootjack, and you know it. Now pipe down so we can get some sleep."

"All right, auntie," Salt answered and, following Pepper's example, he paused only long enough to blow out the candle before tumbling into his blankets.

For more than a week the little scouting party composed of Mosby, Hagan, Salt, and Pepper hung close to the flank of the Union army which was pushing cautiously southward along the Potomac River. During his stay in Washington Mosby had learned that "Little Mac" was being urged by all the officials in the Federal war office to invade Virginia once more and to fight another battle before winter set in. Slowly the big army in blue was creeping forward, the attack was coming—but where would it strike? That was the question that Lee and his generals wanted answered. That was what Mosby, with his little band of scouts, was trying to work out.

The weather was clear and the air was filled with a sharp cold that put life in both men and horses. Often Pepper would forget the grim business at hand, taking keen pleasure in Sunstar's spirited gaits as the horse's hoofs rang sharp on the pebbly roads. The country was bare and rolling, filled with stone walls and icy brooks, with here and there a thick clump of trees left by a Virginia farmer to adorn his fence corners.

"This is the life," rejoiced Salt, riding knee to knee with Pepper through the early dawn, the breath of their horses steaming white in the cold. "I've never had so much fun before."

Before Pepper could answer, a distant voice hailed the little party.

"View-halloo! Wait!"

The scouts checked their horses on the crest of a hill and looked back to see a lone rider urging his horse at a gallop down the slope of a near-by ridge and across the hollow. In a few minutes he drew his panting horse up beside them.

"Why, it's Sam Sweeney," exclaimed Pepper.

"Burn my whiskers," growled Hagan. "What does he want?"

"Hello, Sam," said Mosby. "What's the matter?"

"Nothing, Stuart just sent me out with some orders for you," Sweeney grinned. "I've had a wild time finding you. The Yankees have been nipping at my heels a couple of times."

Mosby unfolded the message.

"Here's good news," he said, glancing up from the paper.

"What is it?" Hagan wanted to know.

"Stuart wants us to continue our present scouting operations until we have definite information where the Yankees will attack. Something seems to have slowed up the enemy's movements and General Lee is worried."

"Hoo-ray!" yelled Salt, his voice echoing loudly against the silent hillsides. "I was afraid he was calling us back to camp."

"You'll be calling the Yankees on us if you yell like

that again," reproved Sweeney. "They're thick over beyond that ridge. Jeb said I should stay with you," he added to Mosby. "The cavalry's too busy to need banjo music right now."

"Good," smiled the scout. "An extra man is always welcome, and no one is ever more welcome than Sam Sweeney. We've got a hard job ahead of us and we'll have to look sharp and ride fast if we want to keep out of the Yankees' clutches. Forward, men! We have work ahead."

They rode toward Fredericksburg, crossing and re-crossing the icy Rappahannock in their efforts to discover the Yankees' plans. Early in November Mosby completed his operations, convinced that the next attack would be around Fredericksburg. Then back toward camp turned the scouting party, sorry that their vacation was ended.

The return trip was nearly finished when the little party cantered down a hill slope and crashed through a dry, tangled thicket. Suddenly Sunstar shied violently, almost unseating Pepper by the unexpected movement.

"Look out, son," taunted Salt. "You'd better learn to ride before you try anything like that again."

"There must be something in those bushes," Pepper said, thinking out loud and paying no attention to Salt's teasing. "Sunstar never shied like that before."

As he spoke, the boy swung the reins sharply, urging his horse into the dense tangle of vines and bushes. Snorting fearfully, and tossing his head nervously, his delicate nostrils quivering, the black horse obeyed his master and plunged into the dense underbrush.

"Careful, boy," warned Mosby.

The words had scarcely been spoken when a sharp pistol shot pierced the silence, cutting through the cold air like the report of a cannon.

Hagan and Mosby plunged forward as a blue-uniformed figure rose out of the thicket. The big lieutenant dived headfirst from his saddle at the Yankee, pinning him to the ground and snatching away his smoking pistol all in one lightning-like movement.

"Pepper! Are you all right?"

Salt's anxious cry attracted the attention of the others from the captured Yankee. Looking up they saw Pepper swaying weakly in his saddle. A wet red stain was slowly spreading across his jacket and his face was colorless.

In an instant Sweeney and Salt spurred their horses to his side. Salt cast an arm around his friend's sagging shoulder while the banjoist swung to the ground and caught Sunstar's dragging bridle.

"That . . . was . . . McGrigg . . . the spy," mumbled Pepper through strangely stiffened lips. "He just . . . plugged me in the . . . shoulder . . . a little. I'll be . . . better in a mi . . ."

The rest of his words trailed off into nothingness for suddenly everything went black and he slumped forward, unconscious, on Sunstar's glossy neck.

"He's hurt pretty bad," Sweeney said, helping Salt

support the boy's limp body. "We've got to get him to a doctor quick."

"There's a camp hospital at the next town, just two or three miles away," Mosby said. "That will be the best place to take him. Sweeney, can you and Salt hold him in his saddle for that distance?"

"You bet we can," both answered at once.

"Yeah, and this blue-backed louse is going along too," Hagan growled, grabbing the captive by the coat collar and yanking him to his feet. "How come he's hiding here anyway?"

"None of your business, you dirty rebel," snapped the blue soldier. "I said I'd get even and I have. I only hope I've kilt him."

The venom-laden voice made Salt remember Pepper's stammered words and he urged his horse nearer the captive.

"Say, that must be Arch McGrigg, the spy Pepper caught last spring," the Georgia boy burst out. "He ought to be shot!"

"Suits me," said Hagan, shaking the captive as he had once before, until the man's teeth rattled. "Get out your pistol, Salt, and I'll hold him."

In spite of McGrigg's threats and curses, Hagan dragged him through the thicket and out into the open.

"Shut up, you murderous skunk," the glowering lieutenant advised.

Salt followed, clutching his big pistol.

Mosby had been examining Pepper's wound, trying

to staunch the flow of blood. Now the high-pitched curses of the Yankee and Hagan's bear-like growls attracted his attention.

"Hey, what are you doing?" he demanded.

"We're going to finish this sneak," answered Salt, his hot Georgia blood clamoring to avenge his comrade.

"Stop! You can't do that." Mosby hurried to the Yankee's rescue.

"But he's a dangerous spy," objected Salt. "And look what he's done to Pepper."

"He's wearing a Federal uniform and we can't shoot him offhand without a court-martial," Mosby answered. "We'll have to take him back with us."

Hagan muttered into his beard and his eyes glittered dangerously. Salt fingered his pistol. Both soldiers realized the truth of Mosby's words—a uniform had to be respected.

"Come on, come on, stop arguing about the skunk," Sweeney called. "We've got to get Pepper to a doctor."

"You and Salt go on," Mosby ordered. "Hagan and I will take care of the prisoner. You take care of Pepper."

"Right!" said Sweeney, swinging into his saddle. Riding one on each side of the wounded boy, bracing him against the jolts, the two soldiers started toward the hospital.

The next thing Pepper remembered was a burning, aching pain in his shoulder. Drowsily he attempted to roll over, only to have a great avalanche of pain sweep over him.

"Careful, son, no gyrations like that if you know what's good for you," a voice said.

Opening his eyes was a difficult task, Pepper found. His lids had never been so heavy before, and there was a strange ringing noise in his ears. At last, after a mighty effort, he forced his eyes open.

A familiar face was bending over him and a cool, friendly hand was holding his wrist. That was strange, Pepper thought. Where was he? His eyes swept inquiringly over the unfamiliar room with its long rows of empty cots before returning in wonder to the face above him.

"Why, it's Doctor Eliason," he whispered. "Where am I? What happened?"

"Don't worry, my boy. Everything is all right. Only you just happened to get in front of a Yankee bullet, that's all." Stuart's staff surgeon smiled reassuringly into the boy's bewildered face.

"Oh, yes. Now I remember," said Pepper slowly, forcing his thoughts backward with an effort. "McGrigg shot at me when I rode into that thicket this morning. Did he hurt any of the others?"

Doctor Talcott Eliason shook his head.

"No, Hagan and Mosby captured him and took him to headquarters while Salt and Sweeney brought you to the hospital. But that was three days ago, Pepper. You've been unconscious ever since."

"Oh," gasped the boy, scarcely able to believe his ears. "Where are they now? How soon can I go back to camp?"

"Now you just calm down and go back to sleep," commanded the staff surgeon, placing a restraining hand on the boy's shoulder. "You need plenty of rest. The more you fuss, the longer it will take to get you back in the saddle."

"All right, Doctor," Pepper said feebly. "But how long will I have to stay in bed?"

"We'll talk about that later," the surgeon answered, stooping to straighten the blanket over the boy's body. "Go to sleep now, soldier."

"Yes, sir."

Pepper smiled weakly and closed his eyes obediently. In a minute he was asleep.

CHAPTER SIXTEEN
Pepper's Yankee Neighbor

A PALE streamer of morning light was falling across the blankets on his cot when Pepper awoke again. Blinking in bewilderment, until a sharp twinge in his shoulder helped him remember where he was, the boy looked around.

The bed in which he lay was pushed into the corner of a long, narrow room that was lined with a double row of empty cots just like the one he occupied. Through the window in the wall at his left Pepper could see the leafless branches of a hedge swaying gently in the breeze. The pale, wintry sunlight that shone down upon him helped drive away the lost feeling that had swept over him when he realized where he was.

"I wonder just how badly I'm shot up," he said to himself. "How long will I have to stay here?"

Since there was no one near to answer his question, Pepper began to shift his body cautiously around between the blankets. His left side had a queer, stiff feeling, and when he tried to move his left arm the surge of pain that shot through his shoulder took all the starch out of him.

"That won't do," he muttered, cautiously raising his right arm and reaching across to feel his left.

After a careful exploration, he found that his left shoulder was swathed in bandages and that his left arm was bent at the elbow and strapped securely across his chest. The slightest movement of the injured arm or shoulder brought out beads of cold sweat on his forehead.

"Reckon I'd better leave well enough alone," Pepper told himself. "Wonder how my legs are."

Carefully bending one knee and then the other, he was relieved to find that both his legs were in good working order. His neck was all right, and there were no sore spots on his head or body. Apparently the only damaged parts were that left arm and shoulder.

Pepper was breathing a sigh of relief when the noise of a door opening and closing caught his attention. Turning his head to the right, the boy saw Doctor Eliason coming down the long aisle between the rows of cots.

"Good morning," the doctor smiled when he saw that his patient was awake. "How do you feel today?"

"Just fine, sir, and hungry as a bear," Pepper answered, returning the doctor's smile.

"That's good," remarked the surgeon, feeling Pepper's pulse and checking the count on his big silver watch. "You're pulling out of it even better than I expected. We'll have some breakfast for you in a jiffy."

"Doctor," Pepper's voice checked Doctor Eliason as he was turning to leave. "Before you came I was sort of exploring around to find out what was wrong. Just how serious is this wound, sir? How long will I have to stay in bed?"

"Well, Pepper, the Yankee's bullet didn't strike any important organs—you were mighty lucky that way— but it did go through your shoulder, breaking the scapula bone and tearing loose a lot of muscles. You won't be able to ride for at least three months, but you should be out of bed in a month if nothing serious develops before then."

"But Doctor, three months! That's a long time—and a month in bed is too much. Don't you think I can get up before that?"

"We'll see," the surgeon said. "Now I'll go and round up some breakfast for you."

"I don't think I've got any appetite left, Doctor."

"Wait and see," the doctor answered, turning toward the door.

After Doctor Eliason left Pepper lay and sourly contemplated his fate. Such rotten luck—a whole month in bed! And three months before he could ride Sunstar again! Three months—they seemed more like a century. Poor old Sunstar, what would he do in the meantime?

That brought a new thought to Pepper. Had the Yankee's bullets done any damage to his gallant black horse? Where was Sunstar now? The wounded boy writhed impatiently until the pain in his arm and shoulder made him glad to lie still again. But his mind raced on in spite of the ache in his body. Where was Sunstar? What would become of him while his master lay useless in the hospital?

"Say, you sure do look cozy and comfortable, Napoleon," a cheery, bantering voice broke in on Pepper's thoughts. "Move over and let a tired old soldier crawl in with you."

"Salt!" Pepper exclaimed, his face lighting up with joy. "Where did you come from, you old loafer?"

"Loafer nothing," retorted his friend. "That's gratitude for you. Here I play nursemaid and bring you a tray full of breakfast, and then you call me names."

"The breakfast can wait," said Pepper testily. "Put it down some place and tell me everything that's happened. Where's Sunstar?"

"Sunstar is all right," Salt answered. "But that's all I'll tell you until you eat this breakfast. Mind now, those are the doctor's orders. You'll have to obey or he won't let me come to see you any more."

"Oh, all right," grumbled Pepper. "Chuck the mess over here and I'll eat it."

"Mess, huh?" protested the young cavalryman setting the tray on Pepper's bed and helping him to get his good arm into action. "I'll bet that's the best breakfast you've eaten since you left the old plantation. No fat back and corn pone for you—you've got real eggs!"

After Pepper had finished the meal he was obliged to agree that it was the best breakfast he had eaten in many months. But, of course, old Aunt Daphne, the darky cook at Magnolia Hill, could have done much better. A twinge of homesickness shot through Pepper. Quickly he began to question Salt who had made himself comfortable on a near-by bench while Pepper ate.

"You said Sunstar was all right," Pepper said. "Where is he?"

"Back in camp eating his head off," was the answer. "You can be glad that every Confederate cavalryman has to furnish his own mount instead of having his horse issued like shoes and bacon, the way they do in the Yankee army. Since Sunstar is your property no one can use him without your permission."

Salt cocked an eye at his friend and then continued teasingly. "Of course, if you want some dismounted trooper in Company Q to use him, it will be all right. It will be good exercise for Sunstar."

"No!" exclaimed Pepper. "No one but myself has ever ridden him—except the time General Stuart tried out his gaits. I don't want anybody from Company Q, or anywhere else, riding Sunstar until I get better."

"Don't worry, pal, nobody will—that's already been taken care of. When you get ready to pull on your riding boots again, old Sunstar will be ready and waiting for you."

"What's happening in the army?" Pepper asked hurriedly, somewhat ashamed of himself. "Has there been any fighting?"

"Oh, a little skirmish now and then—nothing very important. Jeb Stuart has kept us busy watching the Yankees and keeping them from seeing our army. He sent me down this way with a report for General Lee; that's how I happened to be carrying trays for you."

"What are the Yankees doing?"

"Well, they're sort of fumbling around just now. The new commander can't seem to be able to make up his mind."

"New commander," Pepper repeated. "What's become of 'Little Mac'?"

"Oh, he's been removed—like Old Pope was. General Ambrose E. Burnside is now in command of the Union army. Stuart read about it in some captured Yankee newspapers the day after it happened, and now we're waiting to see what whiskery old Ambrose has on his mind."

"I'm sort of sorry to see 'Little Mac' go," said Pepper. "We had so much fun riding around him! We'll miss him."

"Yeah, you and General Lee felt the same way," Salt rallied. "When Stuart reported the news to him, 'Marse Robert' said, 'I'm sorry to see him go. We understood each other so well.'"

"Lee sure did understand him," Pepper agreed.

" 'Marse Robert' could outguess and outsmart 'Little Mac' in every battle."

"Say, I almost forgot about the joke on Jeb Stuart," Salt exclaimed. "I just have time to tell it before I go."

"What was it?"

"Well, Fitz Lee's brigade was having a little scrap with some of Pleasanton's troopers up by Emmittsville day before yesterday. The Yankee fire was pretty hot and Fitz Lee's advance line got driven back to the edge of the woods where the main body was. That made Jeb angry and he rode straight out into the clearing, right in front of the Yankee skirmish line. Of course the staff had to follow."

"That sounds like Jeb Stuart," Pepper murmured. "I don't think he's afraid of anything."

"The staff objected, of course," Salt continued. "Captain Farley said, 'General, this is no place for you. Won't you please—' Jeb didn't give him time to finish. 'This place suits me,' he snapped. 'If it's too hot for you, you're at liberty to leave it.' "

"Say, he must have been really sore to talk like that," marveled Pepper.

"He sure was. Anyway, he kept right on until he was so close to the enemy's lines that the staff could hear the Yankee officers yelling at their men to shoot that big rebel. There was a perfect hailstorm of lead around the General. The staff was scared stiff for fear he'd be hit."

"I don't blame them," remarked the wounded listener.

"All of a sudden Jeb rubbed his hand across his

mouth. Then he turned and rode slowly back to the woods with the queerest expression on his face. When he got beyond range everybody wanted to know what was the matter."

"Was he hit?" Pepper asked anxiously.

"No, but a Yankee slug had clipped off one of his mustaches just as clean as any barber could. He had to have the other one cut off close to match it."

"Whew! Talk about narrow escapes. Wish I had been there to see it."

"Time's up, Salt," Doctor Eliason called, thrusting his head around the hospital room door. "No more excitement for our patient today, or he won't be chasing Yankees in three months."

"So long for now, old sport," said Salt, rising and reaching out his hand. "I'll come and see you as often as I can."

"Thanks," Pepper took his friend's hand in his own uninjured one. "Take good care of Sunstar and tell the gang 'hello' for me."

"Right," promised Salt. "So long."

Sadly Pepper watched his friend walk down the long room and out the door. The three months of separation looked longer now than ever. Well, he'd have to grin and bear it. Gritting his teeth, Pepper resolved to get well just as fast as he could.

The weeks passed slowly in spite of Pepper's grim resolve. Patients came and went but, since the hospital was located some distance from the scene of action, not many of the injured found their way there.

Occasionally Salt dropped in to give glowing accounts of the cavalry maneuvers which consisted mainly of small raids into the enemy lines to snatch prisoners, horses, and wagon trains.

"What became of McGrigg?" Pepper asked one afternoon when and Salt were talking about his mishap.

"Aw, some lunkhead down in Richmond let him get exchanged along with a bunch of other prisoners," Salt answered disgustedly. "Hagan and I wanted him court-martialed and shot right away, but he got exchanged before the court was called. Rotten work at headquarters, I call it."

"He must have a charmed life," Pepper marveled.

"Well, you'd better keep an eye open for him when you come back. He hates you like poison and Hagan said he kept raving about getting even with you the day we caught him."

Pepper smiled grimly.

"I'll be on the lookout," he said, feeling the bandages on his shoulder. "I've got a score to settle with him, too."

Salt's visits were the only bright spots in Pepper's days. Other members of the staff, even General Stuart himself, sent the boy their regards, but they were too busy worrying the Yankees to visit him.

The first snowstorm came early in December. Propped up on his cot, Pepper watched the white flakes falling slowly and gracefully outside his window. His wound was healing, Doctor Eliason told him, but his arm was still strapped to his side to prevent any injury to the knitting bone of his shoulder blade.

Tired of the snow, Pepper glanced disdainfully at the books on the packing box beside his bed. Army hospitals offered little in the way of reading material. He was heartily sick of *A Manual of Surgery*, by J. Julian Chisolm, and of *The Trooper's Manual*, by Captain J. Lucius Davis. The other volumes were equally dull reading.

Early winter twilight was just deepening the shadows in the far corner of the room when the door opened and two hospital orderlies came in, carrying a limp form on a stretcher between them. Doctor Eliason followed them. Telling the orderlies to wait beside the door, the doctor approached Pepper's cot.

"Pepper," he said. "I'm going to put a Yankee next to you. He's hurt pretty badly and I'd like to have you keep an eye on him."

"A Yankee?" repeated Pepper in surprise. "Where did he come from?"

"Stuart surprised some of Pleasanton's cavalry on picket duty not far from here. The Yankees put up quite a scrap and this chap was knocked off his horse. That didn't stop him because he crawled into a thicket and kept taking pot shots at our troopers. Stuart sent a squad of men in after him and they had to get pretty rough before they could silence him. He's full of holes, but he put up such a game fight that Jeb Stuart insisted that he be cared for after the other Yankees ran off and left him."

"General Stuart admires a brave enemy," Pepper said. "Put him in the next cot and I'll watch him, sir."

Doctor Eliason motioned to the orderlies. They carried their unconscious burden to the cot and gently laid him down, pulling the covers up over him. The wounded Yankee was so wrapped in bandages and the room was so dark by this time that Pepper was unable to get a good look at his features. The candle only threw deeper shadows on the near-by bed.

"He can't be any older than you are, Pepper," the doctor said, "and he's a game youngster. He reminds me of my kid brother who died of pneumonia last winter. Keep an eye on him and call me if you need me."

"Yes, sir," said Pepper.

But the wounded Yankee needed no care that night. For a time he lay breathing loudly and unevenly, and occasionally he gave a low moan. Pepper tried once more to concentrate on *The Trooper's Manual*, but he found himself thinking about the Yankee instead.

At last, before Pepper blew out his candle and settled down for the night, the Yankee's breathing changed, becoming deep and regular.

"He's sleeping now," Pepper told himself. "That's good because rest is what he needs. Maybe I can find out who he is in the morning."

Wriggling himself into as comfortable position as his injured shoulder and bandaged arm would permit, the Confederate boy was soon asleep.

CHAPTER SEVENTEEN
Pepper Takes the Yankee Home

"PEPPER! Potter Pepperill! Wake up!"

The words were weak and faint, but they penetrated Pepper's slumbers. He opened his eyes to see the hospital room again filled with winter daylight. The near-by window pane was covered with frosty designs and he could see that snow was still falling.

"Pepper," again the voice whispered weakly. It came from the adjoining cot.

Turning his head on the pillow Pepper got his first

good look at the wounded Yankee. At first he could see
nothing but round upon round of white bandage. He
looked closer. Between the bandages peered a face,
deathly pale, with a pleasant freckled nose and bright
blue eyes. A lock of red hair had worked out between
the dressings that almost covered the boy's head.

Meeting Pepper's eye the Yankee grinned wanly.

"Hullo, Pepper," he said in a weak voice. "Don't you
remember me?"

At the sound of that voice, weak as it was, and the
glimpse of red hair and freckles, Pepper's mind whirled
back to the bright summer morning when he had crawled
out of a Maryland haystack to find a young Yankee soldier feeding his horse in the sunshine.

"Stephen!" he exclaimed, scarcely able to believe his
eyes. "Stephen Reynolds! Where did you come from?
How did you get here?"

"The rebels picked me up and carried me here, I
guess. They surprised us when we were out on picket
and we didn't have a chance. How did you get here and
when are we going to escape?"

"Escape?" repeated Pepper.

"Sure. We've got to get out of here and back to our
own lines. These rebels can't keep us penned up."

"Oh," said Pepper, realizing that Stephen thought
both of them were captive Union soldiers. "You're hurt
pretty badly and I don't reckon you can get up very
soon."

"Pepper, we've just got to escape! There's going to

be an important battle and Burnside needs every man."

"We'll see about that as soon as you're rested," Pepper replied, hoping to quiet the wounded boy. He was afraid the truth would be too much of a shock for Stephen in his weakened condition.

"All right, but you be thinking of some way to get us out," Stephen said. Then another thought occurred to him. "Say, Pepper, why didn't you enroll in Rush's Pennsylvania Lancers like you said you would? I kept looking and waiting, but you never came. What outfit did you join?"

The Confederate boy could stand it no longer. He knew that he must take the bull by the horns and tell Stephen the truth. He only hoped that he could do it as tactfully as possible.

"Stephen," he said slowly. "I reckon I gave you the wrong impression back in Maryland. I did tell you I was looking over the Yankee army—that was the truth. But I wasn't planning to join up. I already belonged to Jeb Stuart's cavalry."

Stephen's mouth dropped open in surprise. His pale face flushed with anger.

"You're a rebel!" he gasped, his voice high and excited. "A traitor and a spy! And I let you go!"

"I hated to fool you after the fine way you treated me," Pepper's voice was low and sincere. "But I'm proud of being a Confederate soldier."

The injured Yankee scarcely seemed to hear. He tossed restlessly on his cot, his blue eyes growing fever-

ish and glassy while his speech became thick and raving.

"A traitor and a spy!" He repeated the words over
and over.

"Please, Stephen," Pepper pleaded, genuinely worried about the sick captive. "Don't take it so hard. I
was working for my country just as you were for yours.
Look at it that way, won't you?"

Stephen shook his head.

"You're an enemy," he said faintly.

"All right, but I'm sorry you feel that way," Pepper
said, half-angered at the other boy's attitude.

The wounded Yankee made no reply. After a time
Pepper raised up to look at him. Stephen lay relaxed,
his breath coming in hoarse, irregular gasps. His face
was white and his lips set and bloodless. Soon his head
began to roll feebly on the pillow and he began to mut-
ter disjointedly.

"Stephen," Pepper called anxiously.

The Yankee only continued his indistinct mumblings.

"He's delirious," Pepper thought in alarm. "I'd better call Doctor Eliason." Reaching for the bell that
he used to summon the surgeon, Pepper rang it loudly.

In a few minutes Doctor Eliason entered the room.

"What's the matter, Pepper?" he asked.

Without speaking the boy pointed to his neighbor
who was now tossing restlessly and mumbling louder
than ever.

With a quick nod of understanding the surgeon knelt

by the bed, took Stephen's pulse beat with his left hand, and with his right he felt the boy's forehead. Stephen continued to toss and rave. Anxiously Pepper watched the doctor.

"Will he be all right?" he asked when at last the surgeon arose.

"He's pretty low right now, Pepper," was the reply. "He is delirious and has a raging fever. He seems to be suffering from a shock, too. What happened?"

"I reckon it's my fault, Doctor," Pepper mourned. "You see, I met Stephen last summer when I was scouting for General Stuart in Maryland. I told him I was looking over the Yankee army before joining up and he was very kind to me. Of course, when he woke up and saw me, he thought I was a prisoner, too. Right away he wanted to figure out some way for us to escape and I had to tell him I was one of Stuart's men. That hit him pretty hard, and soon he began to rave about spies and traitors and rebels."

The doctor made no reply but stood looking down at the sick boy, frowning in a worried fashion.

"Was it wrong to tell him, sir?" Pepper asked. "I didn't know what else to do."

The southern boy was still weak from his own wound, and his keen regret threatened to throw him into a relapse. Seeing this with quick professional eyes, Doctor Eliason seated himself on the boy's cot.

"Pepper, I know how you feel. The shock had to come sometime and perhaps it was best to get it over with at once. Stephen looks strong and he should pull through

all right. Don't worry now, because it will only delay
your own recovery."

"All right, Doctor. But please save Stephen."

"I'll do my best," the doctor promised.

A week dragged slowly by before Doctor Eliason was
able to say for certain that Stephen would recover.
Night after night Pepper lay and listened to the boy's
delirious ravings. Stephen carried on long conversations with his mother and his father. Sometimes he
talked to his little sister and sometimes to his friends
in camp. Pepper came to know the Yankee boy very
well just from listening to these conversations.

During that same week the surgeon gave Pepper permission to get up and walk around the room. At first he
was so weak that he could barely totter across the floor.
By resting between steps and keeping doggedly at it,
Pepper at last was able to walk the length of the room
and back without a stop.

The day after this accomplishment Stephen regained
consciousness and was able to answer the doctor's questions in a faint voice. But the Yankee refused to speak
to Pepper. A whole day passed in this manner and at
last the Confederate could stand it no longer.

"Snap out of it, Stephen," he said. "You're acting
like a kid."

Stephen refused to look at Pepper.

"A spy," he said in a hard, even voice, "is lower than
a snake."

"You were out on scouting duty, yourself, when you

were captured," Pepper answered hotly, stung by the other's tone. "That's just about the same as spying. Think of it that way, you pig-headed Yankee."

Stephen made no reply.

"That's the trouble with you damn Yankees," Pepper continued to storm. "Everybody's wrong but you— that's what started this war in the first place. You stuck your noses into the South's business and tried to tell us what to do. Then, when we objected, you raised an army and tried to force us to obey you. We have to fight back to protect our rights."

Panting and breathless, Pepper ended his tirade, but his angry words had made no apparent impression on the boy beside him. Stephen lay motionless, refusing to reply.

Pepper angrily tossed his covers aside and walked to the far end of the room where he leaned against the window and stared out at the dreary hospital yard. Most of the snow had melted since the last storm, but grayish-white drifts still lay in sheltered places and the bare ground looked hard and frozen. Long, pointed icicles hung from the wide eaves of the hospital building.

Suddenly, from far in the distance, Pepper heard a faint roar. The noise was repeated almost immediately, then it grew into a steady ominous rumbling. The window-panes rattled faintly and the boy could feel the building tremble slightly under his feet.

"Cannon!" he exclaimed, turning swiftly around. "There's a battle going on somewhere."

Stephen, too, had heard and recognized the sound.

Propping himself up in bed, he was listening intently.

"Artillery fire!" he said, his words echoing Pepper's. "I wonder if General Pleasanton is there."

For the remainder of the morning and all that afternoon the distant cannon continued to rumble. Almost bursting with anxiety and curiosity the two boys listened, forgetting to quarrel in their common alarm.

"I hate artillery!" Pepper burst out. "I've seen what it can do to men and horses!"

"Yes," agreed Stephen. "Give me a good clean cavalry fight, man to man, with sabers or pistols. There's nothing sporting about cannon balls and bursting shells."

Toward evening the roar of the artillery died down and only occasionally could the boys hear its faint thunder. Pepper was just getting ready to light the candle when the doctor entered, followed by an orderly with supper for the boys.

"Where was the battle?"

"Who was fighting?"

Both patients shouted at once in their eagerness to hear the news.

The doctor's face was serious. Sitting down on the foot of Pepper's cot, he began to talk while the two boys listened eagerly, too interested to pay any attention to the food on their trays.

"A great battle opened at Fredericksburg today," the surgeon explained. "Lee was on the heights south and west of town. Burnside's attack was across the Rappahannock and from the northeast. They say that the Union losses were terrible, but our own were bad enough. The wounded will be coming in soon and I have much work ahead of me."

"Was Burnside defeated?" Pepper asked.

Stephen said nothing.

"No, General Lee expects another attack tomorrow," answered the doctor.

"Have you any news of Stuart?"

Doctor Eliason shook his head.

"My only information comes from a courier who was carrying the news to Richmond. He stopped here just long enough to change horses and he told me just what I've told you."

The doctor reached into his pocket and pulled out a sheaf of papers.

"Pepper," he continued, "I'm going to need every bed I have here so I've arranged a two months' sick leave for you. You can be moved now and I'm sending you home to convalesce under your mother's care. I've already sent for your horse, and I'll lend you my own rig and will send a man with you to see that you get home safely."

"What about Stephen?"

The surgeon shook his head solemnly.

"I don't know. I suppose I'll have to send him to a war prison because I simply must make room now for our own wounded boys."

"But you can't do that, sir," objected Pepper. "He's too sick to go to prison. It would kill him."

"Don't worry about me, rebel," Stephen broke in hotly. "I'd rather be with my own people, even in prison."

Pepper paid no attention to the words of the wounded prisoner.

"Doctor Eliason, can't you send him home with me? I'll see that he doesn't escape, and my mother will be glad to take care of him. I owe it to him because he helped me once. Besides, I want to show him how folks live in the South. He thinks we're some kind of heathens and savages. Please let him come."

"Why, Pepper, I couldn't do that. It would be very irregular and not according to army rules," the surgeon objected.

"But he'll die if you send him to prison, wounded as he is. I promise to see that he doesn't escape. Aw, Doc, let him come," Pepper pleaded.

"I'll see if I can arrange it," Doctor Eliason said, rising. "Now I must go and get ready for the ambulances. I'll see you before you leave tomorrow."

"Why did you do that, Pepper?" Stephen asked when the doctor had gone.

"Because I can't see you sent to prison while you are wounded. Besides, Stephen, I want you to see how Southerners live and to show you how we treat our slaves. Then maybe you will see things differently. I sure hope Doctor Eliason can arrange it."

Dawn was just breaking when an orderly aroused the boys.

"Your horse and the rig are waiting," he said. "It's pretty cold so you'd better wrap up."

When Pepper was dressed he hurried outside to greet his horse. Throwing his good arm around the glossy neck, the boy buried his face in the silky mane.

"Sunstar, old pal, I'm sure glad to see you," he said. "Have they taken good care of you?"

Sunstar whinneyed softly, reached his sleek head around and rubbed his soft muzzle against his master's shoulder in a joyful greeting.

"Steady there, old chap. That shoulder won't stand rough treatment." Doctor Eliason's voice interrupted the greetings. "Say, he certainly is glad to see you, son."

"Not any gladder than I am to see him," Pepper answered, hugging as much of the great horse as he could reach with his one good arm.

The doctor stepped to Pepper's side and stroked Sunstar's head.

"Pepper," he said quietly. "I've arranged to have Stephen go with you. I hope I don't get cashiered for it because it is mighty irregular. That Yankee is the spit image of my dead kid brother and I can't send him to prison."

"Thank you, sir," Pepper began.

The doctor silenced him with a motion.

"Taking a Yankee into your home is most unusual," he continued. "Of course, I understand why, Pepper. When men have fought each other bravely, a mutual respect sometimes grows up between them. But, on the other hand, war does strange things to people's emotions—and hatred is a powerful thing."

Pepper nodded, thinking of how gruff Lieutenant Hagan felt about Yankees.

"I see what you mean, sir," he said.

"It would be best if you did not tell too many people that Stephen is a Yankee," the doctor continued. "Just say that he is a boy you knew in the army—that is all they need to know. It is for your own good, as well as for Stephen's."

"I understand, sir," Pepper said quietly. "I believe I can manage it."

By this time the orderlies had carried the Yankee boy outside and propped him up in a corner of the buggy. Doctor Eliason pinned the blankets closely around Stephen and assisted Pepper to climb in. The driver mounted his seat and they were ready to leave, with Sunstar hitched on behind.

"I'm going to miss you two," the Doctor told them, "but I have a busy time ahead of me. Take good care of yourselves and keep those blankets up around you."

"We will," the boys answered. "Thanks, Doctor, for everything."

The driver gathered up his reins and clucked to his horse. The buggy started off in a fine swirl of snow and the boys looked back to see the doctor standing in the hospital door, gazing off into the distance. As they swung out of the yard a string of ambulances was just toiling into view. Doctor Eliason would soon be busy salvaging human wreckage from the bloody battle of Fredericksburg.

"Poor devils," said Pepper, his eyes on the lumbering wagons. Then a more cheerful thought struck him and he turned to Stephen with a smile.

"Just think," he said. "We'll get to spend Christmas at home."

CHAPTER EIGHTEEN
Christmas on the Plantation

THE two boys arrived at Magnolia Hill late in the afternoon after a long, tiresome journey from the hospital. When the strange buggy drew up before the great columned porch of the mansion house, all the plantation folk—white and black—came flocking to welcome the returning warriors.

With tears of thankfulness on her cheeks, Mrs. Pepperill greeted her son, her eyes quick to notice his paleness and to see the empty coat sleeve that flapped over the sling and bandages on his left arm and shoulder.

The welcome given by Pepper's aunt and uncle was also warm and hearty. Mrs. Cromartie smiled joyfully while the Judge reached up to help the boy descend from the buggy. The air was filled with noisy greetings.

"Welcome home, son."

"Fine record you've made, boy. We're proud of you."

"Welcome, Pepper! We're so glad they let you come home."

The crowd of blacks, too, was chattering its greetings and its admiration. Dusky faces shone and white teeth flashed between smiling lips.

"How do, Marse Pepper."

"Praise de Lawd dem Yankees didn't hurt him any wuss."

"Lawzy, he sho' do look like a sojer."

"I bet he made dem Yankees run."

"Dere's Sunstar," Uncle Elijah shouted, delighted at the sight of his four-footed charge. "How you like some nice fresh hay, ol' boy?"

"Mother, Aunt Margaret, and Uncle Buford," Pepper said as soon as he could make himself heard. "This is Stephen Reynolds, a cavalry friend of mine. He's been shot, too, and I brought him home to get well."

"Any friend of Pepper's is welcome at Magnolia Hill," Judge Cromartie spoke for his little family. "We are proud to have you and we hope you will like it here, suh."

"Thank you, sir," the Yankee boy said. "It's very kind of you to take a stranger in."

It was not until evening, when Mrs. Pepperill came to her son's room to bid him good night, that Pepper explained about Stephen. Mrs. Pepperill listened quietly while the boy told the entire story.

"Stephen seems to think we're regular savages down here in the South," Pepper concluded. "That's why I wanted him to see for himself. Anyway, I couldn't let Doctor Eliason send Stephen to prison, weak as he is. If it was all right for Jeb Stuart to send him to a Confederate army hospital, it must be all right for me to bring him home."

"You did right, son," Mrs. Pepperill said quietly. "I'm glad you told me about Stephen, but I don't think you should tell anyone else. They might not understand. Your Uncle Buford, for instance, feels very strongly about the Yankees. He and Brian had long arguments about the war. Brian seemed to feel more as you do, but his father is very bitter."

"Thanks, Mother, I was sure you would understand," Pepper said, putting his good arm around her neck.

Mrs. Pepperill kissed her son.

"I'm glad you have come home," she said, rising. "I prayed for you every night and I felt that God would keep you safe. Good night, son."

She pulled the covers around his shoulders, smiled at him and then stooped to blow out the candle, just as she

had done when he was little. Pepper heard her skirts
rustle as she moved toward the door in the darkness.

"Yessuh, Marse Pepper, dis am gonna be one ob de
bestest Christmases we's eber had at Magnolia Hill,"
Uncle Elijah told his young master one afternoon when
he brought the boys their lunch trays. " 'Course it
would be best yet if Marse Brian could be here, but dis
am gonna be a grand one."

Pepper was seated in a big chair before the cheery
fire in Stephen's room. The young Confederate was now
able to be up and about all day but his friend was still
confined to bed.

"What makes you think so, Uncle 'Lije?" the boy
asked.

"Everybody's gittin' ready fo' it jest as fast as dey
kin step," was the answer. "Marse Judge is downstairs
now a-cleanin' his deer rifle to go arter a buck. Yo'
Mammy and Mistiss Margaret is busy plannin' everything and Aunt Daphne and Jane is a-workin' day an'
night a-gittin' ready fo' de Christmas dinner. De silver's done been dug up an' de linen's been aired. I'se
gwine out tomorrow to git some greenery to dec'rate
de house."

"What do you mean, the silver's been dug up?" Stephen asked. A great many of the darky's expressions
puzzled the northern boy.

"Last summer Marse Judge buried de silver out under a rose bush so's none ob dem Yankees could find it.
Come Christmas an' we-all needs it, he has to go out an'

dig it up again. 'Course it has to be all polished bright an' shinin' again."

"Do you mean that Union soldiers steal private property from citizens?" Stephen asked in surprise.

"Yassuh, dem no 'count white trash take everything dey kin lay hands on, Marse Stephen. Dey done walked off wid all de silver plate from de Bradford house down by de turnpike. I sho' am glad Marse Gin'ral Robe't E. Lee done chased 'em out er dis neck ob de woods 'fore dey got ours."

Stephen said nothing. The week he had spent at Magnolia Hill had opened his eyes to many things. Contrary to his former opinion, he found that here the Negro slaves were contented and happy. No heartless overseers drove them to work with whips. If one of them fell sick, the white master or mistress went in person to see that the invalid received proper care. The plantation folk were like one big family—there was no misery or cruelty here. Also, the boy was finding that his own people were not entirely above reproach.

Pepper, too, was silent. He was glad that his friend was having the opportunity to see for himself. Keeping his own counsel, Pepper told no one but his mother that Stephen was a Yankee. His aunt and uncle thought the wounded boy was a Confederate cavalryman from the West. Pepper saw no reason to correct this mistake. There would be time enough to worry about Stephen when the northern boy had recovered. Meanwhile, Pepper was willing to let things drift.

"Lawzy, Marse Pepper, if you two ain't de fightinist

lookin' sojers dat I eber see," Uncle Elijah was rambling on. "You wid yo' arm all slung up and Marse Stephen wropped in bandages an' smellin' like Uncle Snag-
tooth's herb chest. Hit makes me feel right proud ob de
family."

"Uncle 'Lije," Stephen said, "right after the battle
of Antietam, President Abraham Lincoln issued the
Emancipation Proclamation. What do you think of it?"

"Bless Pete, Marse Stephen, if'n you don't use de
biggest words! Emanscumpation Procla——! Lawzy, I
can't eben wrop my tongue around dem words. What do
dey mean? I ain't never heerd ob dat Anteetum battle,
neither. Was you in dat, Marse Pepper?"

"Yes, I was in it, Uncle 'Lije," Pepper answered
quietly, casting a warning glance at Stephen. "Only we
Confederates usually call it the battle of Sharpsburg—
Antietam is the Yankee name for it. Marse Stephen was
just teasing you."

"Was you teasin' me about de Emanscumpation
thing, too, Marse Stephen?"

"No," the northern boy replied. "President Lincoln
did issue an order which he called the Emancipation
Proclamation, saying that all the slaves in the South
were to be free on New Year's Day."

"Dawg-gone! How come he think he kin do dat?"
Uncle Elijah exclaimed indignantly. "Presidumt Lin-
cum ain't de boss ob me. I does what my Marster says
an' dass de onliest man what I takes orders from."

"Don't you want to be free, Uncle 'Lije?" Stephen
asked.

"Free? Ain't I free now as I ever could be? I does mostly what I pleases when I ain't workin'. I'se got plenty to eat and a comfortable cabin. I'se done lived on dis plantation ever since I'se been born, an' dat was 'way back when Marse Pepper's gran'pappy, ole Marster Randolph Cromartie, was jes' a boy. Where could I go if'n I was free? Dat Emanscumpation thing is plum foolishment."

Stephen smiled across the old darky's kinky head to Pepper.

"I guess there are two sides to everything," he said.

All week Stephen could hear the sounds of Christmas preparations going on downstairs. Delicious odors of spices, roasts, and baking bread drifted up from the kitchen.

"What's going on down there, Pepper?" he asked. "Things certainly sound busy and smell good. Seems like the way we carry on back home on Thanksgiving."

"I reckon it is. Just wait until tomorrow when you see how the house has been decorated. Mother thinks you are well enough to be carried downstairs for Christmas dinner."

True to his promise, Pepper burst into Stephen's room early the next morning, followed by Judge Cromartie and the two houseboys, Buck and Cato, who stood grinning by the door.

"Merry Christmas!" Pepper shouted. "Are you ready to come downstairs?"

"Good morning, sir," Stephen said to the Judge,

"and Merry Christmas right back at you, Pepper. You bet I'm ready!"

"I'm glad you're looking so well, my boy," Judge Cromartie said, shaking hands with his guest. "I don't know how they do it where you come from, but we aim to show you what a real Virginia Christmas is like."

He turned to the Negro houseboys.

"Pick him up gently, and see that you don't jar him."

The two blacks carried Stephen down the broad stairs and placed him in a big, comfortable chair in front of a roaring fire in the gaily decorated hall.

"I'm afraid this won't be the kind of a Christmas we had before the war," the Judge continued after assuring himself that his guest was comfortable. "The accursed Yankees have made so much trouble for us. Because of their blockade we can't get half the things we need, and the best of our young men are away in the army."

Pepper knew that the Judge was thinking of his own son, Brian, who would eat his scanty Christmas dinner beside a camp fire in Stonewall Jackson's camp. To cover up a painful silence he said, "Oh, but next year we should be eating our Christmas dinners in Washington, Uncle Buford."

"I certainly hope so," said the Judge.

From outside the house came the sound of many voices.

"The servants have come up to serenade us," Pepper said. "Mother! Aunt Margaret! Are you coming?"

"Here we are," answered Mrs. Cromartie as she and

Mrs. Pepperill entered the room. "Merry Christmas, boys! Merry Christmas, Buford!"

"Merry Christmas to you," the boys answered, while the Judge was busy directing Buck and Cato as they opened the big double doors that led onto the back veranda. When the big doors were opened, the family could see a large group of Negroes gathered on the lawn outside.

"Chrissmus gif', Marster!"

"Chrissmus gif', Mistiss!"

"Hoo-ray fo' Chrissmus!"

The crowd shouted joyfully as the Negroes caught sight of their white folks. Buck and Cato carried Stephen's chair over to the door, and the little group gathered around him.

Uncle Elijah was out in front of the Negroes, with Uncle Eli and his fiddle on one side and Uncle Shadrach and his banjo on the other.

"Git ready fo' de singin'!" the old darky shouted, waving his arms until the long blue tails of his brass buttoned coat flapped in the breeze. "One, two, free, sing!"

Stephen listened entranced as the mellow Negro voices were raised in a well-known old carol. With fiddle and banjo, Uncle Eli and Uncle Shadrach led the song while Uncle Elijah directed energetically, his quavering old voice mingling pleasantly with the strong rich voices of the younger Negroes.

When the carol was ended, the shouting broke out again.

"Chrissmus gif', Marster!"

"Merry Chrissmus, everybody!"

Judge Cromartie stepped forward and raised his hand for silence.

"Thank you, my friends, for your serenade. Merry Christmas to you all. Cato, bring out the gift table."

When the heavily laden table was placed on the veranda, Judge and Mrs. Cromartie took their places behind it and the slaves filed past. Each one received a present—a bright bandanna handkerchief, a barlow knife, tobacco, a doll, a toy, or a pair of shoes. Each foreman also received an envelope with a crisp new Confederate bill in it.

Stephen watched the happy black faces with interest, and Pepper watched his guest and smiled.

Never in his life had Stephen eaten such a dinner as the one served on Christmas day at Magnolia Hill. The Bradfords from down by the turnpike and the Averitts from across the ridge were there. Twenty people sat down at Judge Cromartie's dinner table. Stephen and Pepper were the only young men present—all the others were absent in the army—but the old gentlemen, the women, and the girls were merry and gay.

Dinner for the slaves was laid in the long enclosed portico in the rear of the mansion. The tables fairly groaned with the weight of the food on them.

The men talked of crops and fox hunting. The women discussed housekeeping problems and sewing. But the one big topic that received the undivided attention of everyone was the war. Thoughts of the absent soldiers, however, were not allowed to dampen the high spirits of the Southerners.

"They'll be with us this time next year," everyone said. "The Yankees can't hold out much longer."

"I hope it is over by next year," the Yankee boy said to himself, looking at the friendly faces around him. "And right now I don't much care who wins."

CHAPTER NINETEEN
Jeb Stuart's Telegram

ON THE day after New Year's Judge Cromartie and his wife drove away to Richmond where the Judge had important business. Before returning they planned to visit Brian at Stonewall Jackson's camp. Meanwhile, Mrs. Pepperill and the two boys were left together on the plantation.

"Your uncle certainly is a fine man," Stephen said as the boys sat with Pepper's mother before the fire in the Yankee's room. "Just the same I'd hate to have him angry with me."

"Uncle Buford's temper is still pretty hot," Pepper admitted. "Mother says he was a hair-trigger duelist in his younger days."

Mrs. Pepperill smiled.

"I can remember how it worried my father," she said. "He used to say that it wouldn't be Buford's fault if some young blood didn't put a pistol ball through him at twenty paces."

"Tell us about the time you and Father were out west and the Sioux war party attacked," Pepper asked. Then he turned to Stephen and added, "This is my favorite story. Sometime I'm going out west and see the great plains and wild Indians that Mother tells about."

"Very well," Mrs. Pepperill agreed. "It was in 1850 when Pepper's father and I were on our way to Fort Kearney. Pepper was only three years old and we had left him with his old Negro mammy at Fort Leavenworth. We were riding across——"

"Excuse me a minute, Mother," Pepper interrupted. "I think I hear horses' hoofs on the drive."

He hurried to the broad front window that overlooked the entrance gate. Horses were approaching along the gravel path.

"Why, it's Salt and Hagan and Sweeney!" Pepper exclaimed joyfully. "Say, am I glad to see them!"

"Are you going to tell them about Stephen?" his mother asked quietly as Pepper turned away from the window.

Pepper frowned thoughtfully for a minute.

"No, I reckon I'd better not," he said slowly. "Salt would understand and so might Sweeney. Hagan, though, wouldn't approve of the idea. He has a heart as big as all outdoors, but he is bitter against the Yankees."

"You go down and make them welcome, son," Mrs. Pepperill said. "Have Aunt Daphne fix them something to eat and tell Buck to build up the fire in the dining room. I'll finish telling Stephen my story and then I'll come down to meet your friends."

"All right, Mother."

Pepper rushed away to greet the visitors.

The three troopers were playing a merry tattoo on the big brass knocker by the time Pepper reached the door. Motioning old Julius, the butler, to one side, Pepper threw open the door and, with a wide sweep of his arm, invited the men inside.

"Hello, Napoleon," Salt shouted. "Boy! We've missed you. How soon are you coming back?"

"Pretty soon from the looks of him," Sweeney answered. "Say, he looks like he's been playing 'possum. Never been sick a day, I'll bet. Just plain lazy."

"Hello, youngster," rumbled Lieutenant Hagan. "Glad to see you looking so chipper."

"And I'm glad to see you all," Pepper answered. "Come in and make yourselves at home. Julius, take their hats and cloaks. Then tell Aunt Daphne to fix the biggest snack she ever dreamed of. She's feedin' soldiers now."

Pepper led the way into the pleasant dining room where Buck already had a fire crackling on the wide hearth. The three followed, looking around in admiration and lifting their heavy cavalry boots carefully so as not to scratch the shining floor.

"I've been in the army so long I feel out of place in a home like this," Sweeney admitted. "I don't know just how to act."

"Yes, youngster, you'd better hide anything that's breakable," warned Hagan. "I feel like I'm walking on eggs."

"Don't worry," laughed Pepper. "Pull up to the fire and get comfortable. My uncle and aunt have gone to Richmond but mother will be down pretty soon."

Pepper wanted to hear all the news from Stuart's camp, but he held back his curiosity and played host until his friends were comfortably settled. Aunt Daphne brought in a huge tray loaded with sandwiches, cold meats, and cake. The troopers' eyes fairly bulged at the sight.

"Don't pinch me, Sam, I don't want to wake up yet," Salt told Sweeney. "At least not until I've tasted some of those eats."

"You're not dreaming, youngster," Hagan mumbled, a sandwich already disappearing in the midst of his whiskers. "They taste powerful good to me."

"Go ahead," Pepper urged. "Wrap yourselves around the food and Aunt Daphne will fix more. Hurry up, because I want to hear the news. What have you been doing?"

"Plenty," Sweeney said, his mouth full. "We missed you, Pepper. Say, I'm glad the Yankee's bullet didn't do any more damage than it did."

"Pshaw, it takes more than a little hunk of lead to put me out of commission," Pepper scoffed. "Come on, tell me all the news. Have you had any battles or gone on any raids? How's the General? How's everybody at camp?"

"Whoa there, youngster," Hagan chuckled. "One at a time. Military handbook says never confuse the command by giving too many orders at once. Slow up until we can fire and then reload."

"But what have you three been doing?" Pepper urged. "I suspect there's been a raid. Come on, tell me about it."

"All right, nosey," Salt answered. "Sure there's been a raid, a fine one. We started out on Christmas Day."

"That's a funny way to spend Christmas," Pepper interrupted. "Didn't you have a big dinner, or anything?"

"Sure we did, youngster, on Christmas eve," Hagan rumbled. "I spent a whole week collecting food for it. We even had some turkeys, 'though the Texas regiment across the ridge got away with most of them beforehand. I had to rustle up some more at the last minute."

"I'd count on you for that, Lieutenant," Pepper said. "Go on, Salt."

"Well, it was just like any other raid except that the Yankees hung closer to us this time. We gathered up

a lot of horses and some prisoners as we went—we got
three or four Yankee supply wagons, too. Had quite a
scrap at Dumfries, and then rode north to Burke's Station—that's only fifteen miles from Washington, you
know."

"Yeah, and I wish Jeb Stuart would lead us into
the Yankee capital sometime," Hagan added. "We could
bring the Republican politicians to terms in no time."

"Hurry up and tell him about Jeb's telegram,"
Sweeney urged.

"All right, give me time. We took Burke's Station so
quickly that the Yankees didn't know we were near until
we poked our pistols in their faces. The telegraph officer was busy taking down orders from some Yankee
general and he didn't have time to send an alarm. Stuart
put Jerry Carruthers at the telegraph key and the messages kept on coming, telling the location of all the
Yankee forces out chasing us. Stuart stood there checking the orders and stroking his beard, having the time
of his life."

"I can just see him," Pepper exclaimed, "his eyes
twinkling and his whiskers twitching with laughter. I
wish I could have been there!"

"Wait till you hear the end of the tale," Sweeney
cautioned.

"After Stuart had learned all he could, he sent a
special telegram to the Yankee quartermaster general
in Washington," Salt continued. "He complained because the Yankee mules were so poor that they couldn't

even pull our wagons after we captured them. He signed it 'Major General J. E. B. Stuart, C. S. A.' "

"I'll bet the Yankee hit the ceiling when he got that message," Pepper exclaimed.

"I hope so," Sweeney added.

"After that we cut the wires and started south. We were back in camp the day before New Year's."

"Some adventure," marveled Pepper. "I certainly will be glad to be back with you."

"Take my advice and stay here, youngster," Sweeney said. "It's mighty cold a-camping out in the snow. We're having a hard time feeding our horses—supplies don't come in as they should and the officers are kept pretty worried. Anyway, there won't be much action until spring."

A rustle of skirts interrupted their talk and the four soldiers rose to their feet as Mrs. Pepperill entered the room.

"Mother, these are the friends I've told you about. May I present Barry Salter, Sam Sweeney, and Lieutenant Henry Hagan—the three finest troopers that ever sat in a saddle."

Salt blushed and Hagan shuffled his feet in embarrassment.

"Your son is a better trooper than we are," Sweeney said, coming to his friends' rescue. "He's the gamest youngster I ever met, and he's a son to be proud of."

"Thank you," Mrs. Pepperill smiled. "I am proud of him and I am delighted to meet his friends. I hope he has made you comfortable."

"He certainly has," Salt found his tongue at last. "Makes me sort of homesick for Georgia."

"And I imagine you make him homesick for camp," Pepper's mother answered. "You can all stay for supper, can't you?"

"No, thank you, Ma'am, I reckon not," Sweeney spoke for the others. "We have to be back in camp before midnight and it's a long ride."

"I'm glad you came. Come again if you can," Pepper said as he followed his guests to the door. "I wish I was going back with you."

"You stay at home until you get strong again," Sweeney advised. "And when spring comes we'll have plenty of fun."

"Good-by, Pepper," Salt said as he climbed into his saddle. "I sure do miss you."

"Thanks for those eats," Hagan added. "I never foraged any that tasted better."

"From you, Lieutenant, that's a big compliment," Pepper laughed.

"Good-by, Ma'am," said Sweeney, touching his hat to Mrs. Pepperill who appeared at the door to watch them depart. "We're proud to have met you."

"Good-by, good-by," called the other two troopers as they cantered down the gravel drive. "We'll be waiting for you."

"I'll be with you as soon as I can," answered Pepper.

Standing together on the wide veranda, Pepper and his mother watched until the three cavalrymen disappeared over the crest of a ridge far down the road.

The weeks passed slowly. Stephen was almost well by February. The Confederate boy guarded his friend's secret so well that Judge Cromartie never suspected that his guest was a Yankee.

"It's a good thing Uncle Buford and Aunt Margaret were away when Salt and Sweeney and Hagan came," Pepper remarked oné afternoon. "It would have looked funny not taking them up to see you."

"Yes, I guess it would. You know, Pepper, this business hurts my conscience. I wish I could tell your uncle who I am."

"I'm afraid that would upset the apple cart, Stephen. There's no use making trouble because we won't be hère much longer."

"Pepper, what are you going to do with me when you go back to the army?" the northern boy asked. "I am your prisoner, you know."

"That's been worrying me, Stephen. I won't send you to prison, but I can't just turn you loose. You'd never get back across the lines without being captured. I don't know what to do."

"The regular exchange depot is down at City Point on the James River," Stephen suggested. "If you'd take me there I might get exchanged pretty soon."

"All right," Pepper agreed. "I imagine it takes a little influence from the other side. Do you reckon you can get it?"

"I guess so—yes, I'm sure of it."

"We won't have to start until next week. Seems funny

to think that in a few weeks we may be shooting at each other, doesn't it?"

"Yes, and it seems foolish, too. You know, Pepper, I don't think this war would have started if the North and the South had known each other better. Just look at me. Why, I thought all Southerners were terrible. I suppose you thought the same about us."

"To tell the truth, I never thought much about it. When the war started and all my friends took the southern side, I just wanted to follow. I didn't begin to think much about the whole thing until I scouted the Union lines and found that your people are just like ours."

"Too bad everybody couldn't do as we've done," Stephen said. "Do you suppose people will ever think twice before they start fighting?"

"That's hard to say. When the bands start playing and the soldiers go marching by, they sort of sweep you off your feet. Your feelings paralyze your brains, I reckon. Say—how did we get started talking like this?"

"I don't know. I feel all serious, like I do in church. Let's change the subject, Pepper."

"I know, let's go down to the stables and take a look at Sunstar," the Confederate boy suggested.

"Good. I'll race you there."

Before Stephen had finished his challenge the two boys were off, tearing across the lawn and down the slope toward the barn in the bright February sunshine. Laughing and panting they pulled up at the stable door.

"Lawzy, Marse Pepper," Uncle Elijah exclaimed, popping his head around the corner of a stall. "You and Marse Stephen am as frisky as a pair ob squirrels. Magnolia Hill done fixed you up, even if dem Yankees did shoot holes in you. 'Pears like you'll be a-shootin' back at dem mighty soon."

"I reckon so," agreed Pepper. "How's Sunstar, Uncle 'Lije?"

"As spry as a bobcat and mighty near as hard to manage. He'll be ready when you is, Marse Pepper. I'se gwine miss you powerful bad. I hopes you kin lick dem Yankees right smart and den come ridin' home to stay."

"So do I, Uncle 'Lije," agreed Pepper, feeding an apple to his glossy black steed. "What do you say to that, Stephen?"

The Yankee returned Pepper's grin.

"Well," he said. "I hope whoever is going to win will hurry up and do it."

CHAPTER TWENTY

Sunstar Is Captured by the Yankees

"HOW does it feel to be back in camp, Pepper?" General Stuart asked his young courier one morning soon after the latter's return from sick leave.

"It feels natural, sir," was the answer. "I'm sorry I missed the Christmas raid. Barry Salter told me all about it and I wish I could have seen the Yankee quartermaster's face when he got your telegram about the mules."

"So do I," said the cavalry leader, grinning at Hagan who stood close by. "It is high time someone was jacking those Yankees up. None of their mules is worth anything. It scarcely pays us to waste our energy in capturing them."

"Are we going on another raid soon, sir?" Pepper asked eagerly. "I hope so because I feel pretty much out of practice, and I'd like to take a crack at old General Burnside."

"Burnside," repeated Stuart. "Why, son, you're 'way out of date. Fighting Joe Hooker has been in command of the Union army since back in February."

"Those Yankees certainly change generals fast," marveled Pepper.

"No, we just wear them out fast," the cavalry leader corrected. "Now, Pepper, if you really want to have another try at the bluecoats, I'll send you along on a little scouting trip. I am detailing Hagan, here, and Sweeney for the job and sending you and Salt as aides. You are to ride up toward Morrisville and see how things look. Keep a sharp watch for blue patrols—the country up that way is thick with them."

He turned to Hagan.

"Do you understand, Lieutenant?"

"Yes, sir," Hagan saluted. "Pepper, you go rout out the others."

"Yes, sir," said Pepper joyfully.

Saluting, the young courier turned and ran to tell the other members of the scouting detail.

Stuart's camp was filled with troopers, resting from the strenuous activities of picketing the long Confederate lines. Countless little brushes with enemy outposts had kept them busy most of the time since Christmas.

As usual, an interested group was gathered around Sweeney and his banjo. When Pepper drew nearer he could hear the banjoist's pleasant voice and the rhythmic thump of his instrument. The whole company had joined in the chorus, fairly roaring the catchy refrain:

> *"Oh, I eat when I'm hungry*
> *And I drink when I'm dry.*
> *If the Yankees don't get me*
> *I'll live till I die."*

"Sorry to spoil your party, Sam," Pepper broke in when the song ended, "but the General wants us to ride out and take a look at the Yankees. Hagan's in charge, and Sam, you and Salt and I are to go, too."

"That's fine," said Sweeney, springing to his feet and slinging his banjo across his back. "Show's over now, boys. Better clear out before I pass the hat."

Soon the four friends were cantering away, their horses snuffing the bracing April air with as much keen delight as their riders. Sunstar, still fat and frisky from his long rest, danced and capered to show how glad he was to be on the road once more.

"He certainly looks fine," Salt said, running his eyes admiringly over the glossy black steed, "so sleek and well-cared for. Poor old Thunder's pretty much the worse for wear—bad food and overwork. Well—" He gazed sadly at the washboard-like ribs of his own mount and shook his head.

Sweeney nodded.

"Old Thunder needs to be turned out in pasture for a good long rest," he said. "If horses weren't so hard to find in the South almost every cavalryman would be re-mounted. Our horses are almost worn out."

"Dismounted Company Q is fuller than it's ever been before," said Hagan. "About the only way a man who's lost his horse can get remounted is to have some friend capture a Yankee horse for him."

"Yes, about fifty men were transferred to the in-fantry last week, just because they couldn't get more horses," Salt added. "It's hard on an ex-cavalryman to have to hoof it himself."

The other three troopers nodded in solemn agree-ment, riding in silence for a time.

The gently rolling Virginia hills were just beginning to show tiny patches where new green growth was push-ing up through the brown winter carpet. New buds on the oak trees were swelling to give promise of summer's foliage.

The four Confederates paused at the foot of a little hill to water their horses in a clear bubbling brook that flowed merrily along the edge of a densely wooded thicket. Pepper dismounted to tighten his saddle girth while the other three troopers sat their steeds easily, waiting for them to finish drinking.

Suddenly, and without the slightest warning, a shrill

yell split the soft spring air. Pistols cracked and balls spattered into the brook or chipped fragments of rock from the hillside as a company of bluecoated riders burst out from the cover of the thicket.

"Get 'em all, boys," one of the Federals shouted. "There are only four of the rebels!"

Instantly the place was filled with confusion. Sabers flashed and more pistol balls kicked up little spurts of dust in the valley. Flying hoofs and heavy bodies milled around Pepper, sweeping him away from Sunstar.

"Run for it!" he heard Hagan's deep voice bellow.

"Wait! Wait for me!" Pepper shouted.

"Where are you, boy?" the lieutenant roared.

"Here!"

Pepper's voice was almost lost in the mad confusion. There were so many Yankees milling around in the tiny valley that each one got in someone else's way. No man was able to see just what he was doing. Pepper tried desperately to avoid the trampling hoofs and the rearing horses. One rider swung his mount sharply, tossing Pepper to one side like a feather. The boy cast a terrified look over his shoulder to see another horse rear up, lashing out toward him with iron-shod hoofs. Then a heavy hand seized him by the collar of his leather jacket, snatching him backward so that the murderous hoofs missed him by a hair's breadth. He was slung roughly over a saddle and his rescuer spurred madly away, soon leaving the wild confusion to die out in the distance.

"That was a close call, sonny," Pepper heard Hagan's gruff voice say as the lieutenant checked his horse and lowered the boy to the ground. Being slung across a saddle like a meal bag had knocked the wind pretty well out of Pepper.

Soon Salt and Sweeney came galloping up, breathless and excited. In the confusion caused by the Yankees' headlong charge all four of the Confederates had escaped.

Sweeney took off his hat and looked ruefully at the bullet hole through the crown.

"That was a mighty fine hat," he mourned. "It cost me twenty-five dollars of good Confederate money, back in Richmond last month. And now look how those Yankees have spoiled it."

"Listen, you should be thankful that the hole's just in your hat and not in your head, too," Hagan said positively. "Lucky for us there were so many Yankees. They got in each other's way."

By this time Pepper had caught his breath and his brain began to function again. He looked around wildly.

"Where's Sunstar?" he gasped.

The three troopers exchanged glances.

"I'm afraid the Yankees got him," Sweeney said at last. "We couldn't bring him away."

"I know," Pepper nodded dully. "Now it's Company Q for me."

"I'll see that you get another horse, sonny," Hagan promised gruffly. "I'll bring you the best Yankee nag I can capture."

"Thanks," said Pepper, fighting hard to keep the

tears back. "But I certainly am going to feel lost without Sunstar. I hope the Yankees will take care of him."

"Come on, mount behind me," Salt said. "We'll have to get back to camp and report this party of Yankees. I'm sorry about Sunstar, Pepper. Maybe you can capture him back again."

After that the days dragged slowly for Pepper. Life in the dismounted Company Q was drab and uninteresting. The energetic troopers fretted endlessly and the lazy ones spent most of their time loafing and sleeping. A week of this life found Pepper almost desperate.

One afternoon, about ten days after Sunstar had been captured, Lieutenant Hagan came riding into camp leading a fat brown horse that was conspicuously marked with the Union army brand. Mud and dust covered the lieutenant from head to foot, but his face wore a look of triumph.

"Here's that Yankee mount for you," he called, tossing the reins to Pepper. "The best one I could find this side of Maryland. He's not much for speed, but at least he'll keep you out of the infantry."

"Thanks, Hagan," Pepper's voice was hoarse with gratitude. "I sure do appreciate it. Honestly, I think I'd go crazy if I had to stay here much longer."

"I know, sonny," the big lieutenant nodded, his bushy whiskers bobbing up and down against his gray collar. "A good man eats his heart out in Company Q. Whew! The weather's getting hot."

Hagan took off his hat and mopped a coat sleeve

across his damp forehead. As he did so, Pepper caught sight of a dark clot of blood that had dried in the thick hair over one temple.

"Hagan," he exclaimed, "the Yankees shot you—there's blood on your forehead."

The big lieutenant touched the place tenderly with one huge hand.

"Just a scratch," he grinned. "My head's hard enough to make any bullet bounce. You know I promised to get you another horse, and I try to keep my word."

Pepper smiled as he swung a leg over the back of his new mount.

"I'll remember that," he said. "Your promise is a valuable thing to have."

Next morning General Stuart called the four friends to his tent. Silently they stood before him while the cavalry officer added two or three lines to the long report he was writing. Then he looked up at them, chewing thoughtfully on the end of his pen.

"I have a dangerous mission for you," he said slowly. "It will take careful and accurate scouting almost in the teeth of the enemy. I know that I can depend on you four. That is why I chose you. Are you willing to undertake it?"

"Yes, sir," the four answered, speaking almost as one man.

"Good. I want to find out what Hooker is up to. I understand that he is pushing south and I must know where he plans to strike. You four ride north and get as close to Washington as you can. Try to intercept any message from the Federal war office to General Hooker. Take a week if necessary, only bring me the information. Is that clear?"

"Yes, sir," again the words were spoken in chorus as the four saluted smartly.

In a short time they were riding northward. Pepper soon found that his Yankee mount was far from being a matchless horse like Sunstar. As the miles rolled behind the boy found himself wishing, more and more, that he could feel the glossy black steed's tireless body between his knees. Almost unconsciously Pepper sighed deeply.

"What's the matter, Napoleon?" Salt asked curiously.

"Oh, nothing. I was just thinking about Sunstar."

"That's what I thought. You miss him, don't you?"

"Yes," said Pepper quietly. "I don't want to seem ungrateful to Hagan, but this horse can't even be compared to Sunstar. By the side of Sunstar, this nag's nothing more than a plow horse."

They rode northward all day, splashing across the muddy Rappahannock at Grady's ford and continuing on across the narrow strip of land that separated the Rappahannock from the Potomac. Dusk was just falling as they topped a gentle rise and saw the broad Potomac stretching before them. On the horizon, far to the north and east, they could see the last rays of the setting sun gleaming on the great dome of the Union capitol.

"There it is," said Sweeney. "Too bad we can't drop in and have supper with 'Father Abraham.' I reckon we'll have to bunk in the woods and live off the country for the next few nights."

"I hope it stays warm," added Hagan. "We don't dare build a fire here or we'd have half of the Washington garrison down on us before morning."

"There's a nice windbreak over there in the thicket," Salt announced.

The four scouts fastened their horses securely, giving them enough freedom to graze, and then threw themselves on the ground to eat the cold rations stored in their knapsacks.

"I'll take the first watch," said Hagan, yawning. "Sweeney, you take the second, Salt the third, and Pepper last. Does that suit you?"

"It's all right by me," agreed Sweeney, busy spreading out his blanket. "Call me when you're ready to turn in."

"Suits us, too," chorused Salt and Pepper.

The big lieutenant propped his broad back against a tree, draped a blanket over his shoulders and prepared to keep watch. Tired by their long ride, his companions rolled up in their blankets and soon were asleep.

CHAPTER TWENTY-ONE
Pepper Invades Washington

WHEN his turn came to keep watch, Pepper sat gazing up at the bright stars, trying to stay awake. His thoughts flew back to that other time he had kept watch in the early dawn, when Jeb Stuart's troopers were out on their famous ride around McClellan.

Pepper thought of how his gallant black horse had come and stood watch with him. Sunstar was more than a horse to Pepper—he was a faithful companion and friend. The boy gulped hard to swallow the lump that rose in his throat when he remembered how Sunstar had been captured.

"I wonder if I'll ever see him again," he whispered. "I hope the Yankees will take good care of him. I wonder if he misses me half as much as I miss him?"

There was no way of answering these questions. Pepper sat keeping guard over his sleeping companions while the sky grew light in the east and the broad surface of the Potomac took on a rosy glow, reflecting the morning sky above. Somewhere across the river a rooster crowed and a dog barked sharply.

Behind him, Pepper could hear his friends beginning to stir. Leaves rustled and dry twigs cracked as they unrolled their blankets and sat up, yawning.

"Any signs of the Yankees, youngster?" Sweeney asked.

"Nary a sign," Pepper answered. "Not even a boat on the river."

"I reckon the Federal gunboats are all busy blockadin' our ports," growled Hagan. "I can't see why 'Marse Robert' and General Stuart don't try attacking the Yankee capital, instead of letting the bluecoats invade Virginia and march on Richmond."

"I wish so, too," agreed Sweeney, "but I reckon the officers know best. Come on, you all, and swallow your rations. We've got to be moving."

"What are we going to do?" Pepper asked, his mouth full of corn bread.

"Sam and I will scout the roads and back country," Hagan said. "You boys stick to the river shore. If you see any Yankees, get them. They'll probably be carrying dispatches."

"Stay close to the woods where the sentinels won't see you," advised Sweeney. "We're a heap too close to the Yankee lines for comfort, so watch your step or you'll end up in Old Capitol Prison for the duration of the war."

"We will," promised Salt.

"You bet," echoed Pepper. "We'll watch the river like a couple of hawks and meet you here at dusk."

Sweeney and Hagan mounted their horses, riding quickly down hill and disappearing in the wooded valley. The two boys stood for a time watching the Potomac, eyes alert for signs of Yankee activity.

"We might as well start," Salt said at last, tightening the girths on Thunder's saddle.

"Yes," agreed Pepper. "Let's get off this hilltop before somebody sees us."

The boys climbed into their saddles and cantered down the hill, keeping close to the dense thickets along the shore. Spring was well on the way and the late April air was soft and pleasant. The alders were covered with young green leaves and red-winged blackbirds twittered in the grass along the swampy shore. The sun shone warm and bright and all nature seemed eager to help complete the perfect spring morning.

"Seems funny to think of fighting on a day like this," said Pepper. "I'd rather go fishing."

Salt laughed.

"Wouldn't General Lee's army look funny marching

off with fishing poles instead of rifles over their shoulders?"

"Sure," grinned Pepper, "but I'll bet they'd like it better."

When noon came the boys rode to the crest of a hill overlooking the Potomac. Dismounting, they tied their horses behind a clump of bushes and lay down to watch the surrounding territory. The sun was warm and pleasant, and soon Salt began to grow drowsy.

"Pepper," he murmured, "are you sleepy?"

"No, I'm not."

"Then you keep watch for a little while and let me catch a nap. I can scarcely hold my eyes open."

"All right," said Pepper, stretching out on his stomach and propping his chin on his hands.

Salt tipped his hat over his eyes and soon his deep breathing showed that he was fast asleep. Idly Pepper lay watching the land across the river. It was open and gently rolling and a well-travelled road ran parallel with the water on the opposite shore. A few cows grazed in the pasture across from him. A buzzard soared serenely above in the blue spring sky. For a long time nothing happened.

At last, far down the road to his right, Pepper glimpsed a small cloud of dust. He eyed it curiously. Since the river lay between, no matter who or what it was, the scout could do nothing but look on.

Nearer and nearer came the dust cloud until it was almost directly opposite the Confederate watcher. He could see that the cloud was being made by a single

PEPPER INVADES WASHINGTON

horse and rider, but the dust was too thick to let him see more. Suddenly a gust of wind swept up from the Potomac and dispersed the cloud. Pepper's eyes grew wide with recognition.

"Salt! Salt!" he cried, excitedly shaking his friend's shoulder. "Wake up!"

"What's the matter?" Salt sat up and blinked owlishly.

"I just saw Sunstar! Some Yankee is riding him just across the river. I'm going after him!"

"Hey, you can't do that!" Salt was wide awake now. "The Yankees will be sure to capture you."

Already Pepper had unbuckled his long saber and was halfway into his saddle.

"I'm willing to risk it," he answered. "Take care of my saber and wait three days for me. I'm going to try it."

Still protesting, Salt watched his friend ride down the hill and urge his horse into the water. The rider on the opposite bank was just disappearing over a ridge toward Washington and the river shore was deserted. Salt frowned and shook his head.

"He's crazy to try it," he muttered, "but I don't blame him for going after Sunstar. I reckon I'd do the same thing myself."

Meanwhile Pepper had urged his horse out into the Potomac, digging his heels into the animal's flanks to make him hurry. A few splashing steps and the horse was swimming against the sluggish current. The opposite shore looked a long way off as Pepper slid from the saddle and swam with one hand on the pommel to relieve the horse of his extra weight.

At last they scrambled, panting and soaked, up the northern bank of the river. Pepper turned to wave a hand to Salt on the opposite shore before setting off after Sunstar.

"I'll have to be careful," he thought, "so no one gets suspicious. I'm just a poor boy from the country and I don't know my way around. That story worked for me once, and I hope it's still good."

Urging his horse forward as fast as he could, Pepper, outwardly calm, rode toward Washington, his gray eyes ever watchful for danger. Once he caught sight of the great black horse he sought, just topping a hill in the distance. Already Sunstar was entering the outskirts of Washington. Pepper's heart beat faster at the thought of braving the dangers of the enemy stronghold, but he kept steadily on.

When he reached the first Yankee outpost he gave a clumsy salute to the blue soldiers on guard. By this time his clothes were dry enough to escape notice. Pepper was glad that he didn't have to concoct some yarn to explain his swim across the Potomac.

"Howdy, boys," he drawled. "I'd like to get into town and do some tradin' for my maw. Can I go past?"

"Where you from, youngster?" asked the sergeant of the guard.

Pepper waved a hand over his shoulder.

"From back that way," he answered. "We live on a farm near Broad Creek. My maw wants me to buy her some thread and buttons. My kid brothers just natch'lly lose the buttons off their britches as fast as maw can sew 'em on."

The Yankee sergeant laughed.

"Sure, kid," he said. "Go on in. Be sure you get back out of the city before dark."

"Thank you, mister," Pepper touched his hat brim and rode off, scarcely noticing the poorly dressed civilian standing near by.

Pepper had gone only a short distance down the road when the man knocked out his pipe, put it carefully away in his pocket, and turned to the sergeant of the guard.

"Did you notice anything strange about the horse that boy was riding, Sergeant?" he asked.

"No sir, Major Pinkerton," was the answer. "It looked like any old brown farm horse to me."

"It had a U. S. army brand and it looked mighty like the horse the rebels stole from Captain Garstand not long ago. I'm going after that boy."

Major Allan Pinkerton, head of the Federal secret service, swung into his saddle. Soon Pepper observed a shabby-looking, short-bearded man riding beside him.

"Nice day isn't it, sonny?" the man said.

"It sho' is," Pepper answered, careful to use his farm-boy drawl. "I'm glad to see spring come again."

"Ever been in Washington before?"

Pepper did some quick thinking. He had told the sentry that he lived not far away, and yet his obvious ignorance of the capital city might betray him. Better make his stories hang together as well as he could, the boy decided.

"No, sir," he answered. "I've never been here before. Paw usually does all our tradin', but he's sick and I had to come this time."

They were well within the city now and the streets were crowded with teams and carriages. The sidewalks swarmed with hurrying pedestrians.

"There sure are a lot of folks in Washington," remarked Pepper, busy watching the streets in hope of seeing Sunstar. All around him were strange faces and the boy's heart beat fast when he remembered that every one was an enemy.

Meanwhile the stranger had been watching the boy narrowly through shrewd eyes. He noted the soldierly carriage, the worn leather jacket and the faded homespun trousers. His mouth twitched slightly when his eyes fell on a bulge beneath the boy's jacket that might mean the handle of a pistol. From the rider, Pinkerton's eyes swept over the brown horse, lingering thoughtfully on the "U. S." branded on the left flank.

"Where did you get that horse?" he snapped suddenly.

Pepper stared at him in surprise for the new tone was totally different from the man's former lazy drawl.

"I brought him from home," the boy answered. "He belongs to my paw."

"Then why does he have the U. S. army brand on him?"

"Paw bought him from the quartermaster last winter," Pepper answered. "It's none of your business anyhow, mister."

"Oh, yes it is," the stranger retorted. "You're a rebel spy, and you stole that horse from Captain Garstand a few days ago!"

"That's a lie," stormed Pepper, his heart thumping wildly. "This horse belongs to my father."

"We'll see about that." The man reined close and thrust a pistol against Pepper's ribs. "I'm Major Pinkerton of the secret service. Come with me and don't make a fuss. I'll put a ball through you if you resist."

Resistance was useless, Pepper realized that, and it would only get him into more trouble. The best thing to do was to keep on bluffing. But Major Pinkerton—cold chills ran up and down the boy's spine when he remembered the stories he had heard of this famous Yankee detective.

"All right, I'll come, mister," he said, "but honestly, you've made a big mistake."

"We'll see," said the detective grimly. "Come along."

Pinkerton kept his pistol muzzle trained uncomfortably close to Pepper's ribs during their short ride through the city to the military headquarters.

"Get down and march ahead of me," the detective ordered sternly. "And remember, my finger's on the trigger."

Pepper entered the dingy office with Pinkerton at his heels and together they stood before the desk of the officer in charge. Pepper was about to protest his innocence when a hatefully familiar voice interrupted him.

"Well, by gad, Major Pinkerton, you've finally got that rebel where he belongs. He's been dodging a firing squad for a long time."

It was the high, sneering voice of McGrigg, the Yankee spy and agitator. Pepper recognized it immediately and his heart sank.

"Do you know him?" Pinkerton demanded.

"Know him?" McGrigg arose from his chair in a corner of the room and slouched over to thrust his rat-face close to Pepper.

"You bet I know him," the spy's thin lips curled. "This is the meddling rebel who got me captured twice. First time was just before my buddy, Ed Buckett, was shot while trying to escape from Libby prison with me. Second time I thought I'd settled his hash with a pistol ball, but these slave-beating Southerners are hard to kill."

"Just as I suspected," Pinkerton told the officer in charge. "I thought something was wrong when he rode into Washington on a horse with a U. S. brand."

"He's a spy, that's what he is," shrilled McGrigg. "He ought to be shot."

"No." Pinkerton said slowly. "That's outside my department."

"President Lincoln is not so keen about having men shot offhand like that," the Federal officer said doubtfully.

"But I can identify him," McGrigg broke in eagerly. "I know he's a rebel spy."

"Then he'll have to be court-martialed," the officer

answered. "I'll send him to prison until the court meets."

He wrote briefly on a paper and handed it to an orderly.

"Take this man and lock him up," the officer said.

"You'll get yours this time, rebel," McGrigg's satisfied voice followed Pepper as the guard led him away.

A few minutes later Pepper found himself pushed into a big, gloomy room on the second floor of a rambling old brick building. The grimy, whitewashed walls were covered with cobwebs, and the floor was littered and dirty. Only a faint light filtered in through the broken, dusty panes of a great arched window that had wooden slats nailed across it.

The room contained about twenty other prisoners, men who paid little attention to Pepper, after a single curious glance at the newcomer. Some of them were busy playing cards, others played dominoes or read newspapers. Still others merely sat and stared at the floor.

Pepper first walked to the window, hoping for a breath of fresh air to relieve the heavy, sour smell of sweat, stale cooking, and sewage that had filled his nostrils from the time he first entered the prison. But only a little air came in through the broken panes, and soon Pepper turned and threw himself on a wooden bench where he sat with his head in his hands.

Events had happened with such speed that the boy had been unable to open his mouth in protest, and McGrigg's malicious hatred made the future look dark and forbidding.

"Now I'll never see Sunstar again," he thought sadly.

Someone sat down beside him and a kindly voice said, "What's the trouble, my boy?"

Pepper raised his head and saw a chubby little man smiling at him. A fuzzy fringe of white whiskers ran around the man's face and under his chin, setting off his features in a soft, white frame. Did he dare tell his story, the boy wondered, gazing into the frank blue eyes.

The man seemed to understand.

"You can trust me, son," he said. "I'm a Confederate sympathizer who talked too much. That's why I'm here —and a slim chance I have of getting out, now that President Lincoln has suspended the writ of habeas corpus."

"What's that?" Pepper asked curiously. The man's friendliness made him feel much better.

"It's a constitutional right which prevents the law from keeping anyone in jail without a fair trial. During war time the authorities choose to disregard it."

"Oh," said Pepper. "I reckon I understand. Where are we?"

"In Old Capitol Prison, sonny. Ever heard of it before?"

"Yes, that's where prisoners of war are kept. It's supposed to be one of the biggest of the Yankee prisons. I've often wondered why they call it Old Capitol."

"Because it was once used as the national capitol," the little man answered. "After the British soldiers burned Washington in the War of 1812, Congress met in this building. You're in a famous place, boy. The Senate used to sit in this room. My name is Martin Pressman. What's yours?"

"Potter Pepperill," the boy answered. "How long does it take to get court-martialed?"

"That's hard to say. I've only been here since December."

"Since December! Why, that's five months!" exclaimed Pepper.

"Yes." His companion smiled ruefully. "But many of the men in this room have been here longer. Most of us are political offenders. See that man over there, the one staring at the floor. He has been here a year and a half."

Pepper gulped and said nothing. He sat slumped on the hard bench, staring at a cobweb on the dingy wall opposite him. Things looked blacker than ever for the young Confederate cavalryman.

The hours dragged even more slowly than they had while he was in Company Q. At dusk the prison guard appeared with tin plates of food which they handed around to the prisoners. Pepper accepted his and sat staring at it, his stomach churning at the sight of the greasy slab of bacon from which some black pig bristles still protruded, at the chunk of corn bread that was burned to charcoal on the bottom and left raw in the middle, at the thin sorghum in which several dead insects floated.

Some of the men were eating, but Pepper put his plate on the floor in disgust.

"Better not do that, sonny," cautioned Pressman. "The rats and roaches will get it before you can say 'Jack Robinson.' "

"I don't care," Pepper answered. "I'm not hungry."

Greatly discouraged, he continued to sit on the hard wooden bench until nine o'clock when a sergeant appeared and called the roll of the prisoners. After that, the men began to get ready for bed.

Pepper looked at the three tiers of bunks that lined two walls of the room. Many of the bunks were filled with boxes, pots, pans, and a strange assortment of junk and personal possessions. He wandered over to one and was about to lie down when Martin Pressman stepped to his side.

"Better sleep on the floor like the rest of us, sonny," he advised. "Those bunks are full of bedbugs."

"Oh," Pepper said, backing away distastefully. "Thanks for telling me."

He found a place by the window and stretched out dejectedly on the dirty floor, folding his arms across his face and fighting hard to keep from giving away to the black despair that welled up inside him. At last he fell asleep.

CHAPTER TWENTY-TWO
Pepper Meets a Great Man

DAYLIGHT again filled the prison room when Pepper awoke. At first the boy could not remember where he was, then memory returned with a rush. For a time he lay on his back, staring at the stained ceiling, wondering what his fate would be. At last he sat up and looked around. Some of the other prisoners had already started their card games again.

"Good morning." Martin Pressman smiled at him from a bench near by. "Feeling any better today?"

Pepper grinned sheepishly.

"I reckon so," he answered. "I sure was low in my mind yesterday."

"I know how it is, son. I felt pretty bad myself for the first few weeks I was here. I've got a wife and three children I haven't seen in five months."

"That's too bad," Pepper sympathized. "Don't you have any friends who can help you?"

"They've tried," answered Pressman. "But there isn't much they can do during war time."

While the two prisoners were talking, the jailor and his Negro helpers entered with breakfast rations. By this time Pepper was hungry enough to eat some of the half-cooked beans, stringy beef, and musty-tasting rice that he found on his plate.

Breakfast over, Pepper and Martin Pressman walked to the window and looked out. In spite of the slats nailed across it, the window gave a good view of the street.

"We couldn't do this in some Yankee prisons where captives are not allowed to look out of the windows," Pressman remarked. "Even here the guards will not allow anybody to stop in the street outside, for fear they will communicate with the prisoners."

Pepper leaned against the sill, watching the people passing by the prison. Some looked curiously up at its forbidding brick walls, but no one attempted to stop. The blue-clad sentries pacing back and forth with fixed bayonets made sure of that.

As he watched, a troop of soldiers went marching by, drums rolling and fifes piping shrilly as the blue-uniformed column swung along the dusty road. Teamsters urged their sweating horses with harsh shouts and loud whip-cracks. Negroes trudged by, along with the stream of white pedestrians. Trim carriages sped along carrying gaily dressed ladies and occasionally a blue-and-gold uniformed officer rode past.

For a long time after Pressman had joined some of the group playing cards Pepper watched the ever-changing scene. Suddenly his attention was riveted on two horsemen who were passing. One of them, a lieutenant, was astride a familiar glossy black horse.

"Sunstar!" Pepper shouted.

"What's the matter?" exclaimed Pressman, hurrying to his side.

All the other prisoners were staring.

"That's my horse," Pepper answered excitedly. "Sunstar! Oh, Sunstar!"

The cry attracted both horse and rider. The gallant horse threw up his head. His pointed ears went forward and his feet began to dance. The Yankee officer turned in his saddle. When he did so, the Confederate scout received a second surprise.

"Stephen!" he shouted. "Stephen, it's Pepper!"

"Here you! Get away from that window!" the prison guard shouted angrily through the bars of the door. "Stop that racket or I'll put you in irons."

Pepper paid no attention to the jailor. His eyes were intent on Stephen. But after a single curious glance in the direction of the prison, Stephen looked away. He seemed to be laughing at something his companion said. He put spurs to Sunstar and rode on as if nothing had happened.

By this time the prison guard had unlocked the cell door and jerked Pepper roughly away from the window.

"No yelling through windows," he said harshly. "Try that once more and you'll get a bullet through you."

"What was it, Pepper?" Pressman asked gently after the guard had gone out and locked the door behind him.

The other prisoners, after a short flurry of interest, returned to their cards and newspapers.

"I saw my horse and a fellow I thought was my friend," Pepper answered dully. "But he didn't even look at me. He just kept on talking to the man who was with him, 'though I'm sure he recognized my voice."

"I'm afraid you must be mistaken, Pepper. I saw the young man. Don't you know who he is?"

"Of course I do. His name is Stephen Reynolds," Pepper replied, surprised at Pressman's tone. "He's my friend."

"Did you notice the man with him?"

Pepper shook his head.

"That was his uncle, Edwin M. Stanton, the Yankee Secretary of War. There are few men in the North who dislike the South as much as Stanton does. As Secretary of War he has a great deal to say about the fighting, and he is bitterly opposed to the Confederacy and all who sympathize with the South. You couldn't possibly be friends with his nephew."

"Oh," said Pepper, dropping down on his bench. "I didn't know that."

For a long time Pepper sat motionless, thinking of the happy months he and Stephen had spent at Magnolia Hill. He smiled bitterly when he remembered how kindly his mother had cared for the wounded Yankee, and also how he himself had tried to have Stephen see both sides of the war. It made him squirm to think how neatly the northern boy had tricked him.

Pepper recalled Stephen's parting words, spoken at the exchange headquarters at City Point. "I never will be able to thank you for all that you have done for me," Stephen had said. "I hope that sometime I'll have a chance to repay you. Remember, Pepper, war or no war, I will always be your friend."

Now Stephen had denied him, scarcely a month after speaking those words. He was as bad as the spy, McGrigg—worse even, for at least McGrigg never had made any promises of friendship. Pepper felt bitter and disillusioned. He hated himself for ever feeling kindly toward the Yankees.

And, to make matters worse, Stephen had Sunstar. Pepper sprang to his feet and strode up and down the prison room, almost wild with anger and despair.

The second day of imprisonment passed even more slowly than the first. Many of the prisoners became friendly but, when left to his own thoughts, Pepper remembered sadly how he had told Salt to wait three days for him—two of them were already gone. In one more day Salt and Sweeney and Hagan would go riding back to Jeb Stuart, and Pepper would remain behind. The war might drag on for years and it would be ages before he would see the pleasant green hills and winding roads of Virginia—he might never see them again. Meanwhile, Sunstar would belong to a treacherous Yankee. The gloomy thoughts were unbearable.

At last the day drew to a close and night brought sleep and forgetfulness. In his dreams Pepper went galloping along at Jeb Stuart's heels on one of the gay raiding parties. Once more he felt Sunstar's powerful body between his knees.

Early next morning the guard unlocked the heavy door and stepped into the room, taking Pepper roughly by the shoulder.

"Come on, you," he said.

"Am I going to be court-martialed?" Pepper couldn't help asking.

The guard only grunted.

"Good-by, Pepper." Martin Pressman and the other prisoners came to shake hands as though they never expected to see the boy again. "Good luck."

The cell door clanged behind them and the Yankee guard urged Pepper rapidly down the dark stairway and out through the office of the prison commandant. Pepper was still blinking in the bright sunlight when a covered wagon drew up before the prison door.

"You know the orders, Joe," the guard told the driver, pushing Pepper inside and climbing in after him.

"Sure," replied the driver, with a crack of his whip

and a quick jerk at the reins. The covered cart started off with a jolt, rocking crazily over the rutted streets while Pepper and his guard rattled around inside like a couple of peas.

At last the wagon stopped. The guard seized Pepper's arm.

"Come on, rebel," he growled. "Step lively."

Without giving the captive a chance to look around, the guard hurried him out of the wagon, across a driveway, up a flight of stairs and into a dark hall. Pepper was still too bewildered to protest.

Pausing before a high, narrow door, the guard knocked sharply. Immediately the door swung open and a blue-uniformed soldier confronted them.

"Here's the prisoner," said Pepper's guard.

"Good, they're ready for him inside," replied the soldier. "I'll take charge of him now."

The soldier led Pepper swiftly across a bare anteroom, opened another door and whisked him inside, almost closing the door on his heels.

The boy found himself standing in a sunny office, staring into the deeply lined face of a thin, bearded man who sat behind a desk at the far end of the room. There was something strangely familiar about the face. Pepper was searching his mind for the answer to it all when another door opened and a Yankee lieutenant entered the office.

"Pepper!" the lieutenant shouted joyfully, rushing across the room to the prisoner. "Oh, but I'm glad to see you!"

"Stephen!" Pepper gasped, scarcely believing his own eyes.

The Yankee boy was shaking Pepper's hand vigorously before the bewildered Confederate could say more. Pepper tried to draw his hand away.

"Don't try any more tricks, Yankee," he said coldly. "I saw how you acted yesterday."

"Pepper, I had to do that," Stephen protested. "Please let me explain."

Pepper turned away.

"You're Secretary Stanton's nephew," he said. "I'd rather you didn't talk to me."

The bearded man was watching the two boys with interest.

"I think you'd better listen to what Stephen has to say, Pepper," he said in a kindly voice. "You owe him the opportunity to explain."

The man's words, spoken in a quiet and pleasant manner, had a strange influence over Pepper. They seemed to calm his excited nerves and to clear his angry brain.

"All right, Stephen," he said at last. "I'll listen."

"First of all, Pepper, I want to introduce you to the greatest and the kindest man that ever lived," Stephen said, taking his friend's arm and leading him to the desk behind which the thin man was seated.

"Pepper," Stephen continued, "this is Mr. Abraham Lincoln, President of the United States."

Slowly the great man rose to his feet. He seemed to unfold until he towered far above the boys—a tall, un-

graceful man, Pepper thought, until he looked into the man's face again.

It was not a beautiful face, but it was kindly and pleasant, full of sympathy and understanding. It was lined and gaunt. Even the fringe of beard on the thin cheeks and chin failed to hide the signs of weariness and suffering that were stamped deeply on it. The high forehead was topped with an unruly mop of hair that gave a boyish touch to the otherwise haggard features.

The President extended a huge, horny hand toward Pepper.

"I'm glad to know you, Pepper," he said. "Stephen has told me how kind you were to him and I want to thank you personally for it. Every boy in the army is my boy, and I'm grateful to those who are kind to them."

Wordlessly Pepper extended his own hand which was swallowed up in the giant palm of the President. He forgot the strangeness of the meeting, he forgot his anger and resentment toward Stephen. He thought only of the tall, ungainly figure before him, and of the deep light that shone in the tired eyes.

Lincoln smiled and sat down, motioning for the boys to do likewise.

"Now Stephen, I think Pepper should hear your side of the story," he said.

"Yes, sir," answered the Yankee boy. Turning to Pepper he continued. "You see, Pepper, I never dreamed that you had been captured until yesterday when you called to me from Old Capitol Prison. For a minute I was too surprised to speak, and before I found my voice

Uncle Edwin said something about ignoring rebels and traitors."

"I saw him speak to you and I saw you laugh," Pepper interrupted.

"I had to laugh, Pepper, so he wouldn't be suspicious. My uncle hates Southerners as much as your uncle, Judge Cromartie, hates Yankees. After he got me exchanged I told him how kind you had been to me, but he just grunted and said it was probably some kind of a rebel trick. He would have kept me from trying to help you now if I had told him what I was going to do."

"Yes," President Lincoln broke in. "My Secretary of War works overtime at his job. He forgets that God made the rebels as well as the Yankees."

"Because I knew how he felt, I had to ride on and leave you," Stephen continued. "I hated to do it, but it was the only thing I could do. As soon as I could, I came to President Lincoln for help."

"Between my officers who want to shoot rebels, and the friends who want to save them, I haven't a minute's rest," Lincoln laughed ruefully. "Just the same I'd rather save a man than shoot him any day. You can't make me believe that shooting a man does him any good."

"But how did you get Sunstar?" Pepper wanted to know.

"I saw a troop of soldiers bring him in a couple of weeks ago. Of course I recognized him and was scared to death for fear something had happened to you. The men were sure you had escaped and that made me feel better. I bought Sunstar from the quartermaster and was going to keep him until I could send him back to you."

"Then you really did mean it when you said we'd be friends, war or no war," Pepper exclaimed joyfully. "Stephen, I owe you an apology."

The tall President rose and placed a kindly hand on the shoulders of the two boys.

"My young friends," he said in a voice deep with emotion, "if we could only clear up all human misunderstandings as you two have done, there would be no need for the tragedy of war. I hope and pray that this present war may speedily be ended and this great nation made one again, with the North and the South standing side by side to face the future."

Pepper rose to his feet.

"Sir," he said, "when you speak that way, I can't help but feel that your prayer will be answered."

Lincoln smiled down at him.

"Thanks, Pepper. I wish everyone had as much confidence in me as you do."

He stepped back to his desk which was piled high with papers. After clearing a space for his hand, he wrote rapidly for a minute.

"Now all we have to do is slip you out of here before any more of my bloodthirsty friends get hold of you," he told Pepper. "Stephen," he continued, "I want you to see that our young rebel gets back across the Potomac without dodging any Federal bullets. This paper will take you through the outposts."

"Thank you, Mr. President," said the northern boy, his face shining with gratitude.

"Don't thank me," said Lincoln, "thank Pepper, here, for being man enough to make a friend like you in war time. This is only a good deed come home to roost."

Pepper saluted.

"I don't know what to say, sir," he stammered, "but I certainly am grateful for everything."

Lincoln smiled and waved them toward the door.

"Good-by, boys," he called after them. "Just keep on being friends and I'll be satisfied."

The door closed behind them as Stephen led the way across the anteroom and down the dark hall. At the door he paused and motioned to a sentinel.

"Bring the horses, Sergeant," he ordered.

The soldier saluted and disappeared. In a moment he returned leading two horses, a slender bay mare and a powerful, glossy black. Pepper's face beamed with joy. He dashed forward and threw his arms about the steed's arching neck.

"Sunstar, oh Sunstar," he sobbed unashamed. The black horse snorted a delighted greeting.

Stephen mounted the bay mare.

"Come on, Pepper," he urged. "We'll have to hurry. I won't rest easy until you're back in your own lines again."

"All right," answered Pepper, climbing into Sunstar's saddle.

In a moment the boys were cantering through the

streets of Washington, dodging in and out of traffic as quickly as possible. Soon they reached the outskirts where they let their horses out in a gallop, raising great clouds of dust in the warm spring air. Not until the capital was several miles behind did Stephen check his pace.

"My friends are waiting for me across the Potomac," Pepper said. "I can go on alone from here."

Stephen shook his head.

"I want to be sure you're safe," he said, "and I won't be satisfied until I see you cross the river."

"Stephen," Pepper said as they rode side by side. "I never can thank you enough for all you've done—that's just what you told me down at City Point. Do you remember?"

Stephen smiled.

"Yes, I remember. And what I said about being friends still goes, war or no war, doesn't it?"

"It sure does," Pepper answered. "Say, how did you get to be a lieutenant?" he added curiously. "You've really come up in the world since I saw you last."

"Uncle Edwin got me the appointment just after he had me exchanged. I'm on his staff now and, while I miss the fellows in camp, it is interesting to be right in the center of things at Washington."

Stephen paused, and then continued.

"By the way, you haven't told me how you happened to get captured. I heard that you rode straight into Pinkerton's arms."

"It was foolish," Pepper admitted. "But I was scouting along the southern bank of the Potomac and I saw you riding Sunstar on the other side. Of course I was too far away to recognize you, but I knew Sunstar and I set right out after him."

"I might have known it," Stephen said. "That sounds just like you, Pepper."

"I had a good yarn all ready," Pepper continued. "Only Major Pinkerton spotted the army brand on my horse and Arch McGrigg was at headquarters to identify me. You know, I told you how he hates me."

Stephen nodded.

"You won't have to worry about him any more, Pepper. He got into some devilment right after he saw you—tried to pick a soldier's pocket, and the fellow shot him."

"I reckon he only got what was coming to him," Pepper said. "Let's talk about something pleasant."

They cantered gaily onward, talking and laughing as they rode until at last the broad Potomac rolled before them, the reeds along its marshy banks waving in the spring breeze.

"Here's where we part, Pepper," said Stephen.

"I reckon so. There's the hill over there where my friends are to meet me."

"Well then, I guess I stop here." Stephen checked his horse at the river bank. "I'll be looking forward to the time when the war is over and we can be friends again."

"Friends again," repeated Pepper. "Why, Stephen, we're friends now and we'll go on being friends always —war or no war. I am mighty sure of that."

"So am I," said the Yankee. "Let's shake on it."

"Right," said Pepper, and their hands met in a long, steady grip.

"I can't put into words how much I thank you for getting me free and for returning Sunstar," the southern boy continued. "I'll never forget it as long as I live, and I can't see how I could ever have doubted you."

"Don't thank me. Remember what President Lincoln said—it was only your good deed coming home to roost."

"Perhaps it was," smiled Pepper. "And it sure came home in good shape. I must go now, Stephen. Good-by, and thanks."

"Good-by," answered Stephen. "Forget the thanks."

The young Union soldier stood watching while Pepper urged Sunstar out into the Potomac current.

"We're going home, Sunstar, home to Virginia," whispered Pepper, sliding from the saddle and swimming beside his steed. The great black horse snorted in understanding, and struck out vigorously toward his southland home. Soon Pepper and Sunstar were splashing happily through the shallows on the Virginia shore.

As they set foot on solid ground, three mounted figures burst from the near-by woods and rode noisily toward them.

"Pepper!" Sweeney shouted. "Boy, I'm glad to see you."

"Sonny, I was scared those Yankees had you. Are you all right?" Hagan roared.

"Pal, you had us worried," added Salt, thumping Pepper on the shoulder. "I see you got Sunstar. Where did you find him?"

"Yes, where have you been?" echoed Sweeney, and Hagan's whiskers fairly bristled with curiosity.

"Oh, I've been lots of places," Pepper answered airily, turning to wave a final farewell to Stephen across the river. "I've been in Old Capitol Prison, I ran into Allan Pinkerton, and I've talked with President Abraham Lincoln."

Hagan's mouth dropped open and Salt was speechless with surprise.

"Well, all I've got to say," said Sweeney, "is what I've often said before."

He paused a moment and then, grinning, he burst into the jolly old song—

> *"If you want to have a good time*
> *Jine the cavalry. . . ."*

A Note on the Historical Background

ACTION in this book begins a few weeks after the battle of Seven Pines in 1862 and ends shortly before the battle of Chancellorsville in 1863. In writing it I have consulted many accounts of the Civil War written by men who knew and followed Jeb Stuart. Among these works are *Life and Campaigns of Major General J. E. B. Stuart,* written by Major H. B. McClellan, who was Stuart's chief of staff; *Stuart's Cavalry in the Gettysburg Campaign,* and *Memoirs of Col. John S. Mosby,* written by Stuart's famous scout, John S. Mosby. *Memoirs of the Confederate War,* by von Borcke, and *War Years with Jeb Stuart,* by Lieut. Col. W. W. Blackford, C. S. A., were also consulted.

Other books include *The War of Rebellion: A Compilation of the Official Records of the Union and Confederate Armies; Photographic History of the Civil War;* John W. Thomason, Jr.'s *Jeb Stuart;* Douglas Southall Freeman's *R. E. Lee;* J. W. Williamson's *Mosby's Rangers;* and Virgil Carrington Jones's *Ranger Mosby.* These are only a few of the works consulted, but space prohibits the inclusion of the entire list.

In preparing this book the author, the publisher, and the artist all have made great efforts to keep it as historically accurate as possible. However, since *Sunstar and Pepper* is fiction, some liberties have been taken with history.

For example, Hagan did not become a lieutenant until some time after the Peninsular Campaign, and at the time of Stuart's ride around McClellan he still held the rank of corporal. He may not have been the soldier who frightened the Pennsylvania women into feeding him, but one of Stuart's troopers did.

It was Rooney Lee who bluffed the Yankees at White's Ford, but he used Stuart's name in the message. Stuart at the time was elsewhere in the column, looking after the prisoners and captured horses. The cavalry commander told Lee to use his best judgment in the situation, and that is what Rooney Lee did.

Allan Pinkerton, who did great work with the Union Secret Service during the first part of the war, had resigned before the time Pepper is supposed to have visited Washington. Pinkerton was a staunch friend of General McClellan and when "Little Mac" was removed as commander of the Army of the Potomac, Pinkerton resigned also. During the remainder of the war he was employed by the government in examining claims. After the war he returned to his detective work.

For the sake of the story, the time of the action around Mechanicsville has been compressed; Stuart arrives at White House Landing two days before he was actually present. For the same reason, the time occupied by the second battle of Manassas has been cut to three days.

Some of the songs have been changed slightly, to make them fit. The one about Hagan and his whiskers, for example, was written about a captain. But Sweeney might well have changed it to tease the bewhiskered lieutenant.

Of course, Pepper, Salt, and Stephen Reynolds are imaginary characters, but others like them served in the Confederate and Union Armies and had experiences like those ascribed to these characters.

A great many of the people in this book really lived. Some of them survived the war, some did not. For the benefit of those who might be interested, I have listed most of the real characters and a few details about them.

1. Burnside, General Ambrose E., Commander of the Army of the Potomac, U. S. A., November, 1862, to February, 1863.

2. Christian, Lieutenant Jones S., Company F, Third Virginia Cavalry; promoted to captain in 1862; captured in 1864.

3. Cooke, Brigadier General Philip St. George, U. S. A.; Stuart's father-in-law.

4. Dabney, Lieutenant Chiswell, C. S. A.; aide on Stuart's staff.

5. Dandridge, A. S.; owned plantation mansion called "The Bower," near Charlestown, Virginia. Stuart camped near by and was often a guest of the Dandridge family.

6. Eliason, Doctor Talcott; surgeon on Stuart's staff.

7. Farley, Captain W. D., C. S. A.; served as special scout on Stuart's staff; was mortally wounded near Stevensburg, June 3, 1863.

8. Fitzhugh, Major Norman R., C. S. A.; Stuart's adjutant; was captured August 18, 1862.

9. Gibson, Lieutenant Samuel B., C. S. A.; aide on Stuart's staff.

10. Hagan, Lieutenant Henry, C. S. A.; formerly Corporal of Company F, First Virginia Cavalry; was promoted to lieutenant in command of Stuart's escort.

11. Hill, A. P., C. S. A.; became lieutenant general in 1863.

12. Jackson, Lieutenant General Thomas J. (Stonewall), C. S. A.; called Lee's "right-hand man"; was mortally wounded by mistake, by his own men, following the Battle of Chancellorsville; died May 10, 1863.

13. Lee, Robert E. (Marse Robert), C. S. A.; Commanding General, Army of Northern Virginia.

14. Lee, W. H. F. (Rooney), C. S. A.; son of Robert E. Lee, promoted to brigadier general; captured by raiders while recovering from wounds and imprisoned at Fort Monroe; was finally exchanged.

15. Lincoln, Abraham; President of the United States of America.

16. Longstreet, James, C. S. A.; Lieutenant General.

17. McClellan, General George B. (Little Mac), U. S. A.; Commanding General, Army of the Potomac.

18. Mitchell, B. W.; private, Company F., 27th. Indiana Infantry, U. S. A.; found Special Orders 191.

19. Mosby, John Singleton; special scout on Stuart's staff; later famous leader of Mosby's Partisan Rangers; became a colonel.

20. Pelham, John, C. S. A.; major in Stuart's Horse Artillery; killed at Kelly's Ford, March 17, 1863.

21. Pinkerton, Major Allan; Head of the Secret Service, U. S. A.
22. Pleasanton, Alfred, U. S. A.; cavalry general.
23. Pope, Major General John, U. S. A.; Commanding General, Army of the Potomac.
24. Rush, Major Richard H., U. S. A.; leader of the Pennsylvania Lancers.
25. Stanton, Edwin M.; United States Secretary of War in President Lincoln's cabinet.
26. Stowe, Mrs. Harriet Beecher; author of *Uncle Tom's Cabin.*
27. Stuart, Mrs. Flora; wife of General J. E. B. Stuart.
28. Stuart, Major General J. E. B., C. S. A.; cavalry commander in the Army of Northern Virginia; was mortally wounded at Yellow Tavern; died May 11, 1864.
29. Sweeney, Samuel D.; Company D, Second Virginia Cavalry; great banjo player and member of Stuart's escort; died in the winter of 1863–64 at Hanover Court House.
30. Von Borcke, Major Heros; officer in the Prussian Dragoons; ran the blockade to join the Confederate army. He was wounded during the Gettysburg campaign; survived the war and returned to Prussia and served in the Prussian wars; came back to visit the Virginia battlefields as an old man.